ANNA DAUGHERTY

Reaching for Grace

Black Rose Writing | Texas

ISBN: 978-1-68513-469-3
PUBLISHED BY BLACK ROSE WRITING
www.blackrosewriting.com

Printed in the United States of America
Suggested Retail Price (SRP) $21.95

Reaching for Grace is printed in Garamond Pro

*As a planet-friendly publisher, Black Rose Writing does its best to eliminate unnecessary waste to reduce paper usage and energy costs, while never compromising the reading experience. As a result, the final word count vs. page count may not meet common expectations.

Scripture quotations marked CSB have been taken from the Christian Standard Bible®, Copyright © 2017 by Holman Bible Publishers. Used by permission. Christian Standard Bible® and CSB® are federally registered trademarks of Holman Bible Publishers.

Edited by Katy Schlomach

Praise for
Reaching for Grace

"Memorable characters you'll root for until the last page is turned."
–Gail Ward Olmsted, best-selling author of *Landscape of a Marriage*

"*Reaching for Grace* is so well-written, it feels like coming home. This is a story about learning to accept the help and strength of others to accomplish things we could never accomplish alone."
–Barbara A. Luker, author of *I Carry Your Heart*

"Anna Daugherty's adept storytelling takes readers on an emotional journey through this poignant narrative, painting detailed scenes that engage them in the characters' lives. The captivating narrative, filled with themes of faith, love, and family, is impossible to put down. With characters' relationships realistically complex, and emotionally satisfying, *Reaching for Grace* is a must-read for readers seeking faith-affirming and uplifting stories."
–Michelle Caffrey, award winning author of *Desire in Dairyland*

"*Reaching for Grace* by Anna Daugherty is a charming story that will be loved not only by readers of Christian fiction, but also those who like a wholesome and heartwarming tale of how two people overcome the barriers they themselves have erected. I was so invested in these characters that I read this entire book in just one afternoon! A strong five-stars!"
–Diane Nagatomo, author of *The Butterfly Café*

"Anna Daugherty's *Reaching for Grace* is relatable, never predictable, a perfect realization of layered intensity and reflection. A joy to read, the hopeful perspective lingers in the heart and mind. Highly recommended. Five stars."
–Shirley Miller Kamada, Author of *No Quiet Water*

"*Reaching for Grace* explores a little-acknowledged reality within Christian churches and communities: reluctance to truly show ourselves—flaws and all—to others. ... Anna Daugherty's newest book gently covers this terrain—the high cost of hiding who we truly are from others."
–Pamela Norsworthy, Author of *War Bonds*

"Daugherty's latest novel returns the reader to the community she introduced in her debut novel, *Outside of Grace.* Full of real people with familiar anxieties, doubts, and insecurities, this novel offers a potent lesson on what constitutes a truly authentic Christian life. Bravo to Daugherty for her sophomore effort— an uplifting, honest novel, theologically sound and beautifully and compassionately written."
–Cam Torrens, award-winning author of *Stable, False Summit,* and *Scorched*

"He has saved us and called us with a holy calling, not according to our works, but according to his own purpose and grace, which was given to us in Christ Jesus before time began."
–2 Timothy 1:9

Reaching for Grace

Chapter One

Only someone with the name of a bird would show up to a 10K race barefoot in a long yellow skirt, a mauve tank top, and a colorful head wrap. The sun echoed her warm colors as it rose over the horizon to greet the runners.

Hollis walked up to Wren as he pinned his number to his shirt. "Are you running in that, Atwood?"

"Could you not judge my clothes?"

His hands flared out in innocence. "I'm not."

"I don't run, Suits. I'm the water girl, halfway down." She waved a hand toward her ancient Forester, a bright orange cooler sitting next to it.

"Well, I wasn't planning to stop, but since you asked so nicely." Hollis gave her a wink.

"You're a computer guy, Suits. You'll be lucky to make it that far."

"Harsh words from a girl who doesn't run."

She almost smiled, but it disappeared. "Whatever. I have to go set up. Good luck."

Well wishes came rarely from her. Hollis took it as a good sign, heading to the start line to join the others warming up.

As a member of the church hosting the event, Hollis recognized nearly all the other runners and walkers. Between the moms with strollers and older couples in tracksuits, this was clearly a fundraiser and not a serious run, which gave Hollis hope for finishing at the front. He might be the tech geek Wren Atwood accused him of being, but he had trained for this.

Ridley Bay City Park hummed with energy, quieting only when the pastor stood on a temporary platform at the edge of the park and took the microphone. Micah Sanford thanked Grace Church for the turnout and donations for the Romero family. He read a verse about running races before inviting up José Romero, the father of the kid they were raising money for. The kid with stage three cancer.

Romero spoke briefly, then ended with a prayer. Energy buzzed again as everyone lined up.

With a horn blast, they took off. Hollis held the front with a handful of others.

The first two miles were easy enough. As he closed the third, he slowed to catch his breath when he spotted the church's resident flower child.

"Atwood." He joined her behind the water table and reached around her for a cup.

"Wrong side of the table, Suits."

He leaned an arm against the cooler and glanced down at the navy Rice shirt he'd chosen to hide sweat stains. "Does this look like a suit to you?"

"I guess I wouldn't know the difference, would I?" she said, deadpan. Then, with a deep breath, she turned and smiled at another runner as she passed him a cup of water.

Once the runner was gone, Wren spoke without looking at him. "Get back out there."

He would much rather pester her, but if he stood a chance at the top three, he had to go. "Can't wait to watch me walk away, huh?" He shot her another grin before tossing his water cup in the trash and sprinting to make up for the minute he had lost.

Another mile passed underfoot as Hollis caught back up to the lead, realizing now the crucial mistake he had made in training. He ran on a treadmill most of the summer, in a climate-controlled gym. Out here, the Texas coast made it feel like running in a sauna.

"Who plans a race in August?" Hollis grumbled, pressing forward as sweat beaded down his back. Then again, nobody planned to have a child diagnosed with cancer.

When the church planned the event, an "anonymous donor" offered to match whatever money they raised. Everyone quickly made the connection to Hollis, though. Once his Bible study group knew, they doubled down on their fundraising efforts, trying to make it as costly for him as possible. He didn't mind. Matching their funds would hurt less than this race did.

Hollis examined the leads ahead of him. If he slowed, he could finish in the middle with a too-cool-to-care attitude. If he pushed himself, he could possibly make the top three, but someone might have to call an ambulance. Of course, getting fourth was pointless, a forgettable no-man's-land.

One of Grace Church's regulars, Jack Shields, held a steady first place. The guy had run in some of the same college circles as Hollis's twin sisters before he graduated and married the pastor's daughter a few months ago. Hollis tried to remember what sport he had played. Track?

Behind him, a dad who had a couple of kids held second. He had a few extra years on Hollis and a desk job. Hollis could beat him.

Ignoring the suffocating heat that threatened to melt his lungs, Hollis passed the older guy a half mile out and crossed the finish line in second place, a few yards behind the track kid.

Hollis folded forward, hands on his knees, as a small crowd cheered for each runner coming in.

Shields came back to shake hands. "Nice run, Hollis."

God had given the guy a couple more inches. Longer legs. Not fair.

"You too, Shields. Did you run track?"

The kid shook his head and grinned. "Nah, just for fun."

Right. Because any of this was fun.

Looking past Hollis, Shields patted his shoulder as he headed back to the finish line. "I'm gonna wave my wife in. See ya on the stage."

Hollis glanced back just in time to see the kid grab the pastor's daughter in a hug. Shields was faster at everything.

At the water table, Hollis downed two cups. His shirt was drenched in sweat, and the navy didn't hide it as well as he had hoped. With a towel from a nearby table, he wiped his face and neck.

Making his way around the group at the finish line, Hollis shook hands with the Sanford family, Associate Pastor Kaminski, and a few others. The Romeros were there too, and he greeted the dad in Spanish.

"I heard about your matching donation," Romero said, pulling Hollis's handshake into a sweaty back pat. "You have no idea how much it means to us. Thank you."

"Happy to help." Because Hollis did have an idea.

The Romero family had five kids, one with special needs and now one with cancer. Hollis knew what it meant: the doctors' appointments, the travel back and forth to specialists in Houston, the strain on the parents, on their marriage, their jobs, and their children. It was a lonely world, one few people understood. And Hollis knew it well.

Eventually the crowd around the finish line thinned as the last few stragglers walked in. Micah Sanford stepped up to the stage to announce the race winners, waving the top three up. His daughter, Ava, handed out a medal to each, along with a hand-drawn card from the Romero kid.

"Hollis," she said, handing over his.

"Thanks, Sanford—or, Shields, I guess."

She lifted her chin and flashed a smile at First Place. "Mrs. Shields." She was about the same age as his sister Margarita and living a life Maggie never would.

Hollis gave her a quick grin and looked past her. Despite wanting to know the Sanfords better, he needed distance. It was a reflex.

Once the festivities officially ended, the crowd cleared out quickly, driven away by the hundred-degree weather, until only church leadership and the cleanup crew remained. Hollis found Wren emptying coolers next to a truck. She had switched her long, light brown hair into a loose braid, with a dandelion stuck in the headband. A look so natural and raw, he had to admit she fascinated him. Because, yes, he did spend most of his time around suits. And nothing about Wren Atwood was buttoned up for presentation.

"Got second," he said, tossing the silver medal to her.

She watched it fall to the pavement without lifting a hand.

His pride wouldn't let him pick it up now.

"And to think, all the money you spent on the personal trainer, you could have given to the Romeros."

Hollis rocked back on his heels. "I'm giving them a ton."

"Congratulations. Isn't there a verse about giving in secret, not for praise? Or have you not actually read the Bible?"

He blew out a breath. "It was supposed to be anonymous."

She lifted the last cooler onto the truck bed. "I'm sure you were simply devastated that everyone found out."

No, he wasn't. Because the "secret" elevated him in everyone else's minds. But somehow, giving away money disappointed Wren, like everything else he did. And despite decades of disappointing his family, he still hadn't learned how to stop trying.

"Feeling extra salty today, Atwood?" Leaning against the truck, he hoped he didn't stink.

Taking a deep breath, she blew it out slowly. Her eyes met his. "Sorry. I guess so. It's hot. And I skipped breakfast."

He could fix that problem. "I hear you. Want to go grab some food?"

Her eyebrows shot up, and she pressed a hand to her heart in mock surprise. "Why, Hollis, that almost sounds like a normal date."

The running joke in which he asked her out on terrible dates had become a sore spot in his life. He forced a casual grin. "Guess I'm low on ideas."

"You? Never. The invite to a taxidermist was pure creative genius. I almost agreed, just to watch you squirm even more than me."

He laughed. She knew him well, which probably explained her disdain. "Consider it a standing invitation."

Wren shook her head. "As fun as it sounds, taxidermy or lunch, I'll have to pass on both."

"Your loss," he said with a shrug, pushing away from the truck to leave. "Oh and keep the medal. Wouldn't want you to litter." He turned and stepped away, before she could pick up the second-place medal and chunk it at his head.

.   .   .

Once Suits' motorcycle was completely out of sight, Wren climbed into her car and settled shaking hands on the wheel. The heat was getting to her. It had nothing to do with Suits or his stupid medal in her purse.

With a whispered prayer for Gumpy to start, she turned the key, and he responded with his familiar grumble. Breathing deeply, she picked up hints of lavender from her own clothes, sweat, and the salty, humid air flowing through vents that refused to blow cold.

Willfully ignoring the scent of burning rubber, she turned onto the road. "Just a few more days, Gumpy," she whispered, patting the dashboard.

In a few days, she could replace that belt. But for now, she refused to spend a single penny until after she signed the closing documents for her house on Monday morning. She would need every cent to get the bank to approve her. Which meant a free lunch had sounded like a good idea …

Wren cranked a manual window down and blew a breath out, pushing the anxiety away, along with a pesky mental image of Suits and those dark eyes. The gym shorts and worn college tee were different for him. But the single-dimpled, contagious smile was the same. Like a virus, he had infected the church with his charisma. Surely he planned to control local government next. The fact that his running-for-president charm didn't work on her drove him insane.

He had asked her out once, to his company's Christmas event. An utterly superficial invitation, with questionable motives. And for some reason, he asked her in front of their friends, which meant they all saw when she told him off, calling it the worst date ever. But Hollis was an expert at saving his own skin, and he twisted it into a joke, asking her on every horrible date he could dream up since then.

Now, their friends had pitted them against each other like caricatures: the rich boy and poor girl, fated for love. Though they didn't say it in quite so many words. People based her moods on their pseudo-relationship. *"Hollis, why's your girlfriend mad?"*

The phoniness of it all drove her crazy, and he seemed to enjoy that. Nothing Suits did was genuine; he lived for an image, and she wanted no part of it.

But today … today, he had asked her out to a plain lunch, with no one around for the show. And she had thought about saying yes.

Distracted and driving on autopilot, Wren headed toward the docks where Captain Todd carried passengers off to Kinney Island and away from the worries of the mainland. Diverting, she took a left and drove north instead.

Easing onto Florida Street, she soon parked in front of a 947-square-foot house with blue siding and a front porch lined with a white rail. Few people knew this house existed. Fewer still knew Wren was the reason for the *Pending* sign in the front yard.

While she was proud to be buying her first home, she kept it to herself. Telling someone about the house before signing the documents might jinx it. Worse than her superstitions, though, she feared what people might say.

Church friends and coworkers would only see the weeds, the window unit held up by a tilting tower of bricks, and the sheets hanging as curtains. They would try to talk Wren out of it. So would Mavis and Lark, her mother and sister, but for entirely different reasons—cost and commitment being at the top of the list. They would prefer Wren live with them in San Antonio and fund all their habits and addictions.

No one could talk her out of this. To Wren, this house meant more than a project. It was a promise.

Growing up in trailers, apartments, and on friends' couches, she craved a place that lasted. This house, this land, and the enormous oak tree towering over it from the backyard all spoke of permanence. This house wasn't wandering in vain search of hope; it was deeply rooted in the ability to build it. Roof problems aside, this house had been here for decades and wouldn't be erased at the first sign of trouble.

"We can work on each other for as long as it takes," she whispered to the house. Tying herself to this house, in heart and ink, meant Wren was no longer erasable.

She watched as a couple of teenage boys made their way down the street, poking around the cars parked along the curb, their pants hanging halfway down their thighs. They were the kind of kids she had hung out with in high school, looking for an unlocked door and forgotten wallet. An unlikely find in a neighborhood filled with adults who knew those tricks.

Wren raised an eyebrow at them as they wandered past her car and grinned at their backs. Shaking her head and ignoring the protesting squeal from the engine, she turned around and headed to her apartment.

When she reached her apartment complex in the middle of the city, Wren parked and gave Gumpy a quick pat before hurrying into her apartment to avoid picking up the scent of the neighbor's weed on her clothes. Only two more days of that shuffle.

She had graduated from high school on time and completed some secondary education, even if massage therapy school wasn't "real" college. She held a steady job—more than steady, based on the hours she worked. Now all she needed was the key that meant she had overcome the odds.

Come Monday morning, she would have that stamp of approval from society, the one that proved she had broken free from the chains of transience. The home title was a certificate declaring: I Made It.

Once Wren had her certificate, she would be complete.

Chapter Two

Closing on a house, especially someone's first house, seemed like an occasion for shoes. Wren had two options: a simple white sandal or brown ankle boots. Of course, if she was giving the title company this much money, they should let her in regardless—shoes or no shoes. But what if she showed up without shoes and they changed their minds about her? What if the loan officer realized this was a mistake and backed out?

Wren inhaled deeply and reached for the sandals. She could almost imagine the scent of real leather wafting from the imitation straps. Pairing the sandals with a billowing orange maxi dress and floral kimono, she filled in the colors her features lacked.

After flipping off all the lights in the apartment, she stood in the dark, taking a steadying breath. It flowed up from her toes, lifting her head with the apartment's scent of lavender, sandalwood, and her neighbor's weed. She was ready for this.

Gumpy made the drive to the title company as proudly as he had made the drive to the coast six years ago—with a puff and a purr.

The title company operated out of an office in downtown Ridley Bay, which didn't seem fair. Surely they could cut down on the closing costs by having a more modest building somewhere else in Ridley Bay. And now, on the most expensive day of her life, they wanted her to pay for parking? Not happening.

Wren circled the block, looking for a free spot somewhere, while monitoring Gumpy's trusty clock, the only reliable thing he offered.

The Monday morning crowd and all their cars filled the area. The nearest free parking would take too long to walk from, so she pulled into a spot behind a similarly beat-up truck. It was more subtle than taking the high-contrast spot between two sleek, black, look-at-me-I'm-rich sedans.

Within minutes, Wren made her way into the office and sat down at an absurdly long table with only two other people: the loan officer and the title originator. Three, if you counted the stack of papers the size of a small person.

The man with the title company laughed when she eyed it. "You'll feel like a superstar, signing your autograph a hundred times today." It was obviously a rehearsed joke.

Only four papers in, she regretted the bangles on her wrist, jingling with every signature and initial. *Wren Atwood. WA. WA. WA.*

"This one certifies you understand late payments will be charged a 10 percent fee on top of the principal, interest, taxes, and insurance," Mr. Jokes said, pushing the paper toward her.

She had followed an online checklist and a book from the library every step of the way, even asking for her closing documents before the meeting, so she could review them. She knew exactly what she was signing. But doing it still terrified her. Her hand shook, and the bangles only exaggerated the motion.

While Mr. Jokes licked his pointer finger and thumbed to the next page, Wren slipped her hands under the table, silently switching the bangles to the other hand.

The time came to transfer the money from the bank.

What if something went wrong? Maybe someone had stolen her identity this morning and her accounts were emptied. What if the bank made an error—no, what if a second Great Depression had hit while they sat cocooned in this office?

Breathe. Wren closed her eyes and inhaled fresh paper, printer ink, Pine-Sol, and … Axe body spray? *Really, Mr. Jokes?*

"So, you're a masseuse?" Mr. Jokes asked while they waited for Mr. Blue Tie, the loan officer, to return with terrible news.

Wren opened her eyes. "No. I'm a massage therapist."

He shrugged like it was the same thing. It wasn't. "You're buying a house pretty young."

She hadn't felt young since middle school. At twenty-six, she had worked toward this for a decade. "What's a normal age?"

Mr. Jokes twirled his pen around his fingers. "At least thirties, I guess." He looked to be in them himself.

"Why give rent money to someone else when I can invest in something I own?" she asked.

He gave a half smile that made Wren think of words like martinis and money markets. "Most young, single people just prefer something like a condo—gyms, pools, parties." He was clearly "most people." And by condo, he meant anything more glamorous than her Northside shack.

"Not me." *Most people* probably hadn't spent their lives on borrowed couches, craving the day they walked on their own piece of grass.

Thankfully Mr. Blue Tie saved her from any more of Mr. Jokes' observations, though his appearance was about as welcome as a stingray when you're escaping a jellyfish.

Until he spoke. "Everything's cleared."

Something between a strangled sigh and a joyous shout escaped her lips, and Wren tried to cover it with a cough.

The rest of the paperwork flew by, and soon Mr. Jokes dropped a silver key into Wren's hand, along with a branded mug for a housewarming gift, no doubt paid for by the closing costs. Wren clutched the key tightly, thanked both men, and wrapped her arm around the stack of closing documents. Her certificate.

Her heart threatened to fly right out of the room, and Wren chased it. She hurried out of the stuffy building, while John Denver crooned in her mind, "Today Is the First Day of the Rest of My Life." His voice reminded her of the back seat of a station wagon that was at least twenty years older than she was. Gumpy, on the other hand, was nearly her age.

And next to Gumpy stood a woman in uniform.

All of Wren's internal celebration died away. "Wait!" She hurried to the woman's side.

The officer raised an eyebrow at Wren as she slapped the ticket onto the windshield. "This car's been here nearly three hours, ma'am."

"I know, I'm sorry, I had a meeting, and I didn't have any cash—"

"You can pay on your phone," she said, crossing her arms, already bored with the excuses.

Wren couldn't, not without a data plan. Not with years of penny-pinching. "I can move it right now." She reached into her purse, rummaging for the keys.

"Bates!" A male voice called out.

Wren's eyes flicked up to the woman's badge. *P. Bates.* Dread and anticipation flooded her. She knew that voice all too well. If she had a list of the worst possible situations to run into him, this would be in the top five. She'd gone from jellyfish to stingray to shark.

P. Bates brightened at the sight of him approaching from behind Wren. "Hollis, how are you?"

He worked somewhere around here, in one of the high-rises. Suits' hand landed on Wren's arm, and he pulled her into a side hug. "Better now, seeing my two favorite people meet."

P. Bates turned her chin down and gave Suits the look of a scolding mother. She was the right age to pull it off. "Your girlfriend needs to pay for parking."

Seriously? Why does everyone assume—

"She really should, sorry about that," Hollis replied. After going to church together for three years, she could hear the smile in his tone without even seeing it.

"How's Little League going?" he asked.

Mama Bates gave a long-winded answer about her son's incredible fielding and the coach insisting that he learn to slide better. Hollis gave a few apparently welcome tips, from some reserve of baseball knowledge.

Finally, Mama Bates reached over and pulled the ticket off the windshield. She pointed a finger at Hollis and Wren—still a side-hugging unit. "No more freebies."

"You got it. Can't wait to hear how Saturday's game goes."

Mama Bates waved them off and headed down the street, looking for more lives to destroy. And Suits finally let go of Wren, turning to face her instead, with all his black-haired, black-suited pomp. She was only glad for her height that brought them nearly eye to eye; at least he couldn't literally look down on her, whether or not he did metaphorically.

"Are parking meters part of your protest?" he asked.

"I'm not protesting anything."

"I thought you avoided my neighborhood like the plague."

Wren sighed and slipped off her sandals. The concrete was hot and angry, but a salty breeze balanced it, twirling her skirt around her ankles. She unlocked the passenger door of her car and set the nearly sentient stack of papers on the seat, along with her sandals and the mug she hated but would certainly keep. "You can't claim all of downtown as your neighborhood, Hollis."

His boyish, dimpled smile reminded her why he could do things like get parking tickets shredded with only a few sentences. He gestured to the building she had just left. "I work here, and my condo is a block away, what else do I call it?"

These people and their condos. She wasn't sure what he did or how there was enough money in the entire city to pay for his lifestyle, but she wouldn't give him the satisfaction of her asking.

"So, what are you doing over here?" he asked.

Her hand raised of its own accord, dangling the silver key between her fingers. It had been a secret so long, it felt strange to admit it. But it was official, nothing stood between her and her certificate now. No one could take it away. "Closing on my house."

"What? Atwood, congrats!" Suits' face lit up, his dark eyes wrinkling into slits as he pulled her into a hug.

She gave a halfhearted hug back, keeping part of herself firmly in a containment zone. "Thanks."

Hollis let her go with one last shoulder squeeze. "Why didn't you tell me? We need to celebrate."

Wren shrugged and traced the outline of the key. "I wanted to wait until I had it."

"And now you do." He glanced at a fancy, heavy watch on his wrist, halfway hidden under the sleeves of his baby-blue button-up. "Come on, I've got time for a quick lunch to celebrate. You can't say no."

Wren's eyes narrowed. "Not in a cemetery or dark alley or something, right?"

He laughed. "No, a real lunch, on the docks, in a normal restaurant."

"Nobody's here, Hollis. You don't have to ask me out." She didn't want obligatory invitations.

Suits shifted the leather bag hanging from his shoulder, and Wren caught the rich, earthy scent of it. "This isn't a date. It's congratulations."

She couldn't deny the fact that it sounded better than celebrating as a party of one. The house deserved to be celebrated, even with a frenemy. Not to mention, he had just saved her a couple hundred bucks on a parking ticket. "Then we have to split the bill."

"I'll pay and call it a housewarming gift."

"No other gifts, then. No welcome mat or *Live, Laugh, Love* prints or anything." Was she agreeing to this?

Suits scoffed. "Over my dead body." The spark in his eyes said he knew who his killer would be.

Wren couldn't help but laugh in response. An answer slipped out that surprised them both. "Deal."

His face lit into a smile that could sell you a beach house in Kansas. He was more contagious than the flu.

Chapter Three

Hiding his surprise as best he could, Hollis ditched his suit jacket and leather bag in Wren's car. She wanted to walk the three blocks to the docks, which meant he'd be sweating by the time they got there. While she locked the car, he rolled up the sleeves of his shirt.

He didn't actually have time for this lunch, but he would make it. If he suggested dinner, she would change her mind before dinner ever came. Hollis sent off a quick email to reschedule his next meeting and paid for her parking spot on the phone app before she could argue.

"Tell me about the house," he said, as they strolled down the block toward the bay.

Wren twirled the bracelets on her wrist. "You would hate it."

"What? Why would you say that?"

"It's not a condo or a mansion. There's no pool or movie theater. It's just a house."

Hollis snickered and bumped her arm. "You're right, if a house doesn't have a ballroom, I hate it."

She bumped him back. "It's small. Two bedrooms. Blue. There's a giant oak tree in the backyard."

"Sounds cute."

This time she laughed. "Not really. But I'll make it cute."

"I'm sure you will. What's first on the agenda?"

She hummed a cheerful sound. "I just want to go put my very own key in the lock right now and learn the house—its creaks and quirks. I can't do anything to it until I know what it wants."

"The house knows what it wants?"

Her smile flashed brief as lightning. "Yes."

He believed her. She appeared more connected to life than he had ever been. Maybe a house did know what it wanted.

The last block they walked in silence, and Hollis didn't dare break it. They didn't have many conversations last this long without slipping into unfriendly territory. He was going to win her over, if only to prove he could. What he would do with her after that, he wasn't sure.

There were three options for lunch on the marina that ranged from a food trailer to an upscale restaurant. Hollis headed toward the middle ground—a seafood shack popular with the cook-your-catch crowd. Wren slowed, studying the boats anchored along the docks.

"Have you been out on the water?" Hollis asked.

"Almost every Saturday."

That stopped him short. "Really?"

She nodded, leaning over the walkway railing in front of a white yacht. "Kinney Island."

A broken series of islands outlined Ridley Bay, serving as a shield and taking on the brunt of the gulf's wind and waves, leaving their bay calm and relatively clear—at least by Texas standards. Kinney Island was a car-free, undeveloped swath of land, mainly used for fishing, from what he'd heard. And Hollis was not a fish guy. "Never been."

"You can find the best seashells out there, ones you would never see on the bay."

"You go every Saturday?"

"Mostly. Captain Todd operates the ferry, and I found out he has a weak spot for lightning whelks. I give him the ones I find, and he gives me free rides."

Always resourceful.

A gull landed on the yacht and barked at them while the coastal breeze blew Wren's skirt against Hollis's legs. Dressed in something floral and bright, she resembled a garden and smelled like one too—not just the flowers but all of it: sun, rain, and earth. He could get used to it. But this was congratulations, not a date. "Do you like fried seafood?" Hollis asked.

"Love it, but you're vegetarian."

Point to Atwood for knowing that. He couldn't help but grin. "Yeah, they've got some great pasta dishes I can eat."

"Then let's do it."

Luckily it wasn't busy, and they were seated quickly, with a view of the bay through a dirty window. The table still had crumbs on it from the last guests and their server wiped it while taking their drink orders.

"So, Atwood, when are we having a housewarming party?" Hollis asked when their server left.

Her features, all the colors of the earth, pinched. She pulled her bottom lip in. "It's not really a housewarming type of house …"

"What do you mean?"

She shrugged. "Let's just keep it between us for now."

An odd secret. "Where is it?"

"Northside."

Hollis tucked a grimace deep inside. He wouldn't let his sisters drive through that area, much less live there. It bordered the channel and the former industrial area—before the smokestacks were forced out of town by health complaints. He had taken part in a couple of rejuvenation efforts in the area, volunteering with a Perla Tech shirt on, but he wouldn't even dream of visiting the Northside at night. "Do you have any pictures?"

She nodded.

"Well?"

With a sigh, she pulled out her phone. She flipped through several photos before landing on one. Raising an eyebrow in obvious threat, she finally turned the phone around, revealing a tiny house with peeling siding, white windows, and … a wheelchair ramp? Before he saw any more, it was gone. Wren tucked the phone away. "It's not fancy, but it's mine."

"It's perfect then. Is it completely yours? Or still mostly the bank's?"

A flush rose up her neck, turning her cheeks pink as she scoffed. "Do you have to be like that?"

Stupid. He hadn't meant that to be offensive; it was clarification. "Wait, I didn't mean that in a bad way. I was just … Never mind. What are you ordering?"

With a withering scowl, her eyes darted from him to the door, but their server returned with two waters before she could make a run for it.

Hollis ordered a linguine and vegetable plate in creamy crab sauce, sans crab. Wren ordered a shrimp plate.

"So, why vegetarian?" she asked.

He shrugged. "Better for the environment, right?"

Wren's eyebrows pinched, and her eyes danced with a laugh. "That doesn't seem like you. You probably own a private jet."

Hollis raised his hand. "I solemnly swear I do not own a jet." Though he certainly wasn't against the idea …

That earned a genuine laugh from her. "You know, if the guys at church catch wind of this lunch, the girlfriend joke will never die."

He only shrugged and took another bite of pasta. That joke needed to die. Maybe he could pay them off. "Hey, have you been to the wetlands park since they redid it?"

"I didn't think it was reopened yet."

He nodded. "Last weekend, and it's really nice. They added a huge boardwalk for accessibility."

"I'll have to check it out," she said, taking him up on the distraction. "It's the best place for escaping tourists and spotting cranes."

"You're a bird watcher?"

"Well, I have eyes and they're hard to miss." She quirked an eyebrow in challenge. "Why do you like it?"

"Like you said, it's quiet. That can be hard to find when you've lived in this town your entire life."

"Is it really your past here that makes it hard to escape, or is it being Hollis?"

"Both." She had a knack for reading between the lines. Being the founder and CEO of one of the largest companies in Ridley Bay did make it difficult to go undetected.

Time must have warped because before he knew what had happened, their server was back, clearing emptied plates and drinks, and they had talked about everything from the best parks in the city to their favorite songs. The server asked about dessert, and Wren shook her head, looking as dazed as Hollis felt. They had made it through lunch without fighting.

Outside the restaurant, muggy heat hit him like a brick wall, beading sweat at the edges of his hairline. Wren lifted her long hair off her neck, letting the breeze sweep through it as they walked.

"Thanks for lunch," she said quietly, probably reluctantly too.

"You're surprisingly tolerable company."

She laughed and side-eyed him for a moment, genuine surprise on her face. "You stole my line."

When they reached her car, Hollis grabbed his jacket and bag.

"Oh, wait," Wren said, leaning back into the car. "I believe this is yours." She dangled the silver race medal by its red ribbon.

Hollis smirked in defeat as he took it. "Thanks, I think I dropped it."

Wren shook her head with a wry smile. "So careless."

Hollis's phone rang for the third time. "I better go. Congrats again, Atwood." If she were any other girl, he would have hugged her. But she was Wren, so he settled for a wave.

Finally checking his watch, Hollis realized he was more than late getting back to the office. He rarely lost track of time, and it had felt so good, he couldn't muster any guilt over it.

He had been recruited to help with his sister Maggie all day yesterday and dealt with a crashed app all morning today. Taking a solid hour away from problem after problem was exactly what he needed.

Hollis strolled into the office, fielding a few surprised comments about his late lunch and ignoring his partner's huffy attitude. Evan Quincy had been huffy since the day they'd met in college; a late lunch would not change anything.

Settling into his desk, he had to admit he didn't mind the problems here. The problems here could all be broken down into a series of ones and zeros. If life were this simple, he could figure out the bug that had wrenched its way between him and Wren and break that down.

Quincy knocked on the doorframe.

"Hey man," Hollis said, barely glancing up from his screen. "What's up?"

"Saw that email you sent me about the PearlEye updates. I get the changes to the navigation, but why are we phasing it in with half a dozen stages? Why not do it all at once and be done with it?"

"Right." Hollis leaned back in his chair and laced his hands behind his head. "Tell you what, we do it all at once, and you can deal with Mags when she loses it."

"Is that just Maggie, or is everybody like that?"

Hollis didn't care for the way Quincy asked that. No, not everybody was like Maggie. But PearlEye users had similarities. They were all trapped inside their bodies. No one knew exactly how their minds worked, and many preferred to pretend their minds didn't work at all. But Maggie's certainly did. "That's why we have research partners. They'll tell you it's not just Maggie."

"Seems like a waste of time."

"It's not." Hollis stood, truly annoyed now. "Get to know the people we make this stuff for, and you'll believe me. In fact, it'd be better if we didn't even have to do this and got the user-adaptive system in place."

Quincy frowned over a pair of glasses. "Fine. Well. The team got the seizure tracker back online fast."

"If we failed a single user today though, we'll hear about it. Did Vance put out a statement?"

"Not yet. Why we need one is beyond me. Every app crashes sometimes. I'll give you foolproof software when you give me unicorn blood."

"That right there," Hollis said with a finger point. "That's why we have PR. We need you to stay behind the computer."

Quincy grinned. "Exactly." Glancing out the doorway, he whispered a curse and disappeared down the hall.

A second later, the apparition that scared off Quincy appeared in the doorway: Graham Vance, their PR guy. Somewhere in his mid-40s, he was practically ancient in the Perla Tech office. But he brought a dose of reality into their office—a heavy-handed cynicism that a team of IT geeks needed. Otherwise, they all thought they were the next Bill Gates or Steve Jobs, depending on their affiliation. Together, Vance and Hollis whipped out a statement with a bit more panache than Quincy could have managed and settled it.

That was the magic of work. Here, every problem had a solution and Hollis could find it. Outside the office doors, though, he was powerless. He failed to find the answers for Maggie, for his mother, for Wren. Outside of the boundaries of work, the world needed too much, and Hollis was never quite enough for it.

Chapter Four

Gumpy smelled like real leather and a man's suit jacket as Wren drove north. Did she just eat lunch with Suits—and not hate it? Dangerous territory. She had no business spending time with a man like that. They were all the same: arrogant, shallow, judgmental …

The mental image of Hollis's dark hair and matching eyes faded away as she turned onto Florida Street and saw the blue siding of the house— *her* house—come into view.

Approaching the house slowly, she eased into the carport at a crawl. Though she had been inside once with a listing agent and driven by countless times, it all felt different now. The previous owners, whoever they were, had vacated the property before Wren even saw it. It had sat here alone since then, waiting for her. Now, without fanfare or angelic chorus, it was hers.

When she stepped out of her car, the gravelly driveway pricked her bare feet. A wheelchair ramp led up to the front porch, but Wren bypassed it, carefully toeing through the weedy yard, *her* yard. Not caring what the neighbors thought of her, she knelt and ran a hand through the earth beneath her. She had dreamed of this moment for as long as she could remember. A plot of land with her name on it.

Gently tracing the top of the *Pending Sale* sign, she headed toward the three front steps. Wren turned, facing her neighborhood from the front porch.

Neighbors. The word buzzed her blood. For the first time, it meant something good. She wanted to know each one. Which, in this neighborhood, meant brushing up on her Spanish. Having grown up in San Antonio, she had the basics already.

The house across the street held two plastic lawn chairs on its porch, along with dozens of little knickknacks and flowerpots. Maybe one day she would know the names of the family inside, maybe even learn the stories behind some of the decorations strewn around the porch—which ones a grandmother had passed down, which were handmade, which ones the dog had chewed.

Turning from the neighbors, Wren slipped the key into the front door and listened to the click of the lock. When she turned the handle, nothing happened. Wren double-checked the lock, then pushed a little harder. The bottom of the door slipped in a half inch, and she pressed down on the door, giving it a harder press. Finally, it popped open.

The frame was sinking. The inspector had explained it. Despite his dismal report, the place was livable. It was mostly cosmetic issues, or minor annoyances, nothing dangerous. And Wren's standards had been low: cheap and unmoving. Nothing a semitruck would pick up and carry away.

Pink carpet and the scent of cat urine welcomed her into the living area. Those could be fixed. The previous owners had left sheets hanging in the window as curtains. "Roses," she whispered, tracing the tiny pink flowers on the pattern. They clearly belonged to the house, though she intended to replace them with real curtains as soon as she could.

The carpet continued into the kitchen on her left, and Wren trailed her hand along the wall as she walked, closing her eyes and memorizing the steps. At 947 square feet, this would be the largest place she had lived since moving to Ridley Bay.

A tan laminate countertop and white cabinets that had turned yellow framed the square kitchen. It held black appliances and a green backsplash that appeared to be made of floor tiles. Wren opened each door and drawer, imagining pulling a bowl from one, a spoon from another.

Finally, she turned from the kitchen, crossed the living area, and headed to the right side of the house. A narrow hallway held a bedroom on each end and a bathroom in the middle.

She walked to the bedroom facing the backyard first, the one that would be hers, and felt the emptiness of the space, letting it tell her where her furniture would go.

Next, she stopped in the bathroom, where the first thing she noticed was a giant tear in the wallpaper above the toilet. Disappointment gave way to interest as Wren traced a finger over the rip—shaped like a rose.

"Your name is definitely Rosa, isn't it?" she spoke into the empty air. She raised the window in the bathroom and walked back through the house to lift the rest. It would help with the smell and introduce her to the sounds: dogs barking, cars buzzing on the nearby highway, and the occasional cry of a child from somewhere on the street.

Thoroughly satisfied with her perusal and naming, Wren headed out the back door to the small porch and sat on the top of two steps that led into the sizable yard. A beautiful oak stood, tall and permanent, in the center of the yard. If she added a second tree, she could string up a hammock between them and sway in the breeze. Wren inhaled and closed her eyes, letting the tears swim past her eyelashes.

I Made It.

•   •   •

To make up for missing Monday, Wren planned to work long days the rest of the week. She had enough seniority at Renew Wellness Spa to mostly set her own schedule with her regular clients, but she still took walk-ins whenever she could. Walk-ins helped fill the gaps in her budget, even though they didn't tip as well. For six years, she had saved every penny she could for a down payment, with countless setbacks along the way. Now, she wanted the extra work for her renovation budget.

By the end of Wednesday, her muscles were sore from leaning over client after client, kneading out tension and healing whatever she could. Sleeping on the floor at the house last night hadn't helped.

Wren rubbed at her shoulders as she walked into her old apartment. It seemed alive with tendrils that wanted to pull her in and hold her back.

She wanted out of it as quickly as possible. Luckily her coworker Nick had a truck and had agreed to help her move, in exchange for pizza and beer.

She had moved most of the boxes on her own last night. But she needed help with the larger items.

The last few boxes were loaded into the back of Gumpy before Nick finally arrived. He hopped out of the truck with an apologetic look as his girlfriend climbed out of the passenger side. The lady kept tabs on Nick's every move, a classic stage five clinger.

"Thought we could use more muscle," he said with a shrug. His girlfriend didn't exactly look like "muscle," but Wren welcomed her, fake nails and all.

They loaded Wren's mattress and bed frame onto the truck and piled the small round dining table on top of it. Wren led them through town to her house.

Nick blew out a whistle when they got out of their cars, meeting at the curb. "Fancy place."

Wren grinned. "Okay, so it needs some updating, but it has character."

Once they had the furniture inside and Gumpy unloaded, Wren gave them the tour. It took all of half a minute.

"The lot is a great size," Nick admitted as they walked through the backyard. Even the girlfriend agreed.

"That's what I wanted most," Wren said.

"How close is the channel?"

"About two blocks."

Nick scratched at trimmed facial hair—he always griped about the spa's policy against beards. "What's the flood zone?"

"I don't know, but I didn't have to get flood insurance, so I think I'm fine."

"No?" Nick mumbled something inaudible as he walked around the back base of the foundation and kicked at a sliver in the concrete. "Well, it looks good. There's some work to do, but it's got potential."

His comment was the highest praise. After they had made it through the awkward stage of being new coworkers and feeling out each other's interest levels, Nick had settled into more of a dad-like figure. At least, what Wren assumed was dad-like. Hers had vanished before she even entered the world.

They made three more trips to haul the couch, armchair, dining chairs, and dresser to the house. The last trip involved a washer and dryer. Nearby apartment neighbors were moving soon and had sold their set to her. Now Wren knew why they didn't want to move them. The bulky behemoths were a nightmare without a dolly, but Wren roped in a couple of guys from next door to help, handing them each a twenty-dollar bill.

With everything in the house, Nick and his girlfriend waved farewell, and Wren headed back to the apartment. Her lease was up by tomorrow at five, and she'd be working all day, so she had to have it clean by tonight. She scrubbed and patched late into the night, hoping to earn the security deposit back.

Finally, the apartment looked better than when Wren first moved in. With one last goodbye, she picked up her potted lavender from the front porch and stuck her nose into the velvety leaves of the plant. "No more moving, little guy." With one last shuffle through the dark parking lot, Wren started her car and made the drive home.

•   •   •

As children, Lark had preferred to keep her things in boxes and bags. "You never know when we'll leave," she would say. Wren had always been the opposite. She unpacked immediately, settling in as much as possible, making every new motel room a home, whether for two months, two weeks, or two days. She always hoped each place would last, and unpacking seemed to make that claim for her.

Though she had no deadline now, Wren unpacked every box that weekend. The urgency to establish a home had never left her. She also met two neighbors: Mr. Ortiz to her left, the elderly widower who loved to garden, and Paula across the street, a single mom of two little boys—the sources of many whoops and hollers Wren heard.

Home renovations turned out to be nothing like the TV shows though. Removing the wallpaper from the bathroom took Wren the entire afternoon on Sunday, between realizing she didn't have the right tools and then discovering that no magic tool made it easier after all. Only one wall was mostly free, and it still had bits of papers hanging on, though Wren had even more embedded in her fingernails. She ran out of time for mowing the yard, though it desperately needed it. Not that she had a lawn mower, but she planned to borrow one from Mr. Ortiz.

With the little time she had on Monday morning before work, she attacked the carpet with a thick layer of baking soda to absorb some odor through the day. She would vacuum it up that evening. Though she hoped to replace the carpet eventually, a box of baking soda and a diffuser were a much cheaper solution for now.

While the white dust settled, she headed into the kitchen, opening every drawer and cabinet, committing it all to memory until she could find a spoon or spatula with her eyes closed.

"It's not a race," she whispered, to both the house and herself. "We have all the time we need."

The wallpaper in the bathroom and the stink in the carpet weren't going anywhere because this house wasn't going anywhere. She didn't have to rush through the projects. She wanted to savor them.

Pulling together a simple breakfast of eggs and toast, Wren carried her plate and a cup of tea to the back porch to be savored. The day was already warm, the air still and muggy. The oak tree's shade provided a sweet reprieve over most of the yard.

Seated on the top step of the porch, Wren surveyed the land—the curves, the rises and dips. Rose bushes would look beautiful next to the porch and help Rosa live up to her name, especially with the rose-shaped hole in the wallpaper now missing and the sheet curtains soon to be replaced.

She had just forked down the last bite when her phone chirped with a call. Due to a busy week, she hadn't been in touch with her family as much as usual. And now she would probably hear about it.

Wren pulled on a smile. "Hey, Mavis." Her mother. Possibly the only mother that preferred to go by her first name. Perhaps because Mavis had become a mother at eighteen years old and was never quite ready for a title like "mom." She had never acted as one either, preferring the role of a friend—sharing her worries and woes with her children and checking out when they needed anything more parental.

"Wrenny, it's been so long, I thought your phone must have stopped working. I haven't heard from you all week."

Mavis hated that Wren had left San Antonio six years ago, immediately after completing her massage therapy license requirements. She was supposed to have stayed with her family forever. Lark and Mavis took it as a deep betrayal. Frequent phone calls were their compromise, but they never completely forgave her.

"Sorry, it's been a busy week." Wren took her dishes to the sink, tidying up with one hand while they talked.

"Busy doing what?"

"Working overtime."

"Where are you working now?" Mavis asked, hopeful.

"Still at Renew."

"Still?" Working in the same place for years would be torture for Mavis. She chose transience.

"Yes, still."

"And are you still in that same apartment?"

Wren hesitated. She had wanted to avoid this, but she never could lie to Mavis, or to anyone, really. "No."

"What?" Mavis sounded happy again, hopeful that her daughter would spread her wings and venture further. "Where are you living?"

"A house."

"Ooh, that sounds fancy."

Leaning against the countertop, Wren surveyed her little house that was plenty large enough for one woman. She shared walls with no one, and the living room windows looked out onto a large yard. "It's pretty nice," she said, tracing a finger over the counter.

"Are you renting or staying with someone?"

She blew out a breath and hoped for the best. "I bought it, actually."

"You what?" Mavis's voice pitched higher.

"It's a little thing, in a rougher part of town," Wren said, ready to downplay it all. "I just wanted to have something of my own."

"Wrenny, I'm speechless. I knew being a masseuse was good, but I didn't know it was *that* good."

"Massage therapist. It's good enough, with some tight budgeting."

Mavis scoffed. "Next, you'll tell me how to set up my retirement account. Does this mean you're really going to stay in Ridley Bay?"

As if, after six years, Mavis still thought it was just a phase. "Yes, I love it here."

"Well, I hope you love the house too, since you're tied down to it now."

"Yes, I'm excited about it."

"I guess you can always sell it when you're ready for a change."

Never. "Sure."

"Well, wait till I tell Lark."

"How is Lark?" Wren asked.

"Oh, about the same. I see her here and there." Code for: sober some days, high others. It didn't seem to bother Mavis, or if it did, she ignored it. She talked about it like Lark was visiting a friend. And always welcomed Lark back between "visits."

Two months had passed since Wren last heard from Lark. Two months of opioids and God knew what else. She never knew when her older sister would resurface—or what to do when she did.

Wren had wavered over the years, at times welcoming and friendly, other times hurt and angry. No reaction changed Lark. In the end, Mavis's response was probably best. *Just enjoy what you get.* It summed up Mavis's attitude toward everything. And with an addict, it was true. Wren could only enjoy whatever few moments she got with her sister. She never knew when it would be the last.

Wren buried the pain that always rose when she thought of Lark and sought new territory. "How is your job?"

"Oh, running myself into the ground at that nursing home, cleaning and doing laundry. It keeps me busy. You'd never believe the things I have seen in that place."

Wren set Mavis on speaker and listened to the tales of the nursing home—Mavis's workplace for a solid two months and counting—while she got ready for her own workday. She pulled on a mustard-yellow maxi skirt and a slouchy white tee. Renew Wellness's only dress code was to keep hair out of the way and skin covered.

Sweeping her long hair back, Wren wrapped it into a bun and tied it off with a scarf. "I hate to cut you off, Mavis, but I actually have to head into work now."

"Of course you do, you're funding a high life for yourself."

Wren heard every bit of the insinuation in Mavis's statement. "It's just a little place, honestly. Anyway, I'll talk to you later."

Mavis ended the call with a dejected goodbye. Though she hadn't said it, Wren knew she felt betrayed. Like her daughter had turned into just another one of the common snobs.

Wren pulled the door to her house closed and double-checked the lock.

She was forever caught between two groups of people. According to some, she was turning into a rich snob with a house and SUV. According to others, she lived in a shack and drove a dying car. Both groups were wrong for her. Nobody seemed to understand her.

Gumpy groaned as Wren opened the door. "Wake up, big guy," Wren said, a bit too curtly. She softened the words with a pat on his steering wheel. When he squealed to life, she cranked the radio a little higher than normal and focused on the words of every song, drowning out Mavis and all the wrong groups of people.

Chapter Five

Most of the staff had left for the day by the time Wren finished her last massage on Friday. Indie, their receptionist, stood in the doorway of her room, twirling keys on her finger as she waited for Wren to clean up her space. After wiping down the massage table and tossing the linens in the laundry room, Wren grabbed her purse and the jewelry she had removed for work—donning two small feather earrings and a silver lizard pendant on a long chain.

"My boyfriend and I are going slacklining at the park with some friends," Indie said. "Want to come?"

Wren stretched her arms up and over, lengthening each side. Every muscle protested the week spent working on her house and giving massages. "Sounds fun. I would, but I've got a church thing tonight." The young adults' group had planned a goodbye party for their friend Cora, heading off to Guatemala as a missionary.

"Maybe next week," Indie said, heading for the front door. "Depending on if that storm actually comes through or not."

When they stepped outside, Indie's boyfriend was waiting for her in his car, and she gave a quick wave to Wren before hopping in and driving off.

Wren opened her car door and waited in the parking lot, letting the oven-like heat wave out of the car first. In a few minutes, she would be wishing Cora farewell from the rental house Faith and Bethany shared, and their house was always too cold, so Wren let the heat sink into her skin as if she could save it for later, like a reptile.

Careful not to burn her legs on the seat, she climbed into the car, whispered her usual prayer for Gumpy to start, and turned the key.

Absolutely nothing happened.

Wren straightened, lifted the hair off her neck, whispered the prayer a little louder, and turned the key again.

Nothing.

"Come on, buddy." She took the key out, put it back in, and turned.

Nothing.

Tears sprang to her eyes. She hadn't taken care of him lately. She had given all her time and resources to the house. Gumpy was punishing her, begging for attention.

She popped the hood and rounded the car to study it. She wasn't a mechanic, but YouTube had gotten her far enough. She knew the recent squealing sound indicated a belt problem, but it shouldn't have killed her car … right? Wren stared at the engine—a pile of hot metal.

"I'm so sorry, Gumps."

It had to be a dead battery. There went the budget. Wren could see the new rosebushes and wallpaper wilting before her eyes. What if it was worse than that? What if she couldn't afford to fix it? She lived too far from work to walk or bike. Ridley Bay had a terrible bus system that would never cut it.

Somehow, she deserved this. Wren swiped the back of her hand at hot tears and retrieved a napkin from the center console inside the car to wipe her greasy hands.

Choking down breaths and fighting the rising tears and panic, Wren pulled out her phone and stared at her contacts. Maybe a jump start could get her to the auto shop, where she could buy a battery. But who could she call? Faith and Bethany were hosting the party, Cora was the guest of honor. They couldn't come rushing out to get her. Nick had left work two hours ago. Would he come back? Would his girlfriend be mad?

Wren scrolled through names, up and down, until she landed on Levi McCoy, from their Bible study group. He felt like a big brother to Wren. He should be at the party tonight. Maybe he could stop here first.

When he answered, Wren gave him a quick rundown. She wasn't asking for much. A jump start. Maybe a ride if the jump didn't work.

"I'm so sorry, Wren, I'm out of town this weekend."

"Oh … Okay, that's okay, really, I'll be fine. Sorry for bothering you. Enjoy your trip." She just wanted off the phone as soon as possible.

"No worries. Hey, why don't you call Hollis? He's a car guy."

"Hollis? He has a motorcycle."

Levi laughed. "You know he has a car too."

"I didn't …" But it made sense. A motorcycle was impractical. He had to have a car too. "I don't want to bother anybody."

"Oh, he'll do it for his girlfriend."

"Would you stop?"

"Just call him. Or else I will."

"Don't do that," Wren said quickly. Anyone but Hollis.

"I'm not leaving you stranded in a parking lot."

"It's fine."

"I'm calling Hollis."

"Levi!"

The line went dead.

Wren clicked off the phone call and stared at her phone some more, flipping through names. She should call Hollis and head this off. She had the names of some of the pastoral staff at Grace, but it seemed even worse to ask them. Her stomach twisted around itself. Asking for help made her look stupid. She should have taken care of her car.

Lifting a hand to her brow for shade, Wren stared down the street. If she had a data plan on her phone, she'd be able to search for the nearest car shop and maybe even walk to it. Calling a service company would cost too much.

Frogs croaked out from her phone, and she glanced down at the screen. Suits. *Curse you, Levi McCoy.*

She held the phone an inch from her ear, like it might bite. "Hey."

"Hey, McCoy just called me. You need some car help?"

"No."

"You know McCoy's a contractor, not a mechanic, right?"

"And you are?"

"I know a thing or two."

The air fell out of her lungs. Who else did she have? "I just need a jump."

"Could be the starter or alternator too. I'll check it out. I can head over now."

Wren gave him the address and sat on the curb, leaning back onto her hands as the asphalt left its hot print on her palms. Who flew too close to the sun and burned up? Had she flown too close, bought the house too soon, asked for too much?

Disappointment swirled through her, battling with embarrassment. Suits was coming and he would ask questions that made her feel stupid, like how old the battery was, or why she hadn't replaced the belt. The minutes passed slowly.

With her face to the sun and her eyes closed, Wren heard—and felt—a car approaching. It rumbled low, like a distant earthquake, shaking a tower of dread inside her. Her eyes opened and landed on *a car*. Dread fell and anger surged, bringing her to her feet, her heart racing.

She might not know much about cars, but anyone could recognize a six-figure price tag. Of any snob she had ever met, none held a candle to the absolute vanity of this. Bile rose in her throat when Hollis lifted himself out of the tangerine-orange idol. She had gone to lunch with this person? Any down-to-earth moment he'd had was a lie. She had been deceived, if only for a moment.

The liar showed off a smile designed by an overpaid orthodontist. "What happened to Old Reliable?" he asked.

Bitterness boiled under her skin, bubbling upward. The price of that car could have fed her and her sister for eighteen years. How shallow did someone have to be to buy a car like that? "Forget it, Hollis. I don't need your help."

His entire face dropped half a notch, though it recovered quickly, this time more insincere, like an insurance salesman. "Do we have to do this every time, Atwood?" Without waiting for an answer, he strode to the front of her Forester and started poking around in the engine.

Wren forced a breath. Melted asphalt, salty air, and a touch of starch.

"You know your serpentine belt is nearly shredded too, right?" Hollis's voice was muffled with his head leaning over the engine.

She was tempted to start walking and never look back. "I said forget it."

Hollis walked around to the door and clicked the key, then returned to the engine. "I'm already here. I'll drive you to the shop. We can go ahead and grab a battery and a belt and get this fixed pretty quick."

There were no easy fixes for people like Wren. She had seen families abandon cars for less than this because they simply couldn't afford the repairs. Those were her people. She didn't belong with people like Hollis, floating around in high-rises and supercars, looking down on everybody else. "I'm not riding in that."

Suits' smile finally vanished. "I didn't think you'd want to ride the motorcycle."

Someone nearby whistled, and Wren whipped her head around to find a man walking by on the sidewalk, gawking. Cars like this didn't belong here. She had seen it before in the parking lot at church and ignored it, hoping the dealer or warlord or whoever drove it would find Jesus. Yet Hollis claimed to have already.

He opened the passenger door. "Come on."

She shook her head. "I'm not getting in that thing."

"Why?"

Because that stupid car probably cost more than the house she had saved for years to buy. "I think it's morally wrong."

He started to laugh but stopped himself. "Are you serious?"

"Yes."

Hollis leaned his back against the car and crossed his arms, studying her. "You don't think you're being a little ridiculous?"

"No, that car is ridiculous."

"What are your other options?"

"I'll walk. Or take a bus or something."

"A bus?"

"Do not judge me for taking a bus, or so help me—"

"I'm not judging you for taking a bus. I'm judging you for not accepting help when it's standing right here in front of you."

Help. Like she was a charity case and he needed a tax write-off. "I'm not selling my soul for a ride in a … a Ferrari." She waved an angry hand at it.

He grinned like the cat that caught the canary. "It's not a Ferrari, it's a Corvette Z06."

"Is that supposed to impress me? Does anybody even care about names?"

The cold smile didn't even come close to his eyes. "Yeah, when a car can still drive."

"Excuse me?"

He waved his hand toward Gumpy. "You're the one who wants to talk about names when you have a time machine nobody can even recognize."

Wren scrambled for a reply, but birds didn't fight back. *Birds fly away*, as Mavis liked to remind her. And Wren had nowhere to fly to. Without wings, an open parking lot was as bad as being caged. Crossing her arms tightly, Wren turned her back on Hollis and dialed Indie.

He sighed dramatically and touched her shoulder. "Atwood—"

"Why do you do that?" She wrenched her arm away from him, spinning toward him. The movement sent the lizard on her necklace whipping against her neck. "Call me Wren. Do something normal for once." She didn't even know where that came from.

The flicker across his eyebrows, the loss of words—even Hollis could lose confidence. She had seen it happen one other time. Wren vaguely wondered if she was the only one who didn't swoon over him, the only one who could keep him in check.

Indie's voice came through the phone. "Hey girl, did you change your mind about slacklining?"

"Indie! Yes, I did. I'd love to come. But I need a ride, my car's out. I'll buy dinner to make up for it."

"No worries. I'll send my boyfriend back while I get set up here. See you in a bit."

An escape plan helped Wren stand taller. She squared off with the cat. "You can leave now."

Neither of them moved for a long minute. A staring contest. One last chance for Wren to admit she was the needy wreck everyone believed her to be. One last chance for Hollis to be the salvation he believed himself to be. She refused to give in.

"I'm sorry, Wren."

It jogged her mind to hear him say her name. He was too close, and she wanted him gone. Wren shook her head to shake him off, and all his lies. "No, you're not. You love feeling better than someone else. But I won't be the person you beat down for your ego."

"I don't … That's not true." He stepped back, looking lost, as if he wasn't sure of the truth himself. Finally, he sighed. "Fine. I'll see you later."

With a rumble that echoed in the parking lot, the stupid orange car drove out of sight. Wren dropped to the curb and let out a dry heave, cleansing his aftershave out of her system. She had almost bought into it, nearly believing that a decent person hid beneath the pompous charade. Oh, the things Mavis would have to say about that.

"That's not who we are. We're Atwoods, we're different."

And this Atwood would miss out on the goodbye party tonight.

Chapter Six

It took every ounce of his self-control not to peel out of the parking lot. Hollis gripped the steering wheel too tightly, holding himself back from beating his head on it. Seriously? How had his car started a huge fight? He had thought it a practical choice when he bought it, forgoing a few faster alternatives.

The car didn't matter though. Not when he had caved and said exactly what she expected him to say, harsh words that justified her hatred. She had climbed under his skin, and he reacted. He made fun of her car and hurt her. The look on her face made that much clear.

You're an idiot, Hollis.

He took the long way to the girls' house, climbing onto the highway needlessly and driving faster than he should, wishing he was on his bike instead. It forced his focus.

Exiting before the bridge to the peninsula, he took a U-turn and headed back into town at a more moderate speed.

When he pulled up to Wong and Lehman's place, he leaned his forehead against the steering wheel, whispering a prayer asking for forgiveness. From Wren or God, he wasn't sure, but he didn't want to be a jerk. *Am I?*

People always talked about hearing God like it was an audible experience, and Hollis never knew if that was what they meant or not. He'd love some vocalization from the heavens. But today wasn't his day. No booming voice, no flashing light, no angelic appearance. Just the look on Wren's face.

Atwood was right about him. She saw straight through him. That was why she walked away. Ran away. Along with his dad. Maybe God ran away from him too. Maggie didn't, probably because she couldn't. Maybe he'd ask her if he was a jerk. She never told a lie either.

With a quick glance around the house and street, Hollis edged back onto the road and pulled away as quietly as possible, dialing his mom as he went.

"Amá, is it okay if I bring dinner by tonight instead of tomorrow?"

He owed Cora an extra gift or something to make up for missing the party. A problem for a later time.

•   •   •

Hollis keyed in the front door entry code at his childhood home—a large, Spanish-style house with palm trees in front. He opened the door a crack and slid in sideways. Old habits died hard in a childhood home. He had spent his entire life silently slipping into that door. His entrance didn't escape Maggie's notice though. Halfway down the front hall, he heard his sister's computerized greeting.

"Hello. Hello." The voice came from a tablet attached to the front of her wheelchair. She used his eye-tracking software to communicate through it.

"Hey, Mags."

Parked at the head of the dining table, she had her tablet opened to her favorite art program. Splotches of bright colors formed an arc around the screen.

"Beautiful." He leaned down to kiss her forehead, and she giggled. "Is it a rainbow?"

It took a moment for her to switch from art to the speech program. "Yes."

"I brought pizza," Hollis said, setting the box down on the kitchen counter.

"Pizza?" Amá called from the other room. "Daniel, I told you she's on a Keto diet now."

For the worsening seizures. He hadn't forgotten. "It's a cauliflower crust, from that new Keto place downtown." He caught Maggie's eyes and gave an exaggerated eye roll. She made a series of sounds, squawks, and grunts.

Amá walked into the room, fiddling with an oversized earring in one ear. Her hair was curled, and she wore a full face of makeup.

"Are you going somewhere?"

"You said you were coming over, so I made plans."

"That fast? With whom? When are you coming back?"

She shot him a look. "Am I on a curfew, young man? I think you can spare an hour or two for your sister once a week."

Annoyance churned in his stomach, and he shoved it down. "Yeah. We'll be fine. Are Lilia or Sophia here?"

Amá gave a dismissive wave as she grabbed her purse and headed for the front door. "The twins are never here. Watch Margarita through dinner. Cut the pieces small."

"I know that."

The door clicked shut. It was probably for the best. He and Maggie were happier without her here. Though it would have been nice to have the twins around too.

After spending several years in Houston, he had moved back here for the sole purpose of being closer to his sisters. Now, he could rarely track down two of the three. But Maggie was the star of the show anyway, and they all knew it.

He turned his attention back to his sister. In front of her, a pile of papers and jumbo glue sticks littered the table. Maggie's art therapist would have cleaned it up, which meant Amá and Maggie must have been doing their own crafting. Anything artistic made Maggie happy, but it had likely used up his mother's patience for the day—explaining her mood.

"Let's get this cleaned up while the pizza cools." He reached for the glue sticks, but Maggie grunted a protest, swiping her arms at him.

"I do not like it." She only used the full phrases on the tablet when she was passionate about the topic. "I do not like it."

"Mags … fine. We can leave it. Let's move you to the other side of the table at least."

Hollis pulled a chair away and moved her wheelchair into place. Thankfully she didn't protest when he wiped her hands and face with a washcloth.

He pulled out two plastic plates and cut both of their pizzas into tiny pieces. Maggie liked it when he did things the same way as her.

The pile of papers on the table included a mosaic rainbow of sorts, with chopped pieces of paper forming an arc—her favorite design.

"I like this," Hollis said, reaching for it. "Can I have it when it dries?"

"No."

"Ah, Mags, no love. Your room is already full of them. Can you at least send me a copy of your artwork on the tablet?"

"Yes."

While she ate, her eyes navigated through the tablet screen to another painting—all brown, smeared in a blob. She hit send.

Hollis laughed. "Really? That one?"

She giggled. Even in her own bad mood, Maggie helped him out of his funk. As the two oldest siblings, they'd always had their own connection, though it had changed over the years as Rett stole more of her abilities away.

"Tell me a story." A pre-programmed phrase for one of Maggie's top requests.

He told her about his week, while keeping a close eye on her eating. She gagged occasionally or would miss her mouth entirely. Hollis helped her sip water in between. The whole process stressed their mother to no end, but he didn't mind it. He knew the Heimlich and had done it before. Maggie was always fine.

Once he had caught her up on his week, until today's events, he went quiet. The only thing left on his mind was a girl he had hurt.

"Tell me a story," the tablet said again. Maggie's eyes were on him— she was the only one who got their dad's blue eyes—and flicking around the room, to the pizza, but always back to him. He had her attention. Now was the time.

Hollis gave her the shortest version possible of what happened with Wren. He put it into the simplest terms he could: a girl, a car, a fight. "What do you think? Am I a terrible guy for teasing her about her car?"

"Yes."

"Ouch. Wow. Okay, Mags. Don't pull any punches," he muttered. He could always count on Maggie to tell the truth.

"Daniel ... bad."

If Maggie said it, it was true. Her view of the world was a bit more simplified, and it usually revealed the truth. He sat with the verdict for several minutes. "How can I be a better guy? A good guy?"

"Water."

Hollis moved her drink closer and wiped a paper towel under her chin. "More pizza?"

"Yes."

He cut up a second piece for her and a third for himself.

"Flowers."

"Flowers? You want flowers?"

She grunted, annoyed, as her hands jerked around her face.

"Sorry. Give me a second, I'll figure it out."

"Daniel ... good ... flowers."

It clicked, and he laughed. "That's how I can be a good guy? Give flowers to Wren?"

"Yes."

Hollis squeezed her arm. "You're brilliant, Mags. Thank you. But flowers are kind of romantic, and we're just friends." *Not even that.*

More annoyed sounds. "Flowers. Flowers."

Hollis held his hands up in surrender. "Okay, wow, you're persistent today. Flowers it is."

Pleased with his answer, Maggie focused on eating quietly for a moment before another favorite phrase sounded from the tablet. "God is good."

Hollis squeezed her hand. She used that one often. Maggie was the one who had first convinced Hollis of God's goodness, because if she could believe in a good God despite her condition, so could he.

"Yeah, God is good."

They were both content to eat in silence after that.

After dinner, Hollis put the rest of the pizza in the refrigerator, noting the variety of meal shakes in there. It meant Maggie had struggled with eating lately, which explained their mother's extra protective streak tonight.

"Lilia and Sophia don't come home much, huh?" he called back to Maggie in the dining room. No response. He didn't expect one.

The twins were starting their sophomore year at Texas Gulf University. It was in town, only fifteen minutes from their house, but they lived in an apartment on campus instead. They had moved out as soon as possible. So had he. Their mother wasn't easy to live with.

"How's life with Amá?" he asked, cleaning paint spots from the dining table.

Maggie ignored him again. She looked tired, but he didn't do bedtime. Changing his grown sister into pajamas was beyond brotherly duties.

"Let's watch a movie."

Who knew when their mother would be back. She would take as much time as she could. She deserved a break—full-time caregiving was exhausting.

Ever since his parents had divorced fourteen years ago, his dad had never stayed in town for more than a day or two at a time. He didn't know the first thing about helping with Maggie, which meant it was up to Hollis and the twins to give their mother a break. Hired help never stayed long— they were never good enough, according to Amá. Because Maggie was her baby. Forever her baby.

Chapter Seven

Darkness still blanketed Ridley Bay when Wren pulled up to the docks Saturday morning. Gumpy no longer squealed thanks to Indie's boyfriend, YouTube, and her meager home repair budget, now turned into a car repair fund. It couldn't be counted as a victory though, especially not after arguing in her dreams all night with a man in a suit. She wasn't sure who had said worse things or who owed an apology, but she knew she had been harsh, maybe even petty.

Taking time away from the mainland always healed her wounds, and a trip to Kinney Island seemed more important today than ever.

A single light pole and the faint evidence of a coming sunrise guided her walk from the parking lot to the water's edge. The pavement under her feet clung to the summer heat, even through the night. Wren closed her eyes and breathed the salty air, the morning dew, and last night's catch. Two men headed toward the rusty ticket booth, but Wren went straight to the boat.

The pilot of the tiny vessel stood at the bow of the boat, with one hand holding onto a post in the dock. He chewed on a fingernail on the other hand. He straightened when he saw her, spitting into the water. "Well, I was wonderin' when we'd see you again."

"Morning, Todd."

He resumed the nail biting. "Where you been, kiddo?"

Wren stepped onto the boat, taking the bench seat opposite him. "I bought that house. It's a project, just like you said."

"Keepin' you busy?"

Wren hummed her confirmation as the rhythm of the boat rocked her stresses away. She had known Todd for years now. He was at least twice her age, his features rough and his mannerisms too, but he was honest. And she always enjoyed their conversations. "I heard a storm might come our way."

"Don't have to hear a thing to know that," he muttered.

"Really?"

He raised an eyebrow at her before resuming the chewing and spitting. "Water's rising." He pointed to the pier where the boat was tied. "I know every knot on that wooden post. We're up a couple inches already."

"How bad will it be?"

"I ain't God, but if I were, I'd probably wash this entire city away."

Wren didn't have to ask what that harsh statement meant. Captain Todd was a gloom and doom guy, always prepping for the next disaster.

Two young men with dark features boarded the boat. Todd took their tickets, and they hauled an assortment of fishing rods, one giant tackle box, and a large cooler on board. The man with a full-sleeve tattoo nodded at Wren, slight curiosity on his face. She was the only person who rode the six o'clock ferry without a fishing pole.

When Todd rounded the jetty and picked up speed, Wren always wondered why more people didn't come out to experience this. They headed straight into the sunrise—so bold and brilliant. Old-fashioned fears about sailing over the edge of the earth suddenly made sense. One could almost reach out and take hold of the sun. Wren tried, stretching one arm out toward the bow of the boat. The wind whipped her hair across her face, and she didn't bother to hold it back.

A dolphin jumped in the boat's wake—surely the promise of a good day ahead. Wren couldn't help but laugh at its version of leapfrog, like the wake was its own personal surf.

The trip always ended too soon. Wren let the fishermen clear out with all their gear before she stood, shouldering her tote bag.

"Darlin'," Todd said as she walked past him. She stepped off the boat onto the dock before turning back to him for whatever he had to say. "Better buy some sandbags."

The predawn wind chilled her despite the summer temperatures, and Wren wrapped her arms around herself. "I will."

"Bring me lightnin' if you find it."

"Always," she promised.

Todd gave a tight nod and headed back to his proper post in the boat. Wren walked down the splintered wood of the dock onto the uninhabited island. There was a thin pier here, facing inland, with tame waves lapping at it, water dirtied by the boats that sped through the bay. But several yards away, over the dunes to the other side of the island, the beach sprawled—raw and wild.

No one hurried here, and no one else wanted shells this early. Wren took her time crossing through the dunes as warm sand swallowed her ankles and an orange sun kissed the horizon.

Once she made it across, the mainland was officially gone, its cares untouchable. Here, she had seventeen miles of peace. Wren spread her arms out wide, catching the wind, wishing she were a kite to be lifted into the air. The sun rose, reaching over the horizon, starting a new day. In a few hours, it would be hot and harsh, but right now, Wren adored it.

With the sand glowing orange in the light, she headed to the shoreline and began to search. Simple angel wings and a variety of cockles speckled the shore. Most of them small and nondescript—things a child would collect to fill a bucket. An occasional crab darted out in front of her. Wren searched for perfection. Her house was already decorated with the best shells she had found over the years. They adorned a variety of jewelry pieces, framed a picture on the wall, and filled a jar in the kitchen.

Wren came across a broken sand dollar and scooped it up, studying its delicate lines. Sand dollars were her favorite but too fragile. Of the few whole ones she had ever found, none had survived the trip back to the mainland, no matter how careful she tried to be. They were so delicate, the waves of their own home broke them. Wren lifted it to her ear and gave a slight shake. No sound. All the tiny white doves inside must have fallen out already. She set it back into the sand and continued her search.

Three hours later, the sun had warmed the sand, Wren's stomach growled, and her bag jingled with shells. She hadn't found the elusive lightning whelk, but she had found a gorgeous green marble of sea glass, perfectly smooth and round. Todd would huff at it and say it was somebody's trash, and then, when he thought she wasn't looking, he would tuck it into a small lock box next to the wheel. She had seen the act before. Wren smiled and rolled it between her palms.

The island never got busy, but it began to fill in. Boats ran hourly on the weekends, and by now they had brought in two families swimming and sunbathing, an elderly couple searching for shells, and another half dozen fishermen. The other hundred thousand people that lived in Ridley Bay were still there, on the mainland, dealing with today's people and problems. And it was time for Wren to join them. She had a home that needed some work.

Chapter Eight

Sundays used to be torture. As children, they were dressed and dragged to the Catholic church as often as Amá could manage it. But one by one, as each of her children got a driver's license and a choice, they had stopped going. Only Maggie was still stuck with it, but she seemed to like it.

For years, Hollis didn't go to church anywhere. He had given up on religion entirely. But when he moved back to Ridley Bay to be with his sisters, the twins' social schedule proved too busy for him, and he had to go where they went, which happened to include Grace Church.

After a year of Micah Sanford's sermons, and some encouragement from Maggie, Hollis finally accepted Christ. And the worst day of the week became the best. He woke on Sundays without stress.

Arriving early, he helped transform the middle school where they met into a church for the day, though this job had an end date. The church had broken ground on their own building earlier in the year and work progressed quickly. Flooring went in last week, and Sanford hoped to hold services in the new building by Christmas.

Hollis stayed through both services to help with cleanup too, visiting with familiar faces in between services and catching his sister Sophia after the second service.

"Hey." Hollis greeted her with a hug and looked around for her identical copy. "Where's Lilia?"

Sophia shrugged. "She hasn't been in a while."

He had noticed. "Right. Any idea where she is?" They lived together. Sophia had to know.

"Sleeping, maybe." Sophia turned her attention to Joshua Sanford, Micah's son and her boyfriend, as he joined them. Joshua was the reason Sophia had started coming to Grace, and they were inseparable.

Hollis shook hands with the guy, and they exchanged familiar small talk. Though Hollis wanted to play the role of protective big brother and screen the twins' dates better, he did a terrible job of it. It never fit him quite right.

Somewhere in the time between when he left for college and when he returned to Ridley Bay, the twins had gone from gangly kids still playing with dolls to boy-crazed teens. He had never fully grasped the change. He hadn't even taken Sophia's relationship with Joshua seriously for the first year or so. Now he had some catching up to do.

Just as Sophia and Joshua headed off, Hollis caught sight of Wren, wearing some sort of shawl that reminded him of wings. "Atwood," he said, raising a hand in her direction. *First names.* She preferred first names.

She turned, and she wore her emotions all over her face—defensive, annoyed, maybe sad?

"Hollis."

He aimed for casual as he stepped closer and they edged out of the flow of people. "Wren. If you have a second, I have something for you."

A slight frown wrinkled between her eyebrows. "Is it contagious?"

Hollis snickered. "I won't get that close. Come on." He headed toward the parking lot, double-checking that she was following.

Heading to the Corvette together might be a mistake, but there was no other way to transport the flowers. He reached in and out of it as fast as possible. How someone could hate it was a mystery, but so was she.

Hollis held out a pot of morning glories like a peace offering.

A slight smile turned into a frown and then back upward again. "What is this?"

"Morning glories."

"I know that … I meant why?"

"Part-apology and part-housewarming. I told my sister I was rude, and she said flowers fix everything."

"Your sister sounds smart."

Smarter than most people realized. "She amazes me."

Wren brushed a finger over one purple bloom. "Was it Sophia or Lilia? To be honest, I can't tell them apart, but I can try to thank the right one."

"Ah, the third one," he said, ignoring the familiar roll in his stomach. *The third one* came with so many questions and misunderstandings, he often avoided talking about her. And that alone proved he was a terrible person. "Maggie."

"I didn't know you had another sister. Any brothers?"

"No, just us four. I'm number one. Like, in order. Birth order. Not like … a winner." *Wow.* That got weird fast.

Wren tilted her head, eyes sparkling. "I'm sure your mom thinks you're number one, Hollis."

"No, not really. Anyway, I'm sorry for what I said."

She shrugged. "It wasn't any worse than what I said."

The first hint of remorse. "I don't want to be a jerk. I'm working on being nicer."

Wren sighed and studied the flowers from another angle. "These are lovely, thank you. And I forgive you, but it's not about being nicer."

"What's it about then?"

"Priorities. You can be nice until kingdom come, but if you think you need a car like *that* to get from point A to point B, then your priorities are still wrong."

Nothing would ever be enough for her. He bit back the first response that popped into his mind and tried to stay polite. "I need a cheaper car?"

"Depends. Does driving that make you feel better than other people?"

"No. I drive it because I enjoy it. It's fun."

"You spent a hundred thousand dollars on fun, while Cora is heading to a third world country to help families who live in huts."

He shouldn't have to justify this to her. Nobody else had a problem with his car. "You think if not everybody can drive these cars, then nobody should? Should they just stop making nice cars?"

"They can make the cars all they want, but what is it doing in the hands of a Christian?" She stretched up so their eyes were level, and he wished yet again for another inch or two.

"I don't see the moral problem here."

"Ever heard the story of the rich young ruler? Jesus told him that a camel has a better shot at entering the eye of a needle than the rich getting into heaven. Heaven doesn't take cars like that."

Frustration chugged through his blood. "I've heard it. But I don't think it's about money. I think it's about anything we value more than God. And I think you have something you value too much too."

That earned an eyebrow raise from her. "Really? And what's that?"

"Yourself. You've appointed yourself judge, and I think there's a verse about that too."

Her nostrils flared and she lifted her chin. She pushed the potted flowers back into his hands. "You can take these back to your precious condo. I'm sure you have a spot in your earthly mansion."

"It's a normal condo, and a hundred other people live there too. Are we all going to hell together?"

She was already walking away. "At least you'll enjoy the ride," she said over her shoulder.

The apology flowers wilted before his eyes, and Hollis wanted to pitch the stupid things into the parking lot. Somehow that had gone from "you're number one" to "go to hell" in the blink of an eye. Hollis closed his eyes for a moment and blew out a hot breath before plunking the pot back into his car and striding back to the school, head held high.

Levi McCoy and Emma Foster were standing outside talking, and McCoy gave a huge smirk that meant they had clearly seen the whole thing. Time to divert.

"Anybody want a plant?" Hollis asked. "Apparently Atwood is allergic to housewarming gifts."

"Girlfriend didn't want your flowers? What'd you do this time?" McCoy asked.

"Told her they were from you, the permanent bachelor," Hollis said, mirroring McCoy's smirk.

"Housewarming? Did she move?" Foster asked, interrupting their usual heckling. She didn't like their jokes. Hollis had once taken Foster to a work event, which she took too seriously. After hanging on for too long, she had finally moved her attention on to McCoy, though things seemed equally hopeless there.

"She bought a house last week," Hollis said.

"She told you and not me?" Foster frowned.

Hollis shrugged. "I ran into her on the day she signed."

"Good for her," McCoy said.

Faith Wong exited the school doors at that moment, arms loaded with gear from the coffee table. "Hey guys, can you grab some of this?"

McCoy swooped up the carafes at the top of the stack, and Foster joined him, grabbing the tablecloth. Hollis headed inside to get the rest. Arms loaded with tablecloths, paper cups, and creamer, he joined the others at Wong's car—a Toyota that apparently wasn't driving her straight to hell.

Once the back seat was loaded with things to take to the church storage unit, Wong turned and thanked them.

"We should have a housewarming party for Wren," Foster declared, the self-appointed leader of all twenty-something happenings at Grace.

Wong agreed wholeheartedly. "We can surprise her at Bible study!"

Before Hollis could warn them off, there were plans for cake, decorations, and a gift list. Wren would probably key his car for this.

"I don't think she really wants everyone to know yet," he said.

Foster waved him off. "Everyone wants a housewarming party."

"Maybe she just doesn't want you there," McCoy said, elbowing him in the side.

"Of course she does," Foster said.

"Probably not," Hollis said. "According to Atwood, I'm not even welcome in heaven."

"What?" Wong squeaked.

"She says heaven doesn't take cars like mine."

This time Foster laughed—a sound as full-bodied as her wildly curly hair. "Heaven doesn't take any cars, Hollis. Only souls."

Hopefully it would take his.

Chapter Nine

When Wren woke on Monday morning, the house felt sad. A sunny sky topped the neighborhood, but Rosa had her own personal rain cloud. The blue walls and pink floors held no shine today.

"What's wrong, girl?" Wren whispered, running her hand over the living room walls.

Nothing answered, until Wren walked into the dark kitchen and flipped the light switch. It buzzed a strange response, and before Wren could investigate it, the light overhead popped and went black.

Wren stood there, staring at the burned-out bulb overhead. Staring and staring, as if she could bring it back to life with her eyes. *Please let that just be the bulb and not an electrical problem.*

Did she have time to go buy lightbulbs before work? Could she reach it standing on a chair, or would she need a ladder? The day already felt too hard.

Sinking to the pink carpet on the kitchen floor, Wren pulled her knees to her chest. She didn't know how to do this—how to take care of a house, much less fix it up. What had possessed her to think she had the skill set for this? She was so determined to run against the statistics, to prove them wrong, but they existed for a reason. There was a reason kids raised in poverty, in hunger, and in single-parent homes didn't make it out. There was a reason they turned into adults like Lark.

A fat tear hit her knees. The very thought exposed an ugly side of Wren she wished would disappear. Her sister didn't deserve to be thought of that way. They were both trying to find happiness. Lark in drugs, Wren in a broken house.

With deep breaths, Wren forced herself to focus on her senses—a skill Mavis had insisted they practice together regularly. This close to the floor, the house still smelled like cat. The briefest hint of morning glories floated through her mind as she stood to lean over the oil diffuser on the countertop. She had snagged the diffuser during the spa's clearance event, and an extra for Lark. Did she still have hers? Or had she pawned it off?

Wren stared at the lightbulb again. It looked the same as the one in her bedroom. Maybe she could swap them. She had windows in the bedroom and didn't need the light there. At least this way, she could get breakfast ready. And whatever she did, she wouldn't think about Lark or morning glories anymore. They only filled her with guilt.

•   •   •

Monday night, Hollis arrived at the young adults Bible study early, along with the rest of the group, except Wren. He still wore work clothes, dressed in gray slacks and a white button-up, though he had ditched the tie and jacket.

Faith Wong and Bethany Lehman hosted the group in their rental house. Emma Foster, Nathan Uhland, and Levi McCoy were regulars at the Bible study, and the associate pastor, JP Kaminski, usually led the discussion. Everybody made it tonight.

The girls already had balloons strung around the house and a small stack of presents on the dining table. They were always looking for a reason to celebrate: birthdays, new jobs, grad school graduations, moving. Anything. And Foster always wanted a reason to bake a cake.

Uhland and Kaminski, undeniably the tallest in the group, hung the familiar *Congratulations* banner over the kitchen island. McCoy and Hollis stood off to the side, swapping work stories and jokes while they waited.

Soon a knock sounded at the front door, followed by the creak of it opening, and Wong rushed to the front hallway to pull Wren in. A couple of the girls shouted, "Surprise!" The guys missed it but offered late whoops and congrats.

Wren definitely looked surprised, then horrified and embarrassed by turns. She would probably hate him for this. "I don't … Whose party is this? I didn't bring anything."

Foster laughed. "Yours, silly. Happy housewarming."

"What? How …"

"Hollis told us on Sunday." Wong ratted him out immediately. "Although I can't figure out why you kept it a secret!"

Wren shook her head, fidgeting with the knot tied at the bottom of her floral-printed tee. "Thanks guys. I don't … I can't believe you would do this just because I got a house."

And that started the roll of house questions: Where is it? What's it like? How many square feet? Who are your neighbors?

Wren answered most of them and avoided some. At every turn she seemed determined to downplay the house. "It's small … in a rough neighborhood … lots of road noise … pink carpet …" Hollis couldn't figure out why she had bought the place if she didn't even like it.

"Sounds like the perfect fixer-upper," Foster said dreamily. "When can we see it?"

"Fixer-upper? I guess that's the word for it. It's not really ready for hosting. It needs work."

"You know I work on houses, right?" McCoy asked. "Let me know if you need help, suggestions, whatever."

Wren pressed her lips together, barely hiding a grimace. "Know anything about electrical stuff?"

McCoy raised his eyebrows. "I know enough to stay alive."

She explained the situation with the kitchen light, and McCoy promised to come over the next day and check it out. Apparently, he was allowed into the house.

"I'm sure any of these able-bodied guys would help too," McCoy said, slapping a hand on Hollis's shoulder.

"Happy to help," Hollis said.

Wren raised an eyebrow at him. "I think we've got it."

McCoy snorted. "He doesn't want me alone with his girlfriend."

Wren tilted her head back and blew out a breath. "Are we still doing that?"

"Hollis is nothing if not persistent," McCoy said.

Foster laughed. "How do you think he got to where he is now?"

"I try not to think about it," Wren replied.

"You don't make millions in your twenties without some determination," Foster said.

Hollis interrupted, but he was too late to stop the rain cloud that descended. "Okay—"

"Wow, is that all it takes?" Wren asked. A humorless grin lifted one side of her face. "Gosh, if the rest of us 99 percenters just worked a little harder. Or maybe we don't want to sell our souls."

Foster elbowed Hollis. "It wasn't his soul. It was—"

Hollis stopped her. The last thing they needed was Foster fawning over his resume. But Wren had already plugged her ears and closed her eyes and was humming something that sounded like Bon Jovi's "Livin' on a Prayer."

Kaminski diverted the nosedive with a story about a failed renovation he had once attempted.

After dinner and cake, Wren opened a few small presents. Hollis hadn't brought a gift and hoped it wouldn't be noticed. She had shoved his last gift back into his hands, and he didn't exactly want a repeat. It wasn't the first time she had thrown a gift back at him. It was a repeat offense. He could take a hint. Eventually.

Chapter Ten

When the Bible study ended, Wren loaded a few bags of presents into the car, still shocked and confused by their existence. Hollis had broken her trust, but it had been for the best. She didn't want to hide that part of her life anymore. Sharing the accomplishment left her feeling loved and celebrated, even deserving. Her head spun with warm, fuzzy feelings.

Until she looked at Hollis. Guilt was like a splinter, forgettable until she bumped it. And every time she glanced at him, it throbbed again, reminding her that she had verbally attacked the man behind this party, and not for the first time either.

Now, he was making an uncharacteristically quiet getaway out the front door.

Wren thanked Faith again and slipped out the door with a stack of kitchen towels in her arms. "Hollis," she called as he reached his bike.

He straightened and turned slowly, like he was facing a firing squad. Guilt twinged her side, and Wren realized she hadn't figured out what to say yet.

"Sorry," he said first, when she reached him. Not what she was expecting. "I had to explain the flowers on Sunday, so I told them about the house."

He was apologizing for being rejected. She may have done too much damage here. "You don't have to apologize. I enjoyed tonight. It was sweet, more than I could have ever expected."

Doubt flickered, however briefly, on his face. She had surprised him.

"Actually, I'm the one who should apologize. I was a little harsh about the car."

He only hummed an agreement.

"And I was wondering …"

He leaned back against his motorcycle. "What?"

Deep breath. It was her turn to eat some humble pie. "If you still have those flowers."

His eyes scanned her face for a moment, and it was too dark outside to read them. "I do. But they might be half dead. I have a black thumb. And no patio."

"I can probably resurrect them. They'd be happier on my back porch." The warm air and the dark sky wrapped around them in a rare moment of mutuality, like the most important thing right now was saving those flowers.

Hollis pulled his helmet off the handlebars and turned it in his hands. "The flowers are at my condo, if you're willing to come get them."

A small part of her hesitated. But what alternative did they have? Hollis coming to her house? Meeting downtown? Waiting until Sunday when the flowers would be long dead? Another deep breath. Walking into his condo wouldn't kill or ruin her. And she still needed to make amends. "Okay."

He grinned, that impish grin that would get him access to a bank vault if he asked. "Want a ride?" He held out the helmet.

Wren fought the contagion with all her might. It was nearly impossible. "Um, no … my car. Is here. I should drive it."

Undeterred, he pulled the helmet onto his own head. "Follow me."

The ten-minute drive was barely enough time to prepare herself. They pulled into a parking garage underneath a downtown high-rise, only a block away from where she'd run into him a week ago. He was right; this was his neighborhood.

No matter what happened next, nothing would make her feel bad about her house.

She followed him in silence to an elevator, where he tapped his key ring and it lit green. He hit the fifteenth floor, out of sixteen. The elevator whisked them up, and they stepped out into a brightly lit corridor. There were four doors in the hallway. Hollis unlocked the third and held it open for her.

Wren hesitated. She could already see the large windows facing toward the bay and the inky blackness of the ocean beyond it. From the corner of her eye, she could tell Hollis was watching, waiting for a fight.

Just get the flowers and get out. She stepped inside as Hollis flicked on the lights, drowning out the view and lighting the inside.

It was an absolute bachelor pad. The furniture was probably purchased as one complete set from a catalog. To her left, a leather couch faced a large electric fireplace with an even larger television hanging over it. To her right, four metal barstools lined up at the kitchen counter bar top. Straight ahead, in front of the windows, a bar-height dining table sat bare. And beyond that, the street, fifteen floors below.

"One-bedroom condo," Hollis said. "Not a mansion."

Wren raised her eyebrows, surprised he'd want to bring that up. She would always win, because she was right. "I wouldn't call a downtown high-rise with an ocean view particularly humble."

He sighed, a true, deep sigh. "My mom hates it. Does that help?"

This felt like a different side of Hollis. It felt real, like she was seeing behind the false front. And she wasn't sure what to do with it. "I bet you have a house too," Wren teased. "One you keep secret, and just use this place to look more realistic."

Hollis sent her a serious look without a hint of a smile, killing her own. "I don't."

Pursing her lips, she dared a walk to the windows and looked down. Across the boulevard, boats bobbed in the wharf. She wanted to dive out the window, swoop over the town, and fly home to her mismatched, thrifted furniture that she had worked to earn and learned to love.

Hollis interrupted her vision. "Since you're here, can you at least tell me why you hate me?"

Hate? She didn't hate Hollis. He reminded her of everyone that had hurt her and everything she would never be. She might not like to be around him, but she certainly didn't hate him.

"Is that why you have all this?" Wren asked, sweeping an arm over the space around them. "To earn people's love?"

"No." He joined her at the window, several feet away, hands in the pockets of his slacks.

Wren waited. The palms around the boat docks bent wildly in the coastal wind.

"I have it because I need a place to live and I like not having to commute," he said. "I like having a place I can invite friends to. And yes, I like driving my car. But most importantly, I like knowing I can take care of anything that comes up, any surprise, any need, without stress. Is that so wrong?"

It sounded wonderful. Peaceful beyond her wildest dreams. And it annoyed her to hear him brag about it, to know she would probably never feel that way. "Do you even need a God then?"

Silence filled the condo, slowly suffocating them like carbon monoxide.

Finally giving up on any hope of an answer, Wren paced across the room, watching her steps on the hardwood floors and tracing a hand over the back of his leather couch. She needed to get those stupid flowers and leave. *Breathe.* Leather. Metal. … Sandalwood?

Her head popped up, and she spotted a familiar candle on the side table next to the couch. Last Christmas their Bible study group had held a gift exchange. He had traded a towel set for the sandalwood candle she had brought. Wren had tossed his gift, a bag of Colombian coffee, in the trash. And that was the one other time she had seen his confidence shaken. She'd regretted it for weeks and never said a word.

Wren took another deep breath and joined Hollis at the window, closer this time. "I don't hate you."

Hollis blinked, bringing himself back from somewhere far away. "Yes, you do."

"Not all of you."

He turned to her. "Tell me one thing you find bearable."

Too many things: a confidence and security she envied, a one-dimpled smile, the flowers he gave, the candle he kept, the housewarming party …

"You can be surprisingly thoughtful."

"Surprisingly?"

Wren shrugged. "For somebody who could buy their friends."

Hollis rubbed a hand over his face. "Why is it always about that? Why does it bother you so much?"

"Because growing up, every rich kid I ever met was a total jerk." *Uh oh.* The truth came spilling out before she was ready, and it would be hard to stop now. "They all made fun of me and my sister. We never had the right clothes. We never had the cool toys or tech. We didn't go on vacations. And they acted like we weren't even human because of it."

Yep. Here it comes. "Because people like you look down on everybody with less. As if we don't work as hard. As if we aren't as smart as you. You think you've experienced hard times and conquered them because you caught the flu once. You don't have a clue what it was like to dread school breaks because it meant going hungry. And you think that you're better because of it."

Hollis turned to face her, but Wren couldn't meet his eyes. She knew half the things she was saying were aimed at a general populace and he didn't deserve them. But maybe he did. He at least deserved to hear it.

"I don't think I'm better," he said.

"Well, you drive a car that costs enough to have fed my sister and me our entire childhood."

He nodded slowly, seeming to connect pieces about her that she wasn't sure she should have revealed. "If I could change that for you, I would."

"There's still hungry kids today."

He blew out a breath. "I can't feed every single one, Wren. I can buy a meal for someone I see in need and give what I can, but I don't have to stop enjoying my own life. I mean, what about you? Who are you feeding?"

She turned a hard look on him. "I'm not exactly rolling in cash, Hollis."

"Maybe not, but you have a job, a car, and a house. Why can't you feed someone?"

That question didn't seem fair. She had paid her dues by living through it and surviving on her own now. Did she need to feed someone? She paced away from him, toward the dining table, and took in the same view from a safer distance.

Hollis seemed about to say something when he gave up and walked to the kitchen instead. Through the reflection of the glass, Wren watched as he pulled two glasses out of a cabinet and filled them with ice. He opened his fridge and peeked inside.

"Tea or water?" he asked, as if this were a weekday luncheon.

Amused, Wren wandered toward him. "Tea." She lifted herself onto one of the cold metal barstools at the kitchen bar top.

He filled both glasses with iced tea and slid one to her. "My childhood wasn't particularly easy either," he said.

"Please don't compare them, unless you saw your mom cry at urgent care because the co-pay for your stitches meant no gas in the car, which meant losing her job."

He sighed. "I'm sorry."

"Don't feel sorry for me. My mom did her best. And sometimes it was enough." Not often, but there had been times.

"Then I won't compare because I can't. I don't know what any of that was like." He spun his glass slowly. "But I do need a God. I really need Him. Because I can't buy my way to being perfect, as you like to remind me. Constantly."

Wren chewed on the inside of her lower lip. Maybe constantly reminding him wasn't the most Christian thing to do.

"My dad left too," he said. "Whenever he visited, he bought us stuff. Probably out of guilt, but that's what he did. So sure, for a while, I might have thought I could buy love."

It was one of the most genuine things he had ever said to her; she could see it in his eyes. He was being vulnerable. Even though his version of the past included a dad, she didn't feel the need to point out that advantage right now.

"Since you can't, what are you going to do instead?"

Hollis let out a wry laugh. "I can't earn it either, so I don't know."

"Maybe you don't have to earn it."

The look on his face said he clearly didn't believe her. Without replying, he stood and walked away into another room.

Wren downed the iced tea, unsure of what to say next. She was in Hollis's condo talking about love, like the world had decided to spin in the opposite direction today.

Hollis returned, with the pot of flowers in hand. He set it down on the countertop. "Here."

The purple blooms were sagging, but redeemable. It had good roots. "These are good quality, they'll pull through. Where'd you get them?"

He shrugged. "Small nursery outside of town."

"Madre Tierra?"

His eyes lifted to hers with a frown. "Yeah. How do you know it?"

"There are only two garden centers around here, and Madre Tierra is the best. How do *you* know it, Mr. Black Thumb?"

"My aunt owns it."

The world was absolutely spinning in the wrong direction today, but suddenly everything clicked into place. Hollis's dark hair and the slightest touch of an accent that had slipped through once or twice … a door into his life cracked open ever so slightly, and Wren caught a glimpse that there might be more on the other side.

"There's two in town, and you go to the one where they don't speak any English?" Hollis asked.

Wren held eye contact, curious now about what lay on the other side of the door. "*Soy de San Antonio.*"

His smile came back, slow and sure. "*Mi mamá es de Colombia.*"

Colombia. The mental door swung open and light flooded in. Wren's soul flinched at the brightness of it all. She groaned. "The coffee, last Christmas. It was Colombian."

Hollis gave a slow nod with one eyebrow raised. "Plantation in her hometown."

Wren dropped her head against the countertop. "I'm a pig. I'm so sorry, Hollis." She lifted her head. "Wait—Hollis. That's not … Sorry, it just doesn't sound very… Colombian."

"My dad's English, his last name is Hollis, my last name."

His last name. Wren suddenly realized she was an idiot. Of course his full name wasn't Hollis; he wasn't Madonna. But Wren had kept him at arm's length for so long, she had never bothered to give it a second thought. "What's your first name?"

"Daniel," he said with a Spanish accent.

"Why does nobody know that?"

He grinned. "A lot of people do."

"Why don't you use it?"

He looked around the apartment. "Ah … it started a long time ago."

"I'm waiting."

He shrugged and laughed, looking more than ready to change the subject. Was he embarrassed? If so, too bad. Wren had found a pressure point, and she wasn't going to leave it until the knots were out. She stood from the barstool, taking her glass to the sink as an excuse to stand closer to him.

"My mom insisted my teachers pronounce it the Spanish way, but other kids said it sounded like a girl's name. You know, Danielle. I got teased about it a lot."

"So you told everybody to call you Hollis."

"It was easier than undoing the nickname."

"Kids are the worst."

"They can be cruel. But as long as nobody makes me repeat first grade again, I'll be okay."

Wren couldn't help but laugh. "Again? Did you seriously just say that?"

"I'm serious," he said, with a goofy, self-deprecating grin.

Wren had an absurd impulse to hug him for it. Instead, she bumped her shoulder into his. "You turned out okay for a kid who flunked first grade."

Hollis's smile could have sold snow to an Eskimo. It certainly sold flowers to Wren. She didn't understand this man, and she wasn't sure she liked him all that much. But she definitely didn't hate him.

Chapter Eleven

Tuesdays were Hollis's nights to help with Maggie. His sisters were the whole reason he had moved back home, along with the entire Perla Tech headquarters. While Houston might have been the more popular choice for a medical tech company, Perla Tech didn't need a location. Serving clientele across the nation, they operated remotely. Family didn't.

Hollis started the day earlier than usual, fitting in a workout, a shower, and a car wash before heading into the office. A long line of meetings awaited him, and he had to get through them all before he could get to his sister. And then to Wren's house to fix a light.

Once he was sure Amá had had her second cup of coffee, he dialed her. She gave an unusually warm greeting, probably because she knew she had this evening off.

"I'm helping a friend out this evening, so I won't have a lot of time," Hollis warned her. "But I wanted to take Maggie out to the new city park after work. They have an accessible boardwalk now, I think she'll love it."

Amá clicked her tongue, warmth receding. "You'll have to take the van."

"I know." The hideous white behemoth. But that inglorious creation was Maggie's only ticket to freedom, and she didn't get out enough. "You can come with us."

She was quiet for a moment, considering it, if only to keep an eye on her daughter. "No, I'll clean the house. You two can go. Invite the twins. They haven't seen Margarita in weeks."

He barely saw them either, but their mother's world spun around Maggie. "I will." He clicked off the phone and sent a quick text to Lilia and Sophia, knowing it would be ignored. He only ever saw Sophia at church, next to her boyfriend. Lilia rarely showed up to anything; he only saw her at her cheer meets anymore. And he moved his entire company here for family.

Hollis turned his attention back to the computer screen readily. It made more sense than anything involving the females in his life.

•   •   •

Hollis parked the Z06 in front of his childhood home. Amá hated his motorcycle, so he never brought the bike, though he had a feeling Maggie would love it if she could ride on it. She loved speed; she had giggled through the few rides she had taken in the Z06.

He took the ramp up to the front quietly and eased inside.

According to a panicked phone call from Amá that afternoon, Maggie had managed to knock her tablet off its holder in a particularly bad fit, and the screen now featured a giant spiderweb of broken glass. It was nearly unusable.

Hollis greeted his sister as he removed the broken tablet and set a new one in its place. He had done everything he could to make sure all the settings were the exact same.

"Here you go, Mags," he said, repositioning the tablet. "You ready to go to the park?"

She didn't respond. He waited, checked the device, and showed it to her again. Still nothing. The last thing he wanted was for her to be trapped inside.

"Mags, can you try out the new tablet for me?"

"Yes." A meager reply. She wasn't upset though, so perhaps just feeling quiet today.

"Amá, is she ready?"

"She's ready. She just had a shake for dinner. Not too long, Daniel, she's been getting tired fast."

He ignored his mother's endless fussing and pushed Maggie's wheelchair out the garage door and into the van. Hollis hated the clunkiness of the van and its wheelchair ramp, but designing vehicles was outside of the Perla Tech wheelhouse. Not that it stopped him from dreaming up a few accessible options with a V8 engine.

Eventually, after a few bumps and one angry fit from Maggie, they were on their way.

Within minutes, they parked at the wetlands natural area outside of town. The parking lot was always empty. They both preferred quiet places where no one stared at them or asked rude questions.

By the time he had Maggie out of the van and situated, sweat lined Hollis's brow and neck. The air was still, and the usual breeze missing. Dark clouds on the horizon blocked the sun but thickened the humidity.

They had only taken a few steps on the boardwalk when he heard someone shout their names. "Wait up!"

"Lilia? What are you doing here?" Hollis gave her a quick hug and stepped back to do a scan of the absentee sister. She and Sophia had turned into skinny, crop-topped cheerleaders back in high school, but at least the fake-blonde stage was over and her dark hair swung straight from a high ponytail.

"You invited me, *tonto*. Did you already forget?"

"No, but I didn't expect you to come. At least you still remember your Spanish."

She tossed her ponytail and laughed. "We live like twenty miles from Mexico, how am I going to forget?"

"It's about six times that, but sure."

She poked his head. "Let's go, big brain. Hey, Maggie Moo, I like your braid." She patted her sister's head.

"Is Sophia coming?"

Lilia looked at him like he was a total moron. The twins had mastered that look early on, with big brown eyes that matched his and their mother's. "Sophia? Leave her *boyfriend?* Not a chance. They're probably like common-law married by now. Or maybe the Sanfords adopted her, she's always over there."

The fact that Sophia spent more time with the Sanfords than her own family bothered him, but he tucked it away until a time when he could figure out what to do about it.

Lilia twirled away. Maggie gave a rare giggle, laughing at her silly younger sister. It was good to have his sisters together. His favorite memories had always involved all four of them, but three could have fun too.

Steering the wheelchair toward the inner loop of the boardwalk, he guided them onto the shorter half-mile route. The sun beat down too fiercely for the full mile track. "Okay, so Sophia's practically married. What about you? Are you dating anybody?" He tried to ask it casually, but he knew it sounded lame.

"I was, now I'm not, but I'm still having fun. Maybe I will again." She did a random high kick.

The twins were hard to keep up with. He still remembered them as toddlers overcome with fits of mischievous giggles, faces smeared with beans and fists full of his LEGO bricks. They had been only seven when their dad left and Hollis had stepped into the role, a full fourteen years old.

David Hollis still showed up randomly here and there, dropping off gifts and then jetting out of town again. But he never made it to the piano recitals or gymnastics meets. Amá wasn't there either, usually too busy hauling Maggie to doctors or therapists, so they got by on car pools until Hollis could drive.

But then he left town the moment he graduated, abandoning eleven-year-old twins to the confines of the house with their unstable mother and disabled sister. It was an utterly selfish move he had come to regret. He returned to Ridley Bay in time for their junior year of high school, but by then, they didn't need him.

"Lilia. Daniel." Maggie said.

He stopped the wheelchair to give her his full attention. "What's up?"

"Daniel and a girl. Flowers."

"Ooh, do tell, Danny. Who's the girl who got flowers?" Lilia's tone dripped with irony. She thought the very fact that he worked with technology disqualified him from all relationships.

"Daniel was bad." Maggie ratted him out on the tablet, piecing together words as fast as she could. "Flowers. Daniel was good."

Lilia gave Maggie a blinding smile like they were somehow in cahoots on the entire matter. "Apology flowers? Even better." How she got all of that from Maggie's half sentences would never cease to amaze him.

"Apology flowers for saying something mean," he clarified. "Honestly, the flowers were Maggie's idea."

"And they worked?" Lilia asked.

Hollis glanced at Maggie. Her eyes wandered over the coast while her hands twisted at her mouth, but she was listening. "Well enough." Skipping the part where Wren shoved them back at him, it had all ended up fine. She'd left his place last night with the flowers in hand and slightly less hatred toward him.

"So, who's the girlfriend and when's the wedding?"

"Ha. Ha."

Lilia let out a laugh and skipped a few steps ahead, not interested enough to ask more. He let her gain some distance while he pointed out birds to Maggie. He wasn't sure if she saw them or not, but he did his best.

With pink flowers plucked from a nearby tree, Lilia came twirling back to them. "For your hair, princess?" She gave Maggie an elegant bow. Maggie's hands waved, her head bobbing. Lilia tucked one flower into her hair and handed a second to Maggie for her to pick apart.

Maggie's cheeks were turning red, and his mom would panic if he let her get too hot. The city hadn't added as much shade to the boardwalk as he had petitioned for. Hollis pushed the wheelchair a little faster, keeping pace with Lilia as they walked.

"You should go back to the house tonight, Amá wants to see you."

"No way," Lilia said. "I'm not interested in that guilt trip. However, I am interested in your romantic prospects."

"You first."

She narrowed her eyes at him and decided his love life wasn't worth divulging her own.

Despite dressing in half the clothes a person might normally wear, she was smart. She and Sophia both held perfect grades in college, majoring in advertising and theater, respectively. What Sophia planned to do with theater had yet to be seen. Lilia, meanwhile, had turned down his offers of advertising internships two summers in a row, accusing him of nepotism.

Hollis started the van to get it cooling before loading Maggie into the back. Lilia climbed into the passenger seat and turned the radio to a local Spanish station. "It's in Maggie Moo's best interest," she said, turning Selena up too loud.

Hollis closed the rear door of the van and turned toward her. "What about your best interest?"

She climbed out of the van and shut the door. "What do you mean, tonto?"

"Stop calling me that. You don't go see Amá, I never see you at Grace Church, and you said Sophia spends all her time with her boyfriend. Who are you spending your time with?"

"Ooh, the brains can listen. Congratulations."

"Come on, Lil."

She plucked the pink flower out of her hair and tossed it to the ground. "I have plenty of friends, and the whole cheer squad. Stop making it sound like I'm all weird and lonely to make me hang out with you."

He might feel responsible for them, but that didn't mean he didn't get irritated too. "I'm not. I'm trying to be a good brother, could you possibly make that any harder?"

A devilish grin flashed across her face, revealing a row of perfect white teeth. "Yes."

"Is there any chance we could have a Hollis siblings' night sometime, with Sophia, too? Movies or something?"

"Oh, are we still Hollises too? I wasn't sure, because at Grace, the only Hollis is you now."

He blinked and shook his head in surprise. "Is that why you're not coming?"

"Sophia is dating the pastor's son, and '*Hollis*' is buying them a new church," she said, with air quotes over his name. "What am I supposed to do there?"

"You don't have to do anything."

Lilia laughed and any resemblance of seriousness melted from her face. "I know, so that's what I'm doing. The absolute minimum, *Hollis*." She drawled the nickname out with a laugh, but the humor was flat, missing from her eyes.

"Lilia—"

She waved and skipped away toward her Acura. "Good luck explaining to Amá why Mags is late for dinner," she called over her shoulder.

Hollis glanced at his watch and mentally cursed himself. He would be late to Wren's house too.

Chapter Twelve

Levi was coming over to fix the lightbulb. And possibly Hollis … Daniel? Wren didn't know what to do with the door that had cracked open into his world. It seemed ominous—like a one-way door into an unknown place. She should shove it closed again, but she couldn't deny the temptation to step inside.

Parking under the carport, she ignored the nerves that had built throughout the day. Today would be the first time anyone, besides Nick, came to her house. Though she saw all the beauty and potential in Rosa, she feared others would not. Worse, she feared they might voice their opinions.

As a child, Wren had been jealous of her friends with houses like this—any house was a step up, regardless of the condition or location. They had a home.

Now, Wren had one too. She refused to compare it to anything else. Tracing her hands along the siding around the front door, she put her key in and gave it a firm push to open.

Inside, she tidied the living room and kitchen—unsure if cleaning off the pink floors and laminate countertops made them look better or worse. At least the smell of cat urine was gone by now. Wren lit a candle in the kitchen anyway, opened all the curtains, and turned on the working lights to brighten up the house. It looked—and smelled—more like home every day.

A small bookcase in the living room held more trinkets than books, including a wide, shallow basket on the top shelf with a collection of her favorite shells. The red recliner and yellow couch might have looked mismatched, but a multicolored mandala rug brought the room together. Wren loved the explosion of color. It didn't come from a catalog, put together and designed by a professional who didn't care about what house it went to; this room was living and breathing, carefully crafted for this specific space.

After freshening up in the bathroom and eating a quick sandwich and an apple, the nerves began to dissipate. She loved this house and they could too. Or else they could leave.

A knock sounded at the door before she had cleaned up her dishes. Wren took a deep breath to calm herself—lavender, sandalwood, and ham sandwich filled the air. Rolling her shoulders back, she pulled the door open.

Just Levi. Relief battled with disappointment.

"Hey, come on in," she said with a smile, as if playing hostess came naturally. "Did Hollis back out of a little hard work?"

Levi grinned and hauled a tool bag and short ladder inside. He wore torn jeans, a gray T-shirt that hung loosely around his lanky frame, and an orange ball cap. "Said he had to help family."

"Before or after you sent him the address?"

Levi laughed, his eyes already focused on the single lightbulb in the kitchen. "After."

Soon, her kitchen had no power, missing ceiling tiles, and a tangle of wires hanging down. Levi stood on the top rung of a ladder, the top half of his body hidden inside of the ceiling. He had found water damage inside the ceiling, and it had corroded some of the wires.

"I replaced the corroded ones," he said, pulling his head out of the hole in the ceiling and twisting red and blue wires in his hands. "But we have to figure out where the water damage is coming from or else it's going to keep happening."

"Is that something we can do ourselves?" Wren asked, twisting her own hands as tightly as the wires.

Levi scratched his head. "Maybe. Would take some time though." He pointed to the ceiling tile on the kitchen counter, and Wren handed it to him. He wrangled it back into place and then pointed for the light fixture.

Wren nearly dropped it when a knock sounded on her door. She steadied the light fixture and passed it to Levi before heading to the door.

Tugging the door open, she found Daniel Hollis on her doorstep, in a navy polo and khaki shorts.

"Hey." She frowned, forgetting how to play hostess. "Levi said you weren't going to make it."

"He didn't make it," Levi hollered from the kitchen. "I'm practically done."

Hollis cast his eyes down with a sheepish grin. "Sorry. I had to go help my sister out first."

The hint of morally admirable behavior meant nothing, Wren reminded herself. He was probably helping her choose diamond earrings or a dress for a gala.

He leaned against the doorframe and thumbed back toward the porch. "You bought a house with a wheelchair ramp?"

Wren tilted her head to the side. "Of all the things you want to pick on my house for, you chose the ramp?"

"I'm not picking on it." He straightened and looped a thumb through a belt loop. "I just didn't know if there was a reason you chose one with a ramp."

"Because it was available, and I figured the ramp didn't hurt."

"No, of course not. I like it."

Wren laughed. "You like the ramp?"

"Never mind." Hollis shook out his hands and cleared his throat. "Can I come in?"

At least he had the decency to ask. Wren moved out of the way, waving a hand inside, and he followed. Hollis headed for the ladder in the kitchen. "Anything left I can do?"

Levi twisted in the last screw for the light fixture and climbed down, exchanging a quick back pat with Hollis. "There's water damage up there. And I'm not sure where it's coming from. I think we better take a quick look at the roof before Hurricane Flynn hits."

"Hurricane?" Wren asked. "I thought it was just a tropical storm."

Levi folded the ladder and headed for the door. "They upgraded it. And now I'm booked the rest of the week, because everybody waits for a hurricane to trim their trees."

Trim their trees? Did she need to do that? She had never experienced a hurricane, much less in her own home. Wren turned to Hollis and found him leaning back against her kitchen counter, arms folded, scanning her kitchen and the living room beyond it. Defensiveness sprang to life. "Find what you're looking for?"

His eyes drifted back to hers. "Not really. Kind of wanted a tour."

She usually prided herself on detecting a lie, but it was difficult with Hollis. Nothing he said sounded sincere.

"Kitchen, living room," she said, pointing.

He nodded. "It looks like you."

She wasn't sure whether to take that as a compliment or not. Was she the handmade decorations or the broken backsplash tiles? Before she could decide, a motion by the sink caught her eye—and Hollis's too. A black and white spider skittered across the countertop.

Wren gasped and grabbed at a kitchen cabinet, whipping out a glass cup.

Hollis caught her wrist. "Don't kill it. It's not venomous."

"I'm not killing it." Wren tugged her wrist free and set the glass upside down on top of the spider, trapping it. "I just don't want it in my house."

"Here—" Hollis reached for a piece of junk mail sitting on the countertop and carefully scooted it under the glass. He flipped the cup over and carried it outside just as Levi walked in, earning a grimace when Levi saw the large spider crawling up the walls of the glass.

Levi flipped on the kitchen light and turned to Hollis when he came back inside. "We going to check out the roof or keep playing Crocodile Dundee?"

"Roof," Hollis answered, setting the empty glass in the sink.

Levi headed out the back door while Hollis lingered a moment behind him, reaching into his pocket. He tugged out the silver second-place medal. "I've been meaning to give you this. Bonus housewarming gift." He dropped the medal on her countertop and gave her a grin that would have had her buying more Boy Scout popcorn than she could ever eat. He disappeared out the back door before she could sign on the dotted line.

•   •   •

Wren had been right—it wasn't much more than a shack, but Hollis could see the appeal. The little blue house had an earthiness that spoke of Wren. The inside was entirely her: colorful, mismatched, and ethereal.

Hollis followed McCoy up to the roof, not to help but to learn. McCoy grumbled about Wren's inspector as he ran a hand along cracked and brittle roof tiles. "One good windstorm and half of these are going to break."

"Can we fix it before the storm?"

"Bro, everybody thinks you're smart, don't open your mouth and ruin it."

"That bad?"

"The town's going nuts getting ready for the hurricane. Nothing and no one is available. A tarp is the best I can do."

A door scraped below them. He couldn't see her, but the sound of Wren's voice carried to the roof. "Can I come up?"

Before Hollis could question the structural ability of the roof to hold all three of them, McCoy invited her up. She reached the top of the ladder and stopped. McCoy's status report didn't faze her.

"A tarp then," she said, managing to climb onto the rooftop in a long skirt. Hollis reached a hand out, and she took it, sitting next to him, surprisingly close. He didn't dare move a muscle, less he scare off the wild bird. "I've never seen my yard from this point of view."

McCoy left to hunt for a tarp in his truck while Wren told him the names of neighbors she had met. She was the only person he knew who could make Ridley Bay's Northside sound good.

"By the way, how's your sister?" she asked. "You said you had to go help her."

"Yeah, just needed some tech help." Though that didn't explain the sweat he had worked up at the park, but he hoped she didn't notice it.

"You're the family IT guy?"

Hollis shrugged. "Makes sense, doesn't it?"

"You must be expensive."

"Family gets a discount."

Wren turned to look at him, her lips tugging upward, like she almost believed him. "What do you charge friends for roof repairs?"

Hollis gave half a laugh and decided not to question her use of the term "friends." Things seemed to have improved a little since their talk. "I'll have my people bill you."

Her lightning smile flashed and disappeared. "Good luck, my people have ways of handling unwanted bills."

"Are brass knuckles involved?"

Wren pressed her lips together, but it didn't hide the lift in her cheeks. Hollis heard McCoy wrestling a tarp onto the roof and went to help.

"I've only got one," McCoy said. "But we can cover the section over the kitchen. It looks the worst." They set to work stapling it down.

"What else do I need to do before the storm?" Wren asked.

"It's just a category one," Hollis said. "You'll be fine."

McCoy scowled. "This house needs boards on the windows, sandbags, and a lot of luck. Do you know how far the channel is?" He gestured northeast.

About two blocks. Hollis knew. "We never get more than a little rain."

McCoy sat back on his heels and swung his head toward Wren. "Did you completely ignore the inspection?"

An invisible rod stiffened her back as she lifted her head an inch higher. "I decided I wasn't scared of a project."

Before McCoy could accuse her of any more negligence, Hollis asked what projects she had already done. Wren listed off bathroom wallpaper removal, paint jobs, carpet steaming, and yard work.

"Okay, but next is structural stuff," McCoy said, with an eyebrow raised at her.

Wren lifted her hands in surrender. "Fine."

As if to prove McCoy's point, a breeze rattled the oak tree in the yard, and a few light raindrops began to fall. They all climbed down the ladder, and Hollis helped McCoy pack his things back into his truck with the last of the sunlight. McCoy made a quick exit, while Hollis went back through the house for his keys.

Wren walked him to the door and eyed Hollis's car, parked in the gravel driveway, close behind Wren's SUV. "Didn't trust the street parking?" she asked.

No, not at all. Before Hollis could figure out a more suave answer, she gave a short laugh. "I don't either. Thanks for coming over anyway."

"I don't think I did much. But I'm glad I got to see the place. I can see why you bought it."

She wrestled with that lightning smile. "Even with the ramp?"

"Especially with the ramp."

For emphasis, Hollis crossed the porch and swung down the ramp— a much less efficient route than the stairs. He heard a small laugh. When he reached the bottom, he glanced back up to see Wren leaning against the doorframe.

She shook her head at him and lifted a hand in a wave. "Goodnight, Hollis."

"Night, Wren."

•   •   •

A steady rain started Wednesday morning and continued through the rest of the day, into the night. Rain was healing—it cleansed and renewed. Wren spent most of Wednesday evening wrapped in a blanket, sipping tea, and watching her oak tree dip, sway, and shiver in the rain, with its own unique dance.

When it continued Thursday morning, it began to lose its magic. Rain on the coast usually only lasted a few hours at most. In her six years in Ridley Bay, Wren had only seen a couple of tropical storms come through. Hurricanes always passed farther north. She had paid little attention to them. But when a slight break in the rain revealed an eerie red glow in the morning sky, Wren took note.

She peeked out the window between her first two clients. Todd had warned her to watch the clouds, and she saw now what he meant. They curved strangely, looping toward their little town. Hurricane Flynn had a name, and the walls seemed to whisper it.

In between clients, Wren headed to the reception area, where Indie stayed glued to the news channel all morning.

"How's it looking?" Wren asked.

"They say it's moving slow, which means less wind and more rain. It's supposed to be the first direct hit on Ridley Bay in seventy-three years."

"It'll change direction when it hits the outer islands." Nick huffed, taking over Indie's computer to type in a schedule change. "Meteorologists are just a bunch of drama school dropouts. They're excited for nothing."

Wren prayed he was right.

Chapter Thirteen

JP Kaminski called Hollis Friday afternoon looking for last minute volunteers to prepare the new church building for the hurricane. "Are you still in town?" he asked.

Still in town? A lifelong coast dweller, Hollis had never left for a storm. "Yeah. Are people really evacuating?"

"Some are. They've upgraded it to a cat two."

Nothing more than a good thunderstorm. "Right. What does the church need?"

"A few of us are heading to stores around the city right now to get whatever supplies are left. It's pretty picked over. We're hoping to get to the church this evening to start boarding windows and stuff."

"Okay, I'll be there." At least he didn't have to be on the team running around town like Chicken Little.

They ended the phone call, and Hollis focused on wrapping up at the office. Employees seemed to be getting restless. The energy ran through the building, so Hollis dismissed them all—whoever wanted to finish work from home could.

Within an hour, the building had emptied, and Hollis locked up as he left. As he headed to the elevator, his phone rang, and Lilia's name lit up the screen.

"What's up?"

"You have to call Amá," she snapped.

He had missed two calls from their mother. "Why? What does she need?"

"You have to calm her down. She thinks the storm is going to wash away Maggie or something."

"Right. And I'm the one who can calm her down because …"

"Because you're the man of the house, *Hollis.*" Her words dripped with so much sarcasm, Hollis pulled the phone away from his ear for a second.

"Something going on?"

Lilia groaned. "She's making us stay at the house because she doesn't think our apartment is safe. I've been here since last night, and I'm already going insane."

"I'll call her."

She made a sound that wasn't quite appreciative and hung up.

Hollis weathered through a phone call that was worse than any storm. Amá was worried about Maggie's food and medicine supplies, power outages, and a number of other random thoughts. Hollis reminded her they had a backup generator.

"What good is a generator when your sister is having a seizure and we can't get to the hospital?" Amá asked. "Hmm?"

"Are you really out of shakes and medicine?"

"Not yet, but nobody knows how long this will last."

He sighed. "I'll go to the store for shakes. If you can get a refill in, I'll swing by the pharmacy too." He glanced at his watch. He was going to have to become Chicken Little after all.

"Bring your bags, too," Amá said. "I'll make up the guest room for you."

Hollis nearly tripped on his own feet. "Amá, I'll be staying at my condo."

"What? You have to stay with us."

"I don't, but I'll keep in touch."

The rest of the rant passed as background noise—how he was supposed to be there for them, how distant he was, how work always got in the way. Instead of listening, Hollis mentally planned the most efficient route through the city. He would rather ride out the hurricane in a ship at sea than trapped in the same four walls as his family.

•   •   •

After dropping off supplies on the doorstep, not daring to enter the house and be assaulted by every female in his family, Hollis arrived at the church just in time to help unload the trailer of supplies. There wasn't much, a fact that McCoy and Kaminski seemed pretty upset about. Sanford had a perfect lead pastor face about it all—the picture of peace, going around the area with a handshake, a smile, and a reassuring word.

When his turn came, Hollis grinned and returned it with self-assurance. "You've lived here a while, right?" he asked.

"Almost a decade. Not quite native like you."

He remembered Hollis's background, which scored a few extra points. "Were you here for the last hurricane? Wasn't it Marta, Maxine, something?"

"I was here," Sanford said. "It didn't get a name that stuck."

"A category two shouldn't hurt much."

"You're right. But we're taking some extra precautions with our investment." He waved a hand toward the new building. He knew he was talking to a donor.

"Guess it can't hurt."

"Thanks for coming out to help."

Hollis nodded, and Sanford went on to the next person.

The amount of work they found to do surprised Hollis. Thankfully the steady drizzle and wind held the August heat at bay while they boarded windows, inspected door frames, and checked for anything else that might have been left open on the building. It wasn't quite a finished building, and it was far from storm tested.

With the building secured, they turned their attention outside. Hollis's rain jacket was failing by now, soaking into the black Nike shirt he had changed into earlier. Sick of the sticking material, he took the jacket off and ditched it by the church doors. Sanford had passed out ponchos earlier, but Hollis was already wet anyway.

Hollis joined Kaminski with a ladder as they moved to clear out gutters. Kaminski was tall enough he barely needed a ladder.

"Are you staying in town?" Kaminski asked. A middle-aged guy with ruddy hair thinning around the edges, he mentored most of the young adults. Hollis had always held out on the relationship.

"Of course," Hollis answered, scraping a small pile of oak leaves down the row.

"And your family?"

"Yep."

"How are they? I've seen Sophia more lately, but not Lilia."

"You can tell them apart?" Hollis asked.

"Sure, Sophia is the one on Joshua Sanford's arm."

Hollis hid his grimace with a laugh. Everybody else seemed used to it, so he needed to be as well. And he really needed to get to know the kid better. Maybe if they hung out more, the unease around it all would settle.

Hollis turned to scan the lawn in front of the church. The younger Sanford was here somewhere. Instead of finding him though, he spotted a beat-up Forester pulling into the parking lot. He focused on the gutter again. "I'm not sure where Lilia's been." He hated how it sounded aloud; a better brother would know.

"Must be hard to keep up with those two."

"I wish I were better at it, but they're so busy. They're the whole reason I'm here."

"Here?"

"Back in Ridley Bay."

"I didn't realize you were such a family guy," Kaminski said.

Hollis shrugged. "What else am I going to be?"

Kaminski laughed as they climbed down and moved the ladders to the other edge. "Oh, I don't know, how about tech genius and business owner?"

"I hear that's not the ticket to heaven."

"True. But neither is being a family guy, though it's a good start."

This is why Hollis didn't need Kaminski as a mentor. He knew all his own flaws, and the last thing he needed was someone to point them out to him. Amá pointed out plenty.

"Any other titles I should look to add on?" Hollis asked, hearing the annoyance in his own voice.

"Believer?"

"Got that one already."

"Then I think you're good."

Hollis huffed. "Not everybody agrees."

"You only need the big guy to agree."

"And there's no telling if he does until it's too late."

Kaminski stopped working and turned a slight frown to Hollis. "Yes, there is."

"Right. I didn't mean that." Any mention of disbelief was a Christian slip, like a Freudian but worse. "How's your house? Are y'all prepped?" He turned the conversation back around to Kaminski—anywhere except on him and his family.

They finished the gutters and returned to the front of the church to find half the team trimming tree branches and the other half securing the handful of wooden benches outside. The rain fell more earnestly now, and Hollis stepped under the front awning of the church, wiping his brow while he waited for his next assignment. His shirt stuck to his body, and he ran a hand through his hair, trying to shape the wet mass.

"Don't tell me you're too cool for a poncho." Wren's voice startled him, and he turned to find her crossing through the church doors with a large tote bag. She pulled a towel from the bag and handed it to Hollis.

He mopped his face and hair with the towel before wiping it over his arms, though it was hopeless with the soaked shirt. "Didn't love the idea of climbing ladders in a poncho."

"Should you be climbing ladders at all in the rain?"

"Worried about me?" he asked.

"Worried about the church's insurance policy."

He laughed.

The cool rain hit against ground hot enough to create a light steam, and it swirled over the earth and underneath the awning. The humidity pulled Wren's braid loose, and frizzy pieces waved around her face, too wild to be tamed.

"Thanks for the towel," he said, passing it back to her.

"Sure. By the way, I haven't gotten that bill for the roof yet."

"Decided to let you in on the family discount."

"Very generous of you."

He shrugged. "I might be worth less than you think."

Wren studied him for a moment too long, with hazel eyes that held every color. He wondered what all they saw. "I doubt that," she said.

"Because I'm already at the bottom of your list?"

She only shook her head with a small laugh.

The work on the lawn seemed to be wrapping up, and Kaminski rounded up the mini task force. They headed inside, where Wren continued handing out towels, spreading the extras under dripping feet.

Kaminski thanked everyone for their help. Then Sanford said a prayer and reminded everyone to call him if they needed anything. The group began to disband, and Hollis rounded toward Joshua Sanford before the guy could dart out the door. He never seemed to stick around church as much as Hollis would expect a pastor's kid to.

"Hey," he said, trying to catch his attention.

The younger Sanford turned, eyes darting over Hollis. Joshua looked like a kid version of his father—wiry, with light brown eyes and dark hair curling around his temples. "What's up?" He reached out with a rather stiff handshake. Without Sophia there as a conversational buffer, they never connected very well. It bothered Hollis.

"I haven't heard from Sophia in a couple days," Hollis said. "Just wondered if you knew how she was."

The kid seemed to relax. "Yeah, she's at her mom's—your mom's— house now. She's kind of stressed about Maggie."

Hollis flinched. A horrible reflex, but it happened nonetheless. He avoided using Maggie's name in public. Few of his friends at Grace knew about Maggie, and he preferred to keep it that way. Life was easier to manage when he kept it segmented, divided into small parts he could control.

Now Hollis remembered why he and Joshua didn't talk often. The kid knew too much. Sophia shared everything with everyone. "Right. Maggie will be fine." With a wave that was too curt, he turned and strode out the door to his escape. He *was* worthless, as a brother, if nothing else.

Chapter Fourteen

Renew Wellness made the rare decision to close on Friday, and Wren spent the day working with her neighbors instead. During short breaks in the rain, the residents of Florida Street banded together, like sailors preparing the ship for battle.

In Spanish and bits of broken English, Mr. Ortiz offered to send his son over to help trim back Wren's tree—an offer she gladly took him up on. She stopped at Paula's house to find stir-crazy toddlers running rampant and a war-torn-looking mother single-handedly boarding windows. Wren knew better than to ask where her boyfriend was; she picked up a hammer and joined.

They had just finished when the rain came back with fury, and the sailors scattered back into their houses.

Inside, Wren sat, watching her tree bend in the backyard—a blur in the gray rain. She paced the living room like a restless cat, unsure what else to do, knowing nothing could stop the rain.

The day stretched slowly until she found out about the work going on at Grace Church's new building. Heading into the rain to help, Wren was thankful for the excuse to leave the house.

It ended too soon though, and she was left pacing yet again, with the evening passing minute by minute.

Sometime around nine, a stifling silence settled in the place of the rain. Wren still didn't have internet on her phone, and with no TV, she had no way of knowing what was coming. The silence felt worse than the buckets of rain.

When the staleness continued for an hour, she caved and called Nick for an update on the storm.

"It's been upgraded to a category three," he answered solemnly. Even the stoic seemed shaken.

"But it's all just … drama, right?" She needed the reassurance.

"Depends. How far are you from the channel again?"

"A quarter mile."

Nick huffed. "I won't be surprised if they evacuate you."

Evacuate. Her mouth went dry. What a horrible word. A word for failures, lease defaulters, hiders. Used by city officials who thought they knew best.

Wren stared out at her yard again. Three days of rain had only left a few puddles in her yard. According to Nick, the storm was supposed to blow over town by Monday. Her house could easily withstand two more days of rain.

•　　•　　•

A siren sounded outside of Wren's window in the middle of the night, a sound she could typically sleep through, but tonight it droned on and on, over and over, rising and falling without ever leaving.

When her eyes cracked open, red and blue lights tossed rings around her room, and Wren stood on uneven feet, dizzy and confused. In a haze, she went to peek through the front window—a police car slowly patrolled the street. Finally, the siren stopped.

In its place came a bullhorn.

The voice sounded robotic and distant. The words were jumbled by rain, walls, and Wren's not-quite-awake brain. But she understood enough: mandatory evacuation.

•　　•　　•

Four hours later, dull sunlight struggled to break through the clouds. The wind howled outside, shaking Rosa's very bones. Wren chewed on her thumbnail as she paced from the kitchen to the bedroom and back again.

A police officer had knocked on every door on the street two hours ago, alerting everyone to the mandatory evacuation for their neighborhood. They were too close to the channel, the street too low and her house too unstable to survive Hurricane Flynn, set to make landfall in approximately twelve hours. The puddles in her yard had become small ponds.

Wren called Emma. No answer. Faith, Bethany, and Indie had all left town yesterday afternoon. Nick's girlfriend would kill her if she even asked to stay with Nick. She was out of friends she could stay with. She called two hotels, and both were booked.

How far could Gumpy go? Could he really make it through the rain, wind, and traffic all the way to San Antonio? Wren looked out the front blinds again—the water pooled on the street. She had to leave soon or she would be stuck. *Who am I kidding? I've been stuck since the day I was born.* Panic lodged in her throat.

The police officer drove through again, sirens blaring, megaphone announcing the mandatory evacuation. Surely, he only spoke to her now. The street was empty.

The sound of birds chirping loudly made her jump. Any hope that it was Emma calling back was dashed instantly when she saw her phone. *Daniel Hollis.* Dread pooled in an already over-stressed stomach. He would know exactly how trapped she was. She hated being caged, but for someone else to see it made it even worse. Especially him.

"Hollis."

"Wren, I saw your neighborhood on the evacuation list. Have you left?"

She paced the five steps of her kitchen again before answering. "Not yet."

"You need to leave. Where are you going?"

Somewhere with comfort food. Big, greasy, salty fries that would make her face break out. "I don't know. Everybody's left town, but I don't think my car can make it." Her voice choked on the admission.

"Come stay at my condo."

No way. It was a gut reflex, but another part of her wrestled with it. She was out of options.

"I know you'd rather be abducted by aliens," he added. "But they're busy tonight."

"You would know." Wren traced Rosa's walls like it might be the last time she saw them standing. Her voice shook. "Are you better than aliens?"

"Not much, but I have a better bed."

Wren halted. "Excuse me?"

"What? No—not … no, I meant you can have it. Like, I'll sleep on the couch."

Wren had to smile, though it disappeared quickly. She had nowhere else to go. But if she told the cat he had caught the canary … "Is your condo any safer than my house?"

"It's not on the evacuation list."

She sighed. "Okay."

"Is that a yes? I'll come get you."

"I can drive myself."

"Then I'll come help you pack your car and move stuff higher up in your house."

"My street's already underwater. Don't get your fancy car out in this."

"It'll be fine, I'm heading over now."

Wren sighed and ended the phone call without a goodbye. He would do what he wanted anyway. People like Hollis were used to getting their way. What must that feel like?

Pulling a scuffed-up hiking backpack from her closet, Wren set to work. She rolled skirts and tops and shoved them into the bottom of the bag. Once she had enough to last her a few days, her line of thinking changed. She wasn't packing for a road trip—she was choosing which clothes to potentially save.

Nick had finally admitted he had been wrong. This was the biggest hurricane their town had seen in decades. Grief swept into her with a gust and knocked her onto the bed. Wren clutched the backpack and let out a tearless sob. Would she survive this? Would Rosa?

A knock at the door pulled her from her thoughts. *Deep breath.* Stale, humid air. Old backpack. Dirt. Panic. Suddenly the thought of seeing Hollis was actually a welcome one.

Gray morning light outlined his frame as he stood hunched outside her door in a white rain jacket, and she tugged him inside.

Fighting the wind and the sinking frame, he shoved the door closed behind him and pulled off his soggy jacket, hanging it on a hook next to the door. "Hey."

The part of her that dreaded seeing him disappeared, and she realized suddenly how much she had needed a familiar face. When she wrapped her arms around him, he stiffened in surprise before returning the hug.

"I don't know what to do," she confessed into his shoulder, holding back the tears and knowing they could be heard in her voice.

The pressure of his hands on her back soothed her. "It'll be okay. Let's just get you out of here. You're the last one on your street."

Wren stepped back with a deep breath. "I know. I'm packing."

"Do you have anything that needs to be moved higher in case of flooding? Electronics? Valuables?"

Wren rolled her lips between her teeth. "I don't know."

"I'll take a look around." He stepped around her, scanning her living room, no doubt wondering what century had produced the red corduroy recliner. Wren wondered too.

Pull it together. She walked back to her room and switched her focus to the dresser: the bottom half likely wouldn't survive this. Which meant she was packing some odd things for a couple of days in Hollis's condo. Swimsuit. Quilt. Headband collection. The backpack couldn't hold it all, so she needed to stick to the favorites. She stuffed half of the headbands back into the top drawer.

Grabbing a duffel bag from the closet, she tossed in a few shoes and her more expensive pieces of clothing before facing the rest of the room. Mementos, photos, souvenirs, and seashells lined the shelves and walls. It was like looking at a lineup of children and being asked which one to save. The things on the walls would be fine. Right? As long as the oak tree didn't fall on the house. Panic reached up and wrapped around her throat again.

•   •   •

After calling for her twice with no response, Hollis headed to Wren's bedroom and found her sitting on the bed, staring into nothingness.

"Wren?" No answer. Maybe the aliens had gotten her after all. Hollis knelt and grabbed her hands—they were cold. "Wren. Hey."

She blinked several times before gasping like she had been holding her breath.

"I moved some boxes and books up onto the dining table." He glanced around the room briefly. All the furniture in the house was doomed. He had been wrong about this storm, along with every meteorologist out there. They had upgraded it suddenly, without warning. McCoy's mention of sandbags was no longer an exaggeration.

When Wren still didn't move, he stepped to the side of the bed and unplugged the lamp, lifting the cord onto the bedside table. He grabbed her phone charger and put it in the duffel bag next to her. She watched him without seeing him.

Pulling back a sliding closet door, he examined the floor behind it. Boxes, bags, and a full laundry basket. He moved everything onto the bed. Hopefully the extra two feet of clearance would be enough for them to survive. Hollis hoisted her stuffed backpack onto his shoulder and zipped up the duffel bag.

"Let's check the kitchen." He reached his free hand out to her, and she took it with another deep sigh. "We need to switch your power off. Do you want to grab some food from the fridge?"

She nodded silently and set to work, filling a reusable bag.

Once Hollis had done all he could for the contents of the house, he asked her where to find the breaker box and water valve. She pointed wordlessly. He shut them off, and they used the dingy morning light to finish packing.

Hollis shrugged his wet rain jacket back on to load the bags into her car. "Are you okay to drive?"

She was staring blankly at the living room. "Yeah." It was quiet and unconvincing, but he knew there was no way she was leaving her car here.

When he took the bags outside, an inch of water had climbed up the driveway, heading toward her Forester rapidly. He'd parked the Corvette a few houses away, where the street rose an inch higher. Eerie emptiness surrounded them. No other cars were on the street now. Just trees, bending, waving goodbye.

When Hollis stepped back inside, Wren was exactly where he'd left her.

Nobody had ever needed a hug as much as she did right now. But two in one day would be a stretch for her. Hollis settled for a hand on her arm instead. "Wren, we need to go."

"I don't have flood insurance." Her voice sounded strangled, distant.

Oh, Wren. Why? "A lot of people don't. It'll be okay."

"Believe it or not, I actually like that yellow, floral couch." She nodded toward the piece sitting in the living room.

"My grandparents had one exactly like it. Most comfortable couch I ever slept on."

When she turned to face him, the shock was gone, replaced by silent tears. "I'm screwed, Hollis."

He couldn't help himself. He wrapped her into a tight hug. "It's okay. It'll be okay."

After minute that felt both long and short, she moved and he dropped his arms. Hollis grabbed her keys from the basket by the door and handed them to her, but she hesitated and looked back at the house again. "Can we pray for it? The house? I know that's weird."

"Sure." He grabbed her hand. With their backs to the door, they faced the house together. She stayed silent. Was she waiting for him? He had no idea how to pray for a house.

Hollis cleared his throat and launched into it. "Okay, God. You're the maker of storms, sunny days, and everything in between. Please calm this storm. Protect the people in this city. Watch over Wren's home while she's away and help us remember where our true hope is. In Jesus's name ..."

He waited. Wren said nothing.

"Amen," he finished.

She nodded silently and squeezed his hand. She locked the door behind them, and they made a dash to their cars. The water had already risen on his tires. Only he could ever know that he was genuinely concerned about driving the Z06 through this. It was a shallow thought, in comparison.

Chapter Fifteen

Between the condo and the ocean stood the marina with its few restaurants and abandoned boats, guarding like toy soldiers. The floor-to-ceiling windows acted as Wren's personal big-screen TV. She didn't need the news when she had the storm right in front of her. Dark clouds swallowed the horizon, the sun never fully illuminating the day. Palm trees along the boulevard quivered in fear, begging to uproot and find a safer home.

She had already unpacked and arranged her bags neatly to the side, leaving her with nothing to do in this spotless place.

The wind beat against the windows. When she stood still, barefoot on the wood floors, she could feel the building rock slightly. Was being on the fifteenth floor of a condo safer than her house? At least it wasn't likely to flood.

"Hey." Hollis's voice startled her, and she shook off the thoughts before facing him. "I'm gonna fill the bathtub tonight in case we lose water. Do you want to shower or anything first?"

Shower? In Hollis's bathroom? "Um, sure. Yeah. That would be good." Packing up her house in the smothering humidity had left her sweaty.

After pulling out a couple of towels, he retreated to his room. Wren appreciated the space. He might be a Christian, but she doubted this was the first time a girl had stayed in his condo overnight. And he wasn't allowed to get within a foot of her while she was here.

She dug through her backpack for something to change into. It was just after lunchtime—too early for pajamas, despite desperately wanting their comfort. She settled for something in between: a rose-colored tank top and a loose green jumpsuit.

A hot shower did wonders for her nerves. Wren let it run too long, knowing it might be the last for a couple of days. She scrubbed her hair clean and shaved every square inch of her legs for no reason at all. It was middle school all over again; she was awkward, out of place, and trying too hard.

With one last deep, steam-filled breath, Wren shut the shower off.

Even his stupid towels were fancy. Soft and lush, like wrapping herself in a dead alpaca.

She towel-dried her hair as best as possible. Her hair dryer hadn't made the cut from her house, so she plaited her hair into a long, wet braid and went on the hunt for lotion in Hollis's bathroom. The only thing on the countertop was an electric toothbrush. Because manually brushing teeth was too much work for the elite.

A long row of cabinets lined the oversized bathroom. Wren silently pulled open the cabinet below one of the two sinks, and leaned back as if a snake might burst out of it. She had stayed in plenty of people's houses growing up and learned early on which kinds of people would shout at someone for opening their cabinets. Though she didn't know much of Hollis beyond the false front he displayed, she doubted he was the shouting type.

Wren tried to keep her eyes open only for lotion, but it was hard not to snoop a little. The space was mostly empty, just extra towels and a few cleaning supplies. For Hollis or a maid?

The drawers next to the sink were more revealing. The first held a razor, a shaving soap puck, and the aftershave that gave off Hollis's signature woodsy scent. A nearly full bottle of cologne with an unfamiliar scent sat at the back.

The second drawer held a comb, a few hair products, and a small bottle of unscented lotion. Which meant her hunt had ended, and she had no excuse to open the third drawer. Maybe that was for the best. It probably held gold-encrusted toilet paper and the souls of child laborers.

"Stop it," Wren muttered to herself.

The wall she had built against Hollis had so many holes in it, she was filling it as fast as possible, however unfairly, because if that wall fell, she would get hurt. The fact that she owed him now only made things worse. But she still needed to lay off the insults.

When she exited the bathroom, Hollis was hiding in his room, and she heard computer keys tapping. Work on a Saturday?

She headed into the kitchen and started pulling her food from the refrigerator. No doubt the power would go out at some point during this storm and they would lose it all anyway.

Cooking allowed for more snooping, though kitchens didn't hide many secrets and she quickly found a cutting board, a knife, a pan, and a spatula. The space was decently equipped for a bachelor. Did he cook? How rich would you have to be to hire a personal chef?

The sweet potatoes had just finished roasting, and she had the rest of the ingredients for a Buddha bowl assembled and waiting when Hollis walked out of his room and took her up on her offer of dinner—vegetarian, for his sake.

Wren set two bowls on the dining table before taking one look out the window next to it and returning the bowls to the safety of the kitchen island.

"What's wrong with the table?" he asked.

Wren shrugged. "The wind might throw a shark at the window any minute."

"That would be something," he said, joining her at the island.

"Do you have storm shutters?"

"No, but they're storm windows. They'll be fine." He glanced over at her, and his eyes ran down her. "Are those overalls?"

Wren dropped her fork. "Are you really making fun of my clothes?"

"What? No! It was an honest question." He held his hands up, and the innocence in his eyes was almost comical.

Really, Wren knew he wasn't. But it had happened to her in the past too many times, and it was easy to tease him for it—to fire off all the things she could never say to the kids who had been truly cruel. "It's called a jumpsuit."

"Looks comfortable."

"Better than a suit," Wren said, tilting her fork toward him. He had changed into dry clothes and now wore a blue short-sleeved button-up, tucked into white shorts. Even on a Saturday in his own home, he wore a belt. Always crisp and polished. She used to find it pretentious but now wondered if it was simply him: predictably overdressed Daniel Hollis.

When they finished eating, he moved to the kitchen and started cleaning dishes.

"I can do them," she offered.

"I've got it. There's a race on … Do you mind if I …?" He gestured to the TV.

"Oh, sure, go for it." Sharing this space felt like an awkward dance, and they kept stepping on each other's figurative feet.

He flicked on the massive television, and little cars drove around and around in circles while he watched from behind the kitchen sink.

Two hours later, the race had ended, the kitchen was spotless, and Wren had learned a thing or two about Formula One. The race had provided enough distraction from the storm to calm her nerves for a while. She turned down his offer to watch storm updates on the news. She'd rather not know.

The moment the TV screen went black, the wind howled louder than ever.

"Know any card games?" He stood from the couch and stretched.

"You don't have to entertain me. I can just read a book or something." She had brought a few of her favorites, and Hollis had a small, sparse bookcase in the living room that looked like it was filled with business books, in case she needed help sleeping tonight.

He hesitated with a hand in his hair, looking like he was trying to decide whether to press the cards idea. He was completely off his game tonight, and the human side of him was rather adorable.

Before he could decide, something whacked one of the huge windows facing the bay and sent Wren nearly a foot in the air with an embarrassing squeal. Hollis turned to face the windows and paced in front of them for a minute.

"Was it the shark?" Wren asked.

He laughed, leaning his head on the window and looking straight down.

"Should you be standing that close to the windows?"

"You really are worried about me." He turned back to her with a smile fit for a toothpaste commercial.

She shrugged. "If you die tonight, I'd be the first suspect."

Hollis laughed again, and it was good enough to make her agree to a card game.

•   •   •

They stayed up too late arguing over who would sleep on the couch. Hollis won—or lost, he realized now. His condo, his rules. He had the couch, with a sheet, one pillow, and a quilt Wren had brought with her. He had never bothered with fluffy things like extra blankets and pillows, but he suddenly saw the usefulness.

Even if the couch had been more comfortable, sleeping through landfall of a category three hurricane would be impossible. The entire condo groaned and rattled. He dozed fitfully.

The blaring emergency alert on his phone sent him shooting up from a light sleep. Heart pounding at the eerie sound, he silenced the blasting tone. Bleary eyes slowly focused. The time showed two o'clock as he read the message.

Take cover now in an interior room of a sturdy building, away from windows.

On cue, some projectile smacked against the windows. A cold shiver ran down his spine. If Wren was sleeping through this, she was arm's reach from another large window. Storm windows, he reminded himself. Windows that couldn't shatter.

The siren on his phone sounded again. *Take cover now ...*

Before he could debate it any longer, the bedroom door opened. Wren emerged, clad in an oversized church tee, shorts, and a cardigan. "What was that?" she asked, voice thick with sleep.

"Emergency alert."

"What, is there a storm or something?" She gave him a sleepy grin. Middle-of-the-night Wren was much sweeter than daytime Wren.

Another bang sounded against the window as the hurricane sent debris flying fifteen floors up. They both turned toward it.

"What did the alert say?" Wren asked, more serious this time.

Hollis sighed. "Move to an interior room, away from windows."

"The bathroom?"

"The bathroom."

They stripped the covers off the bed. Hollis brought the quilt from the couch, and they set up a temporary camp on the tile floor of the bathroom, an even worse place to sleep. He tossed pillows next to the tub, closer to the interior, for Wren. Then he sat against the wall, near the door, to give her as much space as possible in the narrow room.

She ended up sitting next to him anyway.

They waited in silence for a moment, listening to the howling wind and beating rain, the room illuminated by a single night-light.

"What's in that drawer?" Wren pointed to the bottom drawer by the sink.

Hollis cocked his head to look at her. In the midst of Ridley Bay's worst hurricane in decades, she wanted to know what was in his bathroom drawer? He shrugged. "Normal stuff. Why? What do you think is in there?"

"Blood diamonds and voodoo dolls?"

Hollis tilted his head back with a tired laugh. He prided himself on being a chameleon—he could fit what anyone wanted him to be—until he met Wren. The one person who seemed more real and honest than anyone he'd ever known was the one person who hated him. And now they were trapped in the bathroom together.

"Don't be ridiculous, Atwood. I keep those in the bedroom. That drawer is for home liens, pink slips, and other greeting cards."

Her laugh warmed the space. He had half expected her to take him seriously.

Hollis stretched his leg across the space and pulled the drawer open with a foot. "It's just a junk drawer."

Wren sat up and peered into it. Hopefully it didn't hold anything embarrassing. He was pretty sure it was random charging cords and half-used hotel toiletries. She leaned back against the wall next to him, shoulder to shoulder.

"Find any ivory tusks?" he asked.

"Not a single one." He could hear the amusement in her voice.

A large crack sounded from the living room, and Wren ducked her head into his shoulder, a move so surprising he forgot about the storm for a second. Her long hair brushed against his arm, and his nose filled with the scent of a garden—floral and earthy.

"I think that was the flying shark," she whispered, sitting upright again. Cool air hit his chest where she had been. "You were right, by the way."

A strange confession from her. "About?"

"The bed," she said. "It's better than an alien's."

"You would know."

She elbowed him in the side, and the moment she did, the night-light went out. Silence took the place of the humming air conditioner.

"Power outage," he said.

They sat there in the dark, heads leaning back against the wall, listening to the sound of a hurricane ripping through their city and the sounds of their own breaths until Wren's voice broke through. "Ever played twenty questions?"

Chapter Sixteen

Feeling as if she had never slept, Wren found herself waking to a dim, cold light coming through the crack under the door. They emerged from the uncomfortable shelter of the bathroom. The storm windows had withheld as they promised, though one in the living room now featured a massive spiderweb crack across it.

The swirling, dark heart of the storm turned into a steady rain pelting against the windows, no longer furious, but incessant.

The power came back intermittently. Hollis said the building had a backup generator strong enough to keep refrigerated food stable and give them an occasional blast of air conditioning.

They spent one fifteen-minute power surge making breakfast. On the next one, Hollis switched on the TV. A swirling red and green graphic covered their city, repeating, twisting over and over. Hanging out. Dumping rain. He turned it off when they started to show the flood damage across the city.

"Should we see if …" Wren started but couldn't finish the question.

"Nah."

She nodded and sat next to him on the couch, listening to the rain and waiting for the hours to pass.

•   •   •

Hollis couldn't remember exactly when the rain had started. It had been raining for days, with few breaks. Hours and hours and hours of rain.

Before the hurricane's arrival, he had watched the bay swell, water rising under the wharf. It took more than your average storm to spill over the channel, yet Hurricane Flynn had succeeded. Not only had it flooded the channel but it had also soaked the wetlands, and the rain had nowhere left to drain. Water rose across the city, backing up, and no one could find the sky's shutoff valve.

The next time they turned on the news, talk surrounded the reservoir system. Not only was the city's main reservoir beginning to flood but they were planning to do a controlled release of the dam, to reduce the risk of collapse. He wasn't sure if Wren understood what releasing the dam would mean for her house. Neither of them brought it up.

Cell towers were either down or overwhelmed—signal cut in and out throughout the day. Hollis used the moments he could to check in on family, friends, and work. He had their remote workers running as much as possible and an apology statement issued to their clients for reduced services in the meantime. His dad called from Boston and wished him well. The twins were still stuck at home with Amá and Maggie.

"Amá will never forgive you," Lilia warned him on the phone. "She thinks you should have stayed here."

"That's why I called you, not her."

Lilia laughed. "I told her I wished I was at your condo."

"How'd that go?"

"She'll never forgive me either."

"We probably weren't forgiven for whatever the last thing was either. What's one more?"

"Good point."

He heard Sophia in the background before she popped onto the line with a voice identical to Lilia's. "Condo crash yet? Bottom floors flooded and buckling?"

"You bet. We're on a life raft right now."

There was a slight pause before both girls spoke at once. "We?"

He didn't want to get into it. "Yeah, me and the rest of the building. We only got one raft."

He managed to distract the girls with their dad's latest adventure in Boston, and they quickly ended the conversation to call their dad and harass him for leaving his precious daughters in a hurricane—undoubtedly a call that would end in a gift being mailed.

Life ran according to the rolling blackouts the rest of the day: fifteen minutes of power followed by forty-five minutes without. Hollis used the intermittent electricity and internet to do whatever work he could.

Eventually, the city's water plant went down, and the flow of water to the condo slowed to a trickle. They had plenty in the tub to flush the toilet, and he had a few gallons of bottled water to drink from, though he now wished he had listened a little more to McCoy's and Kaminski's plans.

There wasn't much to do other than read, play card games, and talk to Wren more than he had ever dreamed. The more they talked, the more their usual taunts and teases subsided, replaced by conversations about weird food combinations and the best kids' cartoons.

They had just agreed that slipping on banana peels couldn't happen in real life when Hollis realized the gray light outside was darkening. He checked his watch. "Power should be back on in about ten minutes. If I get everything prepped now, fifteen minutes should be enough time to cook. How do you feel about vegetarian quesadillas for dinner?"

Wren hopped up from the couch and followed him into the kitchen. "That sounds great, I can make them."

Hollis bumped into her on purpose as he navigated around the kitchen. "You think you can make better quesadillas than me? Mi Mamá es de Colombia, remember?"

She raised an eyebrow and lifted a knife. "And I'm from the Tex-Mex capital of the world."

"Is that a challenge?"

"Loser has to do dishes," she said.

"Deal."

•　　•　　•

Wren had to do dishes, though Hollis insisted on helping anyway. They rationed the water carefully and had just dried the last one in the fading light from the windows when Mavis called. Wren quickly excused herself to the bedroom, shut the door, and answered the call from the far side of the room.

"Wrenny, sweetie, Ridley Bay is all over the news. Are you okay?"

"I'm safe."

"Is your house okay?"

Whatever strength had carried her through the past two days melted and tears formed before she could answer. "I don't know …"

"Oh, dear."

Through tears and hiccups, Wren told her mother about the house, the location, the water drowning everything she had worked for.

"That's too bad," her mother said. "You know, we've never had a flood like that here in San Antonio. Are you sure you want to stay there?"

"Mavis," Wren said, chastising. "Can you at least try to be supportive?"

"Well, sure, I would if you were closer. A family that sticks together can survive anything. But you're so far, what can I do?"

She didn't have to say it directly for Wren to hear the "I told you so" between every line. Her mother always knew disaster would come to those who wanted too much. No comfort would come from Mavis, only an invitation to an old life.

When they finally ended the call, Wren felt no better. If Rosa didn't survive this, maybe she would end up back in San Antonio after all. Her mother would be happy. They would all live together, traipsing from place to place, landing on friends' couches, just as Wren had now.

Was she really any better off here than in San Antonio?

Somehow, when she thought all the tears had been spent, more found their way out. The house she had dreamed of for so long would soon be nothing more than a memory.

Chapter Seventeen

The first thing Wren saw when she woke was more rain. It greeted her with streams running down the windows. She had never known hurricanes could last this long after landfall.

Gray days called for long, slow mornings in one's own bed, but she was Goldilocks, waking up in the wrong bed. Maybe a bear would show up.

Wren climbed out and dressed brightly in a light blue skirt and a sunny yellow tank top, to manifest the sky she wanted. Every rainy-day song she knew battled for mental space, and she fought back by singing the Beatles' "Here Comes the Sun" to herself.

When she finally exited the refuge of Hollis's bedroom—a place she refused to snoop through on moral grounds and simple respect—she found him on a barstool, sipping coffee in a worn Rice tee and red athletic shorts, with mussed hair. It all looked better on him than the suit. It looked real.

"Funny dreams?" he asked, rubbing his neck. "Or do I look funny?"

"Not in the least," Wren said.

"What's the smile for then?"

"Just you."

He blinked, frowning slightly and looking as if he wasn't often the cause for someone's smile.

Wren sat on a barstool next to him and plopped the silver medal from the race down on the countertop. "Of all the things we packed, this sucker survived."

Hollis grinned against his coffee mug. "Of course it did, it's invincible."

"Well, I think it's ready to be back with its rightful owner."

Hollis hummed a sound that let her know it wouldn't last long. He pulled the medal toward himself, then reached up to rub his shoulder.

"How's the couch?" Wren asked.

With a rather bear-like grunt, he tilted his head to each side. She could see the tension on the left. "Not much better than the bathroom floor." He pressed a thumb into the side of his neck in a way that made Wren cringe. He would only make it worse.

"You should see somebody for that," she said.

"You, right? Aren't you a—"

Wren stopped him with a hand up. "Don't call me a masseuse. I'm a massage therapist."

"That's what I was going to say. Masseuse is creepy, who says that?"

Wren shrugged. "People who still use the word 'stewardess' and guys who want happy endings."

A grimace crossed his face. "That doesn't really happen, does it?"

"Do you need me to say no?"

He made a sound of disgust and took his mug to the sink, moving as stiffly as a tin man. When he reached for a bottle of Advil, Wren tucked away a small sigh.

"Sit down," she said.

She had healed dozens of tension headaches for friends of all genders. Nothing was special enough about Hollis that she couldn't do it for him too.

He grinned that Boy Scout grin and took a seat at the couch, Advil still in hand.

Ye of little faith.

She stood behind him, walking her fingers up his neck, feeling out the tension and telling her brain to be professional.

Every sinew from the base of his head down into his shoulders was pulled tight. If she had to guess, it had been going on long before he slept on the couch. The image he held on to so tightly affected his body too.

A silent sigh fell from his back. One of her favorite things about the job was the way people turned into putty at a single touch. Wren always said she chose massage school because it was cheaper than college, but there was more to it. As a child, she had found comfort in Mavis's gentle touch, and it was one thing that never changed, no matter where they were. Massage could heal and bond, anywhere at any time. Not even a hurricane could take that away.

Usually, she let her clients set the pace for conversation, but this was different.

"Did you really sleep on a yellow floral couch like mine?" Wren glanced at the thin pillow leaning against the arm of the couch.

It took him a minute to catch up to the thought. "My grandparents' couch? Yeah. We used to have sleepovers there as kids. The twins got the guest room, and I got the couch."

"Are they still alive?"

"The twins?" Hollis asked with a laugh. She gave his head a slight push, not enough to undo any of her work. "Just my grandpa. He's in a nursing home."

"Mom's side or dad's?"

"Dad's. My mom's parents died in Colombia before she came over."

They were adding onto a long list of things she had learned about Hollis. His favorite holiday: New Year's Eve. Favorite color: blue. Favorite animal: eagle.

"The yellow couch was the first thing I bought when I moved here," Wren said. "I had about fifty bucks and figured a couch could make a bed, somewhere to sit, and a dining chair until I could get the rest. Found it at the Salvation Army." A mental image of the couch sitting in a pool of water flashed in her mind, and she pushed it away just as quickly. "What about your third sister?"

"What?"

"You said the twins stayed in the guest room and you stayed on the couch. What about your third sister?"

Any tension she had relieved sprang back into his neck as he stiffened. He moved away from her, and she dropped her hands.

"You're a good listener." The way he said it didn't sound like a compliment.

"Part of the job."

Hollis stood, still facing away from her. "Let me know what I owe you," he mumbled, heading off to the bathroom, far from his usual suave self.

She had found another trigger point.

•　　•　　•

Hollis hated his own reaction. He was an adult, ten years removed from the taunts of high schoolers. Twenty years removed from irrational childhood fears. Several years into owning an entire company created and named for Maggie. But numbers meant nothing when it came to gut reactions.

Right or wrong, he had spent years protecting Maggie—and himself—by hiding her. She hated stares and questions, and so did he. But she was his sister. And she deserved to be acknowledged. Why couldn't he do it?

Facing the scruffy guy in the mirror, a day past his usual shave, Hollis hung his head, hating his own weaknesses. He flipped on the water, ignoring the boil notice and simply turning it as hot as it would go. Slowly, methodically, focusing on something besides his failings, Hollis shaved and cleaned up.

Finally, he had few excuses to stay in the bathroom and nowhere else to hide from Wren in a one-bedroom condo. Bracing his hands on the edge of the sink, he stared down his reflection, willing one of them to be the better man. Lilia had taunted him just days ago for being the only *Hollis* at Grace Church. He wasn't, of course. They were all Hollises. Including Margarita Hollis.

Forcing himself to re-enter the room, he found Wren seated at the table, facing the windows with a bagel in front of her and another set on a plate beside her.

Hollis sat down and joined in the breakfast. Rain beat the weary palms lining the boulevard below them. High waters washed over the marina's boardwalk. They ate in silence. Wren obviously hadn't forgotten and would not let the topic change until he said something.

"Maggie couldn't do things like sleepovers."

Wren stopped chewing for a moment but didn't look at him, which he appreciated. "Why not?"

She gets homesick. She's really shy. She's not feeling well. He'd come up with a lot of excuses before. The bagel stuck in his chest, creating a tight knot. He hated the truth. "She has Rett Syndrome."

Wren nodded slowly. "I'm sorry, is that … I don't recognize that."

"It's a neurological disorder. She can't … she does most things differently."

"Differently?"

"She can't talk. Or walk. Or use her hands very well. But she's brilliant. She really is. She's the one who suggested I get you flowers."

"But you don't like to talk about her."

He wished it was a question, but it wasn't. "I hate when people talk about her."

"Even yourself?"

"Yeah. I never do it right. And everybody wants to make it all about Rett, but she's not just a disability. She's … Maggie. My funny, artistic little sister who loves to be outside."

"She sounds wonderful."

The knot in his chest loosened. "Did you see the picture in the entryway? The purple arch?"

Wren glanced over her shoulder at the abstract artwork and nodded.

"She did that."

Wren turned in her seat to study the picture. "Really? I figured it was a modern piece you overpaid for."

Maggie would love that; he'd have to pass the compliment on. There was so much he couldn't explain about Maggie though. He couldn't explain how much he loved her, how he had the best memories with her, and the most difficult ones.

"Did she have it from birth?" Wren asked, turning back around.

"Yes, but we didn't know until she was nearly two."

"How old were you?"

"Six."

Her eyebrows raised. "First grade."

"Yeah." His mom had loved Maggie more from the moment she found out she was having a daughter. But the Rett diagnosis had taken Hollis right out of the running. Maggie became the sun his mother's world revolved around, and there had been little room for anyone else. Passing first grade on his own proved impossible.

"How old were the twins?"

"My mom was pregnant with them when we found out."

"That must have been a hard year for all of you."

Hollis gave a short, harsh laugh. "Yeah, becoming invisible is rough."

Her forehead wrinkled. "What?"

"Sorry, I shouldn't have said that."

She held his gaze as firmly as if it were with her own two hands. "Tell me what you meant."

It was better to keep the ugly side of himself hidden, but her hazel eyes seemed to see, and hold, entire worlds. And nothing in her tone sounded pitying or judging; she seemed genuinely interested, empathetic maybe.

"I didn't really exist after that." He shrugged. "My mom poured everything into Maggie and the twins. She really only wanted me around if I was being useful." He had tried to get her attention a hundred ways, tried to help in every way a child could, but soon learned it was best to simply stay out of the way.

Wren let out a heavy sigh and looked out the window in front of them. "But you love them. Your mom and Maggie."

"Of course I do. I mean, my mom probably could have handled things better, but I don't blame her. And Maggie … none of it was her fault. She's my sister, I can't help but love her."

"Mm. You make it sound easy to love difficult people, but it's not."

"Sounds like you know from experience."

Wren inhaled slowly and nodded, staring at her plate. "Nothing like Maggie, though." Then she stood and carried it off to the sink.

If it took a few minutes for him to be able to talk about Maggie, he could wait for her too.

·   ·   ·

Sometime that night, unnoticed as she slept, the rain finally slipped away. Wren woke to the reappearance of the sun shining over an ocean that still sat too high, downtown streets with fallen branches, and a few battered boats. Life here had only been disrupted, not destroyed. They sat in the happy middle, the eye of it all, while north and south of them, Ridley Bay drowned.

According to the news, the streets all over Ridley Bay were a disaster. With every drain, wetland, and river clogged up, the floodwaters simply sat, unable to retreat. It wasn't just on the local news anymore; it was national now. They were the pity project. Millions of dollars in donations poured in from across the country, and Wren had no idea where that money even went.

The desire to rush to Rosa and see the damage fought against her need to run away from it all. Not that it mattered. She couldn't go anywhere until the waters receded.

Wren paced the condo like a caged lion, the walls closing in. *Save the house. Do the work. You can do this. Give it up. Go back to Mavis. You'll never be more.* Thoughts played on repeat, matching the tune of her steps on the wood floor. She couldn't take it anymore.

"I'm going for a walk," she announced, more to the air than Hollis.

"Thought you already were," he said from the dining table, where he had been working on his laptop. Stretching his arms up, he nodded toward the path she had been walking. "Any floor left?"

Wren turned her nose up and headed for the door.

"Wait up," Hollis called, closing his laptop. "I'll come too."

"You have to work." She hadn't asked questions or dared to look his way. The less she knew about his work, the better.

"I own the company. I can take a break."

Wren waved a hand, mentally plugging her ears and playing show tunes to block him out. "Whatever."

Hollis gave that silly, sparkly, half-dimpled smile, and she turned up the volume on the mental show tunes.

The bay front revealed more battle scars at ground level. The tree branches were only the beginning of the debris that littered the sidewalk. To see their city trashed hurt Wren, like the hurricane was a personal attack.

The boulevard that should have been buzzing with traffic and tourists sat mostly silent, save for the occasional blaring siren as an emergency vehicle raced between debris.

A handful of other people had braved their way outdoors. When they crossed paths with one elderly couple, they made small talk for a few minutes, sharing awe over the wreckage this storm had brought. When it turned to talk about the flooded state of the Northside, Hollis ended their chat and moved on.

His protectiveness threatened to destroy the last of Wren's walls against him, and she nearly went tumbling down the other side.

They walked around palm leaves scattered on the sidewalk, listening to another wailing siren somewhere farther away. An overturned garbage can sat in their path, and Hollis righted it, scooping the trash bag back into it, along with various debris he had gathered on their silent walk.

He continued gathering more garbage as they walked, unafraid of touching any wrapper or stray item in their path. Finally, Wren couldn't stop herself. "What's with the nature-guy thing?" she asked.

Hollis looked like he'd been caught with his hand in a cookie jar rather than holding someone's lost flip-flop. "What?"

"The whole vegetarian, spider-saving, litter-pick-up thing."

He chucked the flip-flop and a stray plastic bag into the next bin and shrugged. "I don't know. The turtles make me sad. And every life matters."

"The turtles?"

"You know, the pictures of turtles caught in plastic and stuff."

She had to let that stew for a moment. Hollis definitely had a soft side. "And how do the turtles feel about your car?"

"Well, I try not to drive it into the ocean."

Wren gave in to his contagious smile. Daniel Hollis had an answer for everything. "Let me get this straight. You own a company so that you can take breaks and pick up trash for the turtles?"

Hollis flashed that expensive grin of his. "Nah, I own a company so I can impress pretty girls."

Wren couldn't help it. She dropped her head back and laughed. The air rushed into her lungs like a balm. They had been cooped up inside for too long. "Does it work?"

He raised an eyebrow at her. "Does it?"

"The business, not so much. The turtles, maybe."

As they walked, Wren joined in on the effort, gathering bottle tops and loose netting. They had made it half a mile when a few light drops of rain began to fall. Turning back toward the condo, they moved faster along the sidewalk.

"You call me nature guy, but what's with the bare feet?" Hollis called over his shoulder, pointing out a rusty nail on the ground.

"Grounding, negative ions, improved proprioception and musculature, and you can't judge my shoes," Wren said back, raindrops now running into her face.

Hollis grabbed her hand and pulled her toward one of the many gazebos lining the bay front. Under the cover, they both wiped their faces and shook out wet hair.

"Round two, I guess," Hollis said, looking out at the rain.

"I think it's round thirty-seven at this point."

"People don't judge the barefoot look?"

"That's a vibe, so it doesn't matter."

Hollis tilted his head, studying her. "Fair enough." He leaned against one pillar of the gazebo and watched the rain drip over the bay.

Wren fought his magnetism and took a spot against the next pillar over. The rain clouds were scattered, and sunlight streamed all around them, through the droplets, lighting them up. The rain wouldn't last long this time. "I love when you can see the sunbeams like that." She leaned out of the gazebo. "It feels like a little gift from God. A heavenly hello."

Hollis turned a grin toward her. "I like that."

The sunbeams soon took over and the tiny rain cloud dissipated, but neither of them moved to leave.

"I have a question, but you don't have to answer it," Hollis said.

"Okay …"

"Who's the difficult person you love?"

His question hit like a slap to the back. She'd wondered if he would bring it up again after their conversation yesterday. But he hadn't all day, so she assumed he wouldn't. She assumed he wasn't a good listener and had been okay with that. Now, he turned the tables.

It was her turn to want to lock up the family skeletons. His weren't so bad. Hers, on the other hand, spoke of everything she had come from. If she had ever had a chance with Hollis, she wouldn't once he knew more about her and her family.

She could take the free pass he had offered on the question. But it wouldn't be fair.

"My sister."

Hollis waited. "What's her name?" he finally prompted.

"Lark."

"More birds."

Wren nodded. "More birds."

"Older or younger?"

"Older, by two years." Wren felt the lump in her throat that always showed up when Lark was the topic of conversation. The need to defend her family, always there, irrational and unnecessary, but real.

"Were you close?"

"We used to be best friends. She made my life so much fun growing up."

"And now?"

Wren stared at her toes. "Opioids, mostly. Sometimes a few other things." Lark sounded like a statistic, a storyline, an example. Everyone's stereotype of someone growing up fatherless and impoverished. Lark represented the life Wren desperately ran from, the life she feared, and thinking of her own flesh and blood that way made her feel sick.

"That's hard."

"Yeah." Her voice was caught in her throat. "And it changes her. She's not herself anymore."

"Has she gotten any help?"

"We've tried. She doesn't see the problem though, so she won't stick with any treatment."

"Keep praying, then."

He said it so simply, as if a prayer would have Lark skipping into church, clean as a whistle. Yet underneath the annoyance, Wren felt the sting of conviction because she rarely prayed for Lark. It was an ugly issue to bring to God. Embarrassing, even. Like it could somehow disqualify Wren from heaven by association. "I'm not sure prayer helps."

Turning his gaze back to the ocean, he spoke slowly, choosing his words. "Prayer might not always heal someone, but I still think it helps us handle it. At least, that's what Maggie says." Then, with a loud inhale, he straightened, stretched his arms up, and dropped his hands behind his head. "We'd better keep moving before it starts raining again."

Wren felt glued to the pillar, not ready to lose this moment with him. Not just in the gazebo but all the moments of the last few days. When she reached her hand out to him, he took it and pulled her into motion. Hanging on for a second too long, they headed out of the gazebo and back to the condo. Back into a world where Hurricane Flynn had left, and soon, so would she.

She wasn't ready.

Chapter Eighteen

With a collective breath, Ridley Bay's heart began beating again. The water had begun to recede enough for people to creep out and survey the damage. The noises of the city picked up, with cars on the boulevard and the occasional siren in the distance.

Hollis had flipped off the television the moment Wren emerged from the bedroom that morning, and she knew better than to ask why. The news could only tell terrible stories.

Once they had eaten breakfast, time in the condo seemed to stop. This alternate world they had lived in during the past few days had to end, making its existence all the more valuable. Wren resisted the reality ahead, but finally, time had to continue.

Packing her bag slowly, she held to the belief that she might sleep in her own home again tonight. There was nothing else she could do but believe.

Hollis tried to hide the phone that buzzed endlessly next to him. He had ignored at least half a dozen phone calls during breakfast. Yet he insisted on going with her to the house.

They had to ride together. Neither his bike nor The Car could handle the water.

After loading Wren's bag into her car in the garage, Hollis stepped in front of her and held out his hand. "Keys."

Wren stared at his hand for a moment before understanding his meaning. "What? You can't drive Gumpy."

"I'm an excellent driver."

"He's delicate. If you push him too hard, the transmission will fall to pieces."

"I'll be gentle." He kept his hand out. "But I don't think you should drive."

He must have seen something on the news that he knew would shake her. Or maybe it had come in one of the many texts and calls that vibrated his phone. Whatever his reason, Wren trusted him. She dropped the keys into his hand.

Downtown passed through the window quickly, but the drive slowed as they neared the channel and Hollis navigated around debris and standing water, taking alternate routes and winding slowly north.

Wren kept her hand firmly over her mouth as she saw homes in varying states of disarray. Some roads dipped out of sight, swallowed by miniature lakes that washed against front steps and flower gardens. Some houses might have survived the water, but they hadn't withstood the debris. One looked like it had grown a tree from the inside out, branches waving through the windows.

Finally, they turned onto her block. Wren snapped her eyes shut. "Tell me when we get there." The car stopped too soon. She knew her house was farther down.

He killed the engine. "This is as far as we can go."

Wren opened her eyes and found a place she couldn't recognize.

The street disappeared into water, but the houses around them were mostly dry, the yards rising slightly above street level. She opened her door and slid out, rain boots hitting the murky water. She knew better than to go barefoot in this.

They picked their way toward her house, mostly walking through yards to stay out of the deeper water in the street. Wren kept her eyes down and away from Rosa and knocked on each door along the way to check on neighbors.

Most houses were empty. One crying woman she hadn't met before greeted them. They hugged each other, never exchanging names. Two men stood on top of one house, using a chainsaw to cut tree branches and toss them to the muddy yard below. More sirens blared in the distance. Tears, chainsaws, sirens, dogs barking—the sounds of the Northside.

Mr. Ortiz pushed his way out of his own front door with a black trash bag filled to the brim just as they arrived. He had tears in his eyes. He tried to speak in English but slipped back into Spanish, talking so fast Wren missed most of it. Words about rain and his son and his house. She hugged the frail man while Hollis replied in rapid Spanish. Wren only understood something about help.

"Did you catch all that?" she asked, as they stepped away from the door.

"His son's roof collapsed at his house, while he was inside. He's in the hospital."

Nausea rippled through her. The amount of despair around them was too much. It threatened to choke her.

Wren stared straight down as they made it past one more empty house and to her own front yard. At least two inches of water covered the ground. Hollis held her hand. Wren couldn't do it. She couldn't bring herself to look up.

She turned her back on her house to look at Hollis instead. "How bad is it?"

His eyes scanned the house behind her, and he spoke slowly, like describing it would help take away the shock of seeing it. "There's a waterline several inches up on the house, but it's receded to the foundation. The front door is warped. It looks like some of the roof is stripped."

"Hollis, I know it's a stupid little shack, but I love this house." She choked on every word.

"We'll fix it."

Wren stared into his eyes for a moment longer. If he had ever spoken any truth, she hoped this was it. A deep breath was far from calming—the air smelled of trash, overrun sewage, and pain.

When she turned, her heart dropped straight out of her chest and into the floodwater.

Rosa was dead.

Like at a funeral with an open casket, anyone could see that Rosa's spirit had left. Her eyes were vacant. She had given up, and she had been all alone.

The world tilted sideways, and Hollis steadied her with a hand on her arm. Wren bent over, willing the world back into its place. When she could stand again, she could only stare, unsure if she should step closer or turn and run far away from here. *Fly away, Wrenny.*

Swallowing hard, she took a step forward. She wouldn't run away from her home. She wouldn't give up and search for happiness in the next place. That was an endless search. Mavis was still searching. Lark too.

No, Wren would fight for this home, regardless of how bad it got.

They sloshed across the yard and up the steps onto the porch. Water only reached the base of the house, but Hollis was right—the mark of its presence sat about six inches up on the walls. Enough to ruin everything.

The door was jammed even worse than before, wedged into a new popped position in the frame. It took several body slams against it to push it back. They pressed through the narrow opening, and Wren immediately felt sick. Truly sick. She covered her mouth again.

Everything she had once called her own was now clearly trash, reeking and rotting. With no air conditioning, the house sat sweltering in humidity and the scent of sewage and mold. *Oh, God. Why?*

Was this her destiny? The inevitability of it all seemed clear now. Atwoods were never meant to succeed.

Wren wanted to be alone, to bury the life she had built and to scream at the God she had loved. But the thought of being left here alone terrified her. If Hollis left, every last good thing in her life would be gone. It all came crumbling down around her.

Daring to step away from his side, Wren squished through the house. The carpet oozed murky water under every footstep, the former pink hue now a filthy brown. A dirty line edged her walls, showing where the water had been. The dining table and two chairs were tipped onto their sides, like a wave had washed through. Perhaps through the broken back window.

She traced her hand along the lower portion of the walls—soft like a wet sponge. Some of the wall decorations held on while others had fallen, lifeless in the wreckage. The couch and recliner were swollen and discolored.

Hollis stood stock-still taking it in, watching her take it in.

She wandered into her bedroom, finally alone. Her dresser had fallen forward, spewing contents from every drawer into a tangled, sopping heap.

The dresser was one of the very few things she had moved with her from San Antonio. Now it was soaked, sagging, and breaking apart. It tore into her heart. The piece would have been safer in San Antonio, in her ex-boyfriend's house, than here with her.

Something crunched underfoot, and the vise around Wren's heart squeezed tighter. Warily, she looked down to find the broken pieces of a giant cockleshell.

Wren sank to her knees, letting the muddy floor ruin her clothes like it had the rest of her life. A single sob racked her chest.

They had prayed for this house. Did it mean nothing? They had prayed for the people, yet Mr. Ortiz's son was in the hospital.

Wren tried to piece the shell back together in her hands, but too many pieces were missing—crushed into dust.

Hollis said to pray for Lark like it was as easy as walking up to a vending machine and requesting a soda. She didn't understand prayer. It wasn't a vending machine. But what good was it?

Drip. Drip. Drip. Wren felt her heart beat in time with the continual sound. Forcing her eyes upward, she saw sagging, leaking patches in the ceiling.

Rosa was a death sentence, not a home. And the life Wren had fought for was gone.

She would never recover from this.

•　　•　　•

Hollis ran numbers in his head. Roof repair. Electrical work. Foundation repair. Mold remediation. Drywall. New carpet. New furniture. The numbers ticked upward. It would probably be cheaper to bulldoze it and start over. The city might even condemn it.

The sound of a gasp snapped him out of numbers mode. Hollis carefully made his way to the bedroom. Wren was frozen, kneeling next to the bed, staring at a broken seashell in her hands.

He stood next to her and gently lowered a hand onto her shoulder. A slight flinch ran underneath his fingers. "Wren."

She shook her head, eyes fixed on the seashell. "I don't know what to do." Her sentence cracked and faded away.

And in that moment, Hollis realized he knew her. He knew Wren Atwood, not just her background and favorite things, but her heart. No longer the exotic, mysterious face she had been three years ago, he now knew this strong, passionate, proud woman. And he knew her heart was in this place—a heart breaking more than any numbers in his head could represent.

The house could be saved. FEMA existed for a reason. So did the church. They just had to figure out where to start. A shop vacuum and a fan sounded good right about now, and air freshener.

"I don't either," he said, reaching to help her up off the floor. She took his hand, and he guided her to take a seat on the spongy bed. He didn't trust her ability to stand. "But we'll figure it out."

When he sat next to her, she dropped her head onto his shoulder, her hand still in his. "I always wanted to live by the beach. Look what it's done for me."

"A good tan."

Wren let out a small laugh. "Mostly sunburns." She tilted her head to look at him. "I think I'll tell my past self to stay in San Antonio instead of moving to Ridley Bay."

"But then I'll never get to meet you."

"That's good," Wren said, solemnly. "Emma plans to marry you, if you ever stop asking me out to snail races."

Hollis couldn't help but laugh, despite their circumstances. "Please don't stay in San Antonio, past Wren, I'm begging you." He moved his hand from hers and wrapped his arm around her shoulders. He wanted to take this from her, all the enormity of it.

His phone rang again.

"It sounds like the world needs you," Wren said.

"They can wait." The world needed too much today, and he didn't want to face it. What if he wasn't enough to fix it all? He couldn't fix the house for Wren, and he had a feeling today would add to the list of things Hollis couldn't do.

With a heavy sigh, she stood. "It's okay. I'm ready to go."

"Are you sure?"

"Yeah. I need a break from … this." She weakly waved toward the house. "It's not the most pleasant place to be."

"But it's your home."

For a moment, she only looked around the room. "It used to be."

Chapter Nineteen

After lunch, Hollis didn't see much of Wren the rest of the day. His to-do list rapidly gained steam, from family, coworkers, clients, church, friends, and back again. The list ran into flooded streets, downed networks, emptied grocery stores, and power outages. Several days of work, employees, and clients waited for him, as well as a family of women who were disappointed in him for various reasons and an entire church that needed manpower and finances to get its members back on their feet.

He drove to the office that afternoon instead of walking, in case of more rain. Here, everything physical had survived the storm without a problem, but the far more valuable world inside the computers lagged.

His phone rang before he could hit the elevator button. Hollis braced himself as he answered.

"*¿Sí*, Amá?"

"*¡Gracias a Dios!* I was worried sick, Daniel! I cannot believe you didn't stay with us."

"I was safe."

"Good for you, but what about us? We lost power throughout the storm. We are almost out of shakes for Maggie. There are limbs in the yard, and I don't know how to work the, the, the *motosierra—*"

"Chainsaw."

"You're supposed to be the man of the house, Daniel, and you didn't even bother to check on us."

"I talked to Lilia."

His mom scoffed loudly. "You thought your little sister would know what we needed? Is she the one who makes the food and keeps up with Margarita's medical supplies?"

"What do you need? Do you need me to go get something?"

She huffed. "Food, shakes, anything. She won't eat. But what good is it to ask you? You won't even come."

"I can stop by tomorrow, Amá."

The line went dead without a response. Frustration coursed through him. Hollis shoved it down as he smashed the elevator number harder than necessary.

He'd rather work on the tech company he had founded for Maggie than deal with Maggie herself. At least here, he knew what to do.

Quincy had beat him to the office and greeted him with a long list of complaints, sprinkled with expletives. There were error reports, issues with the off-site servers, and security concerns.

Most of that was Quincy's territory. Since starting Perla Tech, Hollis had focused on growth and development, spending most of his time on the people-facing side of the company, while Quincy stayed behind a screen.

They ran through a list together, prioritizing fires to put out, delegating as many as possible. Thankfully, they had remote employees around the country who had already stepped up, working overtime this week to cover for the headquarters shutting down. Hollis's communication with them was lacking though, and he wasn't quite sure where they stood now.

Once Quincy had calmed down enough to get back to work, Hollis turned his attention to their staff, reaching out to everyone for status updates on who could work and who needed more time.

Then he faced his inbox, filled with client emails—half sending condolences, the other half wanting to know if this would affect services. Hollis didn't blame them. Perla Tech provided lifesaving technology for people with disabilities; they couldn't wait around for support, regardless of any act of God.

Long past his usual quitting time, a phone call from Micah Sanford interrupted Hollis's workflow. After confirming Hollis had weathered the storm just fine, Sanford filled him in on the church.

"Levi went by the church earlier today and said there's damage," Sanford said. "I haven't made it out myself yet, we only just cleared a tree from the end of our street."

"Is your house okay?"

"Yes, thankfully we're all fine here. But I'm getting a group together to go out to the church tomorrow, first thing in the morning, to meet and check on it. We'd love for you to be there as we come up with a plan to support our members."

Support meant dollar signs, but Hollis didn't mind. It included him in the bigger picture, and he wanted to be part of it. "I'll be there."

When he got off the phone, he glanced at the time. He had missed dinner by a long shot, so he might as well keep working at this point.

·   ·   ·

The alarm on his phone sounded too early, and Hollis heaved himself out of bed and dressed. He had gotten back late last night, nearly waking Wren as she slept on the couch—having stolen the spot in his absence. Honestly, he couldn't claim to be disappointed about sleeping in his own bed again. Though for some reason, he still woke with a headache. If he hadn't agreed to be at the church at the crack of dawn, he would wait around for another massage.

Slipping out of the condo in silence, he headed to the church. Their new building was located in the middle of town, near the university, and the roads there were easy enough to navigate.

Hollis slowed as he approached the property. The church was built out, waiting for paint and flooring, only a couple of months away from being ready. But now this new building, full of hope and promise of the future, sat littered with oak branches, broken window glass strewn about and roof shingles torn away.

Sanford looked like a wreck—ten years older since Hollis last saw him. He pulled Hollis and everyone else who showed up into hugs. Soon they were gathered in front of the building while Sanford gave a rundown of how many church members had been affected, who needed help most urgently, and the service day they had planned for the church.

"If we had plumbing and air conditioning connected, the church would be a shelter," Sanford said. "At it stands now, it's low on the priority list."

The list of needs sounded insurmountable. But McCoy said the only thing anyone could. "I guess we'd better get to work."

Sanford prayed them out, and they disbanded, off to help friends either get back into their homes or find other arrangements for now.

McCoy caught up to Hollis. "Wren called me yesterday. She got hit pretty bad. I'm heading over there now if you want to come."

"I've already been." Hollis ignored the slight eyebrow raise from McCoy. "It'll be hard to save."

"Is it even worth saving?" McCoy asked.

"It's worth it."

"Where are you heading now?"

Hollis rubbed at the growing scruff on his face. "Work." There had been a time it hadn't even felt like work. He missed those days.

"Good luck."

"You too."

•   •   •

Wren hated being alone at Hollis's condo. It felt sterile, so far separated from the world below, like a personal fortress. Without Hollis there, her restlessness grew unchecked. When she woke to find him already gone, she threw her things into her car and left.

She drove down to the docks first, but Todd wasn't there—of course. Standing by the water's edge for a while, she absorbed the ocean's strength before driving back to Rosa to meet with Levi. Though it hurt her pride to call him, she needed someone to tell her what to do next.

Florida Street had already awoken for the day when she arrived, with some neighbors hard at work. The others hadn't returned yet.

Squishing through the little house, Wren brushed her hand along the surfaces that still stood. The place she had tried so hard to memorize now felt foreign. Truly, she had lived in other places longer. This was no more home than any other she'd had. She could fly away and build a new nest. Then again, she had sunk every dime into this house. Where could she go?

She was stuck, like a bird in a cage. "Since the day I was born," she whispered.

With a heaviness in her chest, Wren stepped into the backyard, wandering through the muddy mess and fallen branches. She slogged through it, looking over each branch to acknowledge its story.

It wasn't until Wren reached the oak tree that she finally registered its presence.

"You didn't fall," she said, running a hand up the bark.

This is what she had bought—a promise. Potential. Leaning her forehead into its rough sides, Wren let the bark imprint on her skin. The sound of a chainsaw somewhere on the street signaled yet another cleanup job, another attempt at redemption.

The roar of a truck engine sounded and stopped just in front of her house. Levi McCoy.

She met him at the front door. He took one look around the place and lifted off his ball cap, rubbing his short brown hair underneath. "This is pretty bad," he said, twisting his cap on and off his head, like a cat trying to find the right place to sit. "One of the worst I've seen so far. The city might pay you to condemn it."

"Great pep talk."

He laughed. "Well, you have flood insurance, right?"

Wren's defenses raged upward like a rogue wave. This was why she didn't want help—it always came with judgment. This was why she didn't let anyone in. She gritted her teeth. "No, I don't."

Levi let out a sound between a scoff and a curse. "Wren ..."

"Sorry, the biggest storm in Ridley Bay's history wasn't exactly on my radar. Did you come to give me a lecture?"

Levi's cap finally settled into place. "No, I'm here to help." He gave Wren's shoulder a squeeze for emphasis. "Let's figure out what we can do and what needs to be hired out. There's a lot of emergency funding available."

Wren forced the rogue wave back down. Honestly, Levi looked too much like a brother to her to be a threat. A brother who was just as overwhelmed by the job in front of him as she was.

Pulling out a notepad, he began a slow walk through the house and directed Wren to take photos of everything. Though she didn't have flood insurance, a lot of damage had been caused by roof issues, and he said it might be covered. Despite the floodwaters only rising a few inches, the water damage from above had affected nearly everything.

When they had finished, Levi mapped out a plan of action for her: contact insurance, apply for emergency funding, remove furniture, pump the remaining mud and water out of the house, dry it out with fans, check for mold … It all started to blend in Wren's head, but he jotted it all down on the notepad, marking what he thought church volunteers could help with and what required an expert.

The fight for the house had only begun. How long would it take? How hard would it be? It seemed every day of her life would be a fight. Nothing could be easy for an Atwood.

Levi promised to be back tomorrow with volunteers to get started on the basics. "Do you have somewhere to stay tonight?"

Wren paused. Did she? She had loaded her bags into her car yet again, and it no longer felt right to go back to Hollis's condo. She hadn't even seen him last night. Maybe he avoided her. Surely he wanted her out by now. "Um, I'm not sure."

"Where were you during the storm? Not here, were you?"

"No, I was at Hollis's place."

Levi's eyebrows shot up, and his mouth dropped an inch before snapping shut. He appeared to change his mind on whatever he was going to say and simply nodded. "So, there again?"

"I don't think so. I don't want to wear out my welcome." Something she had watched Mavis do time and again. It always made people resentful.

"With Hollis?" Levi laughed.

"It's possible."

He stuck his hands in his pockets. "Well, pretty much everybody at church is offering spare rooms and couches. I know Bethany and Faith have a pullout sofa. Why don't we call them?"

It felt so familiar. Sleeping on friends' couches. Calling to ask for favors. Bags packed in the car. So sickly familiar. Nausea waved through her. "Actually, I can get a hotel."

"Wren, you won't be back in this house for … a while. A hotel will get expensive. I mean, we can find out what the city is offering for temporary housing, but—"

"No, thanks. No temp housing. I'll call Faith." Anything to stop him from mentioning temporary housing. She wasn't homeless. She refused the title.

Levi stayed around until she called. Faith said she was welcome to use their sofa. So much for a new start; Wren's life officially hit repeat.

Chapter Twenty

Hollis headed back to his place for a late lunch—all of his usual spots downtown were still closed and he needed medication, or a neck massage, for the headache that wouldn't leave.

He exited the elevator and stepped into his condo to find an empty space—exactly what he had walked into for the last several years, yet now it was emptier than ever. Wren should be here, and he felt her absence like a ghost. He hadn't realized how much he wanted to see her until now.

Pulling out his phone, he tapped her name and waited for her to answer. While he waited, he looked around, realizing none of her things were here. Even her quilt that had served as a cover on the couch was gone.

"Hey," she said.

"Hey. Are you at your house?" he asked, though he immediately registered the sound of other voices near her.

"No … I'm at Faith and Bethany's house, actually."

"Oh. Are you coming back?" He sounded like a lost puppy.

"No. I'm staying with them for a few days."

No goodbye. "You didn't have to leave."

"Thanks, Hollis, but I can't keep accepting your help."

"Why not?"

"Because I can't repay it."

"I would never ask you to repay anything. It isn't even helping, it's just being a good friend."

"I know, and you are. I appreciate it."

It sounded like a programmed message and nothing like the girl he had gotten to know over the last few days.

"Are you okay?" he asked. "Did I do something wrong?"

"No, you're great. I just … had to."

No reason, just rejection. The simple instinct others had to leave Hollis when they got close enough to realize he wasn't worth much of their time.

"Right. Okay. Well … call if you need anything."

"Thanks, I will," she said.

"Okay. I guess I'll see you later."

"Yeah, later."

And just like that, it all ended.

•   •   •

That evening, Hollis found an open café and picked up a smoothie for Maggie before heading to his childhood home, bracing himself for the verbal lashing from Amá. By now, a steady throb had settled into his temples.

Palm leaves littered the front yard, along with one large branch from the neighbor's tree, but no other sign of the storm lingered here. Amá stepped outside before he even reached the front door—a bad sign.

"Where have you been?" She wagged a finger at him and slipped into Spanish, asking if he would ever help, if she had to pay the landscaping company to come fix the yard, and so on.

Somehow every trip back here made him feel sixteen again, like he should be mowing the lawn on the weekend, instead of owning and operating a multi-million-dollar assistive technology company.

He interrupted her tirade with a kiss on the cheek. "Sorry, Amá."

She shook her head slowly, disappointment clear on her face. Only a kid who failed first grade got that look. "You don't even care."

She walked inside, and Hollis followed, not bothering to defend himself. His mother disappeared toward the back of the house, and he found Maggie at her usual spot near the table, a stack of jumbo-sized crayons and untouched paper in front of her. There was no sign of Sophia or Lilia, though he knew by their cars out front they were still here.

"Hey Mags, I brought you a smoothie."

Her head rolled back against her wheelchair, and she didn't bother looking at him. Her hands waved spastically around her.

Hollis knelt in front of her and gently straightened her. "It's chocolate and banana, your favorite." He held it toward her, but she jerked away. "Come on, Mags, just a sip."

After two more failed tries, footsteps and voices on the stairs interrupted him.

"She isn't eating," Sophia said. "Whatever Amá forces on her comes back up. She has to get a tube again."

The headache built, pressing behind his eyes and wrapping around his head. He looked again at Maggie and began to see the evidence: less responsive, thinner, paler.

It wasn't his fault, but it was his job to protect her. He had failed.

Hollis despised the feeding tube. It felt like one more thing that dehumanized Maggie. Rett Syndrome was just a cover. She was a real person, with the ability to taste and enjoy food like anyone else. She deserved a chocolate banana smoothie. He set the drink on the dining table and pressed a hand into the side of his pounding head. "Nobody was going to tell me?"

Lilia skipped down the steps behind Sophia, her hair swinging free from its typical cheerleader ponytail. "Uh, well, it looks like nobody remembered to get *us* smoothies, so no."

Sophia joined in. "Seriously, where are ours?"

Though he rarely broke form, even he had a limit. Frustration ripped through him. The twins didn't need smoothies. They had two good hands and a perfectly good digestive system.

Stalking to the refrigerator, Hollis yanked out a handful of fruit and a gallon of milk and slammed them onto the granite counter, headache flashing alongside his temper. "Here's yours."

Sophia and Lilia froze at the bottom of the stairs, their eyes wide.

Lilia slowly raised both hands in front of her. "It was just a question."

Hollis gripped the kitchen island and hunched his shoulders over it. He was turning into Amá. He had only thought about Maggie, and just like their mother, he had assumed the twins should be fine on their own—more than fine, they should be helping as much as he was. Pressure threatened to drown him. He swallowed hard against it. "I'm sorry." *I'm sorry I will never be enough to rescue you all.*

"Next time, tell us when you're PMS-ing," Lilia said. "And we'll lock the front door."

"Very funny."

The next thing he knew, Sophia was beside him, silently returning the fruit and milk to the refrigerator. "Have you eaten dinner?"

He shook his head.

"How about something more filling than smoothies?" Sophia pulled out deli meat and a block of cheese. Sandwiches didn't sound particularly appetizing, but it was all she knew.

Hollis grabbed his keys on the counter and moved towards the front hall. "Actually, don't worry about me. I'll pick something up on my way home."

"Wait." Lilia joined them in the kitchen. "You don't have to leave."

Hollis turned, exasperated. They should want him to leave. Instead of annoyance though, he found sheepish expressions on their faces.

"I know Amá took the stress out on you," Lilia said, looking at her feet. "It's not really fair. You take more heat than you should."

"Please stay," Sophia added.

If he wasn't his mother, he was his father—wanting to walk away from it all. Wanting to escape the pressure. Hollis had to be better than them both. He was all his sisters had.

He waved a hand toward Maggie. "Guys, if you're going to hide, you've got to take Mags with you. She feels all the stress too, and I'm sure that's why she can't eat."

Lilia nudged Sophia in some secret message, and Sophia jumped to their defense. "We tried! A little."

"Amá doesn't let her out of sight for long," Lilia added.

It wasn't their fault. It wasn't anyone's fault. Hollis forced himself to set his keys down. He was in Ridley Bay for three reasons, and all three were in this house. He couldn't leave. Closing his eyes for a second, he pulled in a breath and forced his shoulders down. "I'll take a grilled cheese."

Sophia grinned. "I'm not your cook, Danny. Make your own sandwich."

· · ·

Amá stopped Hollis on his way out that night. They stood outside under a dark sky. A light sprinkle of rain fell.

"We have to get a feeding tube for Maggie," Amá said, squeezing her hands over and over. "But everybody's booked. The hospitals are overrun, and her doctor said he can't get her in until next week. The only doctor who can see us sooner is in Houston."

"Maybe she's just stressed, give it a couple more days."

"A couple more days?" Her hands flew out and dropped to her sides. "It's already been four, Daniel. Four days. Could you go four days without food? Mm?"

The frustration that rose in his chest was squashed back down. It was a constant rise and push, so familiar he barely noticed it anymore. "No."

"Next week would make ten. What about ten days, Daniel? Can you go ten days without food?"

"No." Not that his answers mattered. She didn't hear them anyway. "I guess she'll have to go to Houston then."

"Can't you do something? Pay somebody here?"

Hollis huffed. He was supposed to pay off doctors now? Have one on payroll? "Not exactly."

Amá sighed and sank onto a patio chair. "You know she hates long drives."

"If it's the drive versus ten days without food …" he countered.

"I can't take her alone."

That's what it really came down to. Amá hated the drive herself. "Can one of the twins go with you to help?"

Amá waved the suggestion off. "Their classes start back on Monday, I can't ask them to do that."

Right. But she could ask him to take a day off work. Quincy would have a heart attack over this. It was another day away that Perla Tech couldn't spare. But what did that say about his priorities?

These were the moments he wondered where his dad was. David Hollis should be more responsible for Maggie than Daniel Hollis. Yet his dad was in Boston. Far, far from hurricanes and daughters needing feeding tubes.

"Fine. I'll help drive her," he heard himself say.

Amá grabbed his arm. "Really?"

He covered her hand with his own. "Of course."

His mother reached up and patted her approval on his cheek.

Chapter Twenty-One

The last week felt like a secret world to Wren, one in which Hollis wasn't an image anymore. He was Daniel. The unofficial, invisible ending of that world left Wren feeling unsettled and sleepless. It all seemed wrong.

Sitting up in the sofa bed, Wren took in her surroundings, her mind churning through the fog. Somehow, in just a matter of days, she had grown accustomed to the condo and expected a high-rise view and a disheveled businessman. Instead, she found herself in Faith and Bethany's rental house, with a whitewashed living room and a dozen inspirational quotes on the walls.

After an awkward breakfast, Wren headed to her house. She had to leave as soon as possible, to escape the familiar world in which she slept on couches belonging to "friends" who weren't quite such. For some reason, staying with Daniel hadn't reminded her of the past as strongly as this did.

Slowly approaching Florida Street, Wren watched for news trucks. She had seen several on another block when she left her house yesterday and passed one on her way in today. This was their feeding ground—perfect for shooting videos meant to incite pity and sideways glances. Wren wanted nothing to do with it.

Halfway down the street, she spotted Mr. Ortiz struggling with a roll of carpet. Wren threw Gumpy into park in her driveway and hurried to Mr. Ortiz's house. He looked exhausted as she lifted the other end, and they hauled it to the growing trash piles on the curb.

With a mix of their broken languages, he told Wren his son was still in the hospital. The small hospital system in Ridley Bay was struggling with their own losses, damage, and the influx of patients—another news topic. The news loved pain.

She tried to encourage him to wait for his son before continuing repairs, but the elderly man only shook his head and murmured about "work, work, work."

Wren picked up broken branches in the yard until Levi's promised volunteers arrived. The pastor's daughter, Ava, and her husband, Jack, were there, along with Emma and Nathan from her Bible study group. So many people to traipse around Rosa's corpse. Levi left them with tools and instructions and then rushed off to the next house.

"Thanks for coming," Wren murmured as they began to pull swollen, rotting furniture out of the house. Thanking someone for tearing apart your house didn't feel natural, but she didn't know what else to say.

"Of course!" Emma's perky voice replied. "I heard your house was damaged, and I begged to be on the team to come and help you." Her curly hair splayed, wilder than ever and barely restrained in a thick ponytail and with a cheeky bandanna tied over it, like she had searched "renovator chic" on Pinterest.

Soon the yellow couch, her dresser, the recliner, and more piled into a heap of trash. As her life gathered on the street, she couldn't help thinking she had come from the street and was headed back for it now.

Once the worst of it was out, they took all the salvageable pieces to her car: some wall art, a few clothes, some shelf-stable foods, and bathroom toiletries.

Ignoring the heat and the weight that settled on her chest, she continued, because people were here. She couldn't break down now.

They pulled out a shop vacuum Levi had left, and the girls set to work sopping up the remaining water in the carpet. The guys headed outside to cut up branches too large to carry to the curb.

It was dirty work—filthy water that had to be emptied into a filthy yard. The carpet she had slaved over deodorizing would eventually have to be torn into pieces.

By lunchtime, Rosa sat empty, with fans and dehumidifiers running in every room, all connected to a generator outside. They couldn't turn on the electricity until a professional cleared it, and that could be weeks. It also meant no air conditioning, and despite the fans and open windows, the air inside turned stale by midday.

They had accomplished more than Wren ever could on her own. She should be grateful. Instead, she felt sick. She would never be able to repay this. The distance between her and the rest of the church just kept growing. She needed their help but couldn't seem desperate, needed to thank them but wished she didn't need them at all. Heat and stench flooded her mind.

Levi came to pick up supplies and move the group on to the next project. Wren made sure to thank each individual person.

"We just want to help you," Emma said, with a pouting face that made Wren's internal ick factor climb upward.

"Thanks," she said. How many times would she be saying that?

•   •   •

Enormous black waves crashed over Hollis's head as he fought for another breath. From the bay, he could see the Perla Tech office building crumbling, falling, brick by brick. His mom watched him from the shore, unmoving. The dream wouldn't stop. Every time his legs finally gave out and a wave took him under, the dream started over.

By the time Hollis woke Friday morning, he was exhausted. A dark cloud hung around the edges of his mind as he went through the motions to get ready for the day.

He had worked late yesterday, trying to prepare for taking most of today off, but never catching up.

Now, he had media interviews and PR meetings to fill his morning. As one of the wealthiest companies in Ridley Bay, their charitable arm, the Perla Foundation, had created an emergency fund for hurricane relief. It provided a great opportunity to build awareness and rapport with the community, since many people didn't take time to understand assistive technologies. But it meant very little actual work would get done this morning.

Hiding the dark cloud as best he could, Hollis made it through the morning with coffee and the help of Vance, their PR guy.

He didn't have time for lunch before heading to the house to get Maggie and drive to Houston. Amá had been nervously checking in every half hour throughout the day to make sure he would be there in time.

"You made Perla Tech for her, it can wait for her too," he told himself. It didn't help much. His priorities blurred, and everything claimed utmost importance and asked too much of him, all at once.

Pushing harder against the cloud, he drove to the house. As he navigated through a still-flooded street just outside of downtown, the Z06 hit a pothole hidden under the water, slamming the front bumper into the asphalt. With a curse under his breath, Hollis jerked his attention back to the street.

He had also gotten a faint scratch on the passenger side from squeezing by a pile of debris earlier this week. Beaten and bruised, it needed a good wash, buff, and touch up. A Z06 was no hurricane rescue vehicle. It wanted to be on the highways of Houston, not trapped in the tight waterways of Ridley Bay.

When he arrived, Hollis did his best to argue for Maggie to ride in the Corvette. It required an elaborate harness install, but Maggie loved his car and loved to go fast. He had once gotten an actual giggle out of her when they raced down the highway. But Amá was adamant: Maggie was weak and had to be in her wheelchair. Hollis finally caved to driving the joyless behemoth to Houston.

Maggie seemed to hate it as much as he did, with a screaming fit starting at the city limits. Hollis put in noise-canceling earbuds and cranked up his music, leaving Amá to deal with it. His car could have drastically shortened this drive.

He let his mind wander on the drive. He needed no map—he could drive to Houston's medical district with his eyes closed. Houston was better equipped for special needs like Maggie's, and they had been there for many therapies and operations in the past.

Maybe that was why he chose Rice University. Houston already felt like a second home. And he had needed to get away from Ridley Bay.

At one point, he thought he'd never come back to his hometown. But after his first serious relationship ended and his first app sold, life had stalled out in Houston. Ridley Bay had cheaper real estate for Perla Tech to set up its offices, and Hollis knew he needed to get back to family.

Eventually, he might even have to become Maggie's primary caretaker—something he didn't look forward to but had accepted from an early age. Nobody really knew what to expect from Rett Syndrome.

Within a couple of hours, they arrived at the hospital with plenty of time to spare before Maggie's surgery.

Seeing no point in wasting the afternoon waiting at the hospital, Hollis dropped off his mother and sister and left. Perla Tech had key investors in Houston, and Vance had already set up a couple of meetings to make the most of today. Anything was better than the hospital.

•   •   •

By the time Hollis made it back to the hospital that evening, Perla Tech's favorite investors had renewed confidence in the hurricane-hit business, and Maggie was out of surgery, with a tube in place. The recovery room was small, sterile, and cold, both in temperature and decor.

"She's lost too much weight," Amá said. "The doctors want her to stay overnight and make sure her body responds well. We can't leave until the morning."

"This was supposed to be an outpatient procedure." Hollis, anxious to leave as soon as possible, studied the chart next to Maggie's bed, where she slept.

"Well, it wasn't," Amá said without looking at him.

Hollis could feel his heartbeat rising—hospitals always did this. Once you entered, they never wanted to let you go. But he couldn't lose another day. He had promised to help at the church service day tomorrow and planned to check on Wren's house after that and to try to fit in some time at the office as well. Another day in the hospital would be torture.

"I can't stay," he said.

"And I can't drive Maggie back by myself tomorrow."

"I'll fly one of the twins up."

She picked up a flyer on the countertop, advertising the latest medicine for Parkinson's disease. "They have cheerleading practice all day tomorrow."

Cheerleading practice. Thousands of people relied on his company for their survival, but the twins had cheerleading practice. The hospital's fluorescent lights beat down, straight through his corneas and into his brain. Stress and the smell of antiseptic wrapped around his lungs, suffocating him.

"Let me see what I can do," he muttered, pulling his phone out as he stepped into the hallway.

Hollis stared at the phone. He didn't have a plan. But the white lights overhead were crushing him. With quick steps, he wound through the maze of the fourth floor and found an elevator.

Outside, the muggy Houston air wasn't much better. The oil and gas metropolis wasn't exactly a treat for the lungs.

The sky had turned dark, but hospital lighting kept the courtyard bright. Hollis headed for a cement bench and took a seat, head hanging, rubbing his hands back and forth. He wanted to be everything for everyone, but there just wasn't enough of him. He wasn't enough.

Wren's voice rang out in his head. *Do you even need a God?*

He did, of course. But people needed him too. Shouldn't God give him the strength and ability to be enough?

"Why am I not enough?" he muttered.

A sermon Sanford had recently preached came to mind, full of verses about boasting in weakness. Sanford claimed everyone had missing pieces, and it wasn't a flaw in the design—each missing piece was meant to point a person to God.

Hollis ran a hand over his face. Perhaps God meant for him to not be enough. But he didn't see how the magical God piece came in to fill the gaps. How could letting down his family, his church, his friends, and his company point to God?

"I'm looking, but I'm not finding anything," he whispered.

With a deep breath, Hollis stood from the bench. Whatever the next step was, it wasn't here in this courtyard. He headed for the doors, walking past two doctors on the way.

"Daniel Hollis?" a voice rang out.

Tucking away a groan and putting on a smile, Hollis turned, realizing he recognized one of the young doctors. His mind raced for the matching name as he reached a hand out. "Kyle Pence," he said. Pre-med student, same chemistry class at Rice.

Pence returned the handshake. "What's up, man? It's been a few years."

"Seven or eight, right? How are you?"

"Good, good. Hey, you're in Ridley Bay, right? I've been watching the reports on Hurricane Flynn. I hope that's not what brought you here."

"No, just—" *Visiting a friend. A check-up appointment. An elderly aunt.* The lies came so easily, and he hated it. He wanted to give them up, to finally be imperfect and be okay with it. "Actually, my sister needed something, and the hospitals in Ridley Bay were packed." His own truth sounded strange aloud.

"I heard, man, that's rough. Some of the doctors and nurses here are heading down there tomorrow to help at the emergency centers."

Hollis knew what he needed to do, but it churned in his stomach like a sickness that had to be released. He had to ask for help. "Hey, this is probably a long shot, but do you know anyone who would be willing to drive a van there? My mom and sister could use an extra set of hands, and I need to go before they're out."

"Really? We have a couple people who still needed to find transportation, so that'd be great."

Hollis simultaneously wanted to hug the man and hide under a rock for the rest of his life. Within a matter of minutes, he had the names and numbers of a couple of nurses and found one who was happy to catch a ride to Houston, even if it meant possibly listening to a temper tantrum from a twenty-three-year-old.

Hollis offered to pay for her time, but she refused. He offered to fly her home, but she said she'd get a ride back with another volunteer. He was about to offer to sponsor a hospital brick in her name when she told him she had all she needed.

Kyle had left before the phone call, and now Hollis stared at the empty courtyard. God did answer prayers after all. Though he hadn't fixed any of Hollis's weaknesses, he had provided a way out. Hollis blew out a silent praise before remembering the next thing on his list: he had to break the news to Amá. She wouldn't like this.

On his way back inside, Hollis rehearsed his words in his head, perfecting a short version of how it all came to be.

When he walked into the room, Amá shushed him immediately. Maggie was still passed out in the bed, despite the bright lights overhead.

"Can we talk?" Hollis whispered.

Outside of the room, he quickly recited his speech and braced himself for the onslaught of guilt, the questioning about why he didn't love his family and why he had traded his soul for his work, just like his father. Instead, Amá shrugged. "Fine."

"Fine?"

"I don't like to drive alone with Maggie. Now I don't have to. Fine."

Something sank deep inside of him. Hollis crossed his arms to stop it from dragging him all the way down. Amá wasn't going to load him with guilt because she didn't care if she was riding with her son or a stranger. Not only was he not enough, his mother didn't care if he even tried. Where freedom should have been, he only had rejection. "Okay."

"Are you leaving tonight, then?"

"Yeah." He had already requested a pickup from a nearby rental car company.

"Yes," she corrected.

"Yes."

She sighed and for a split second seemed to soften. "Don't drive too fast, Daniel."

"Sí, Amá."

She pulled his face down to plant a kiss on his cheek, then slipped back into Maggie's temporary room.

Alone in the endless white hallway, his shoulders dropped, and Hollis slipped away quietly, leaving his family in the hands of strangers.

Chapter Twenty-Two

Pastor Micah Sanford stopped by Wren's house late on Friday afternoon, letting Wren know the church was putting together an emergency fund. He also gave her a list of city and national resources. In a moment, Wren was nine again, with a teacher pulling her aside and letting her know about the summer school lunch program.

The push and pull of needing the church, yet feeling so far separated from it, caused a vertigo that wouldn't leave. Wren seemed to watch it from outside of herself. She realized she was doing exactly what she had always accused Hollis of: playing a part, being whoever she needed to be to get what she wanted.

She spent most of Friday afternoon at the library computers researching grants and emergency funding. Most of it didn't make sense, seeming to go in endless loops. File here, after applying here, but only after you've contacted these people ...

Maybe twenty-six-year-olds shouldn't buy houses. Surely there was another level of adulthood where this would make more sense. Though Wren had been surviving mostly on her own for nearly a decade, she became a helpless child in the face of a hurricane.

Wren dragged her feet back to Faith and Bethany's house that evening. She forced Gumpy's windows down and ignored his protesting groans as she drove along the bay front. She passed by Renew Wellness slowly, missing the comfort of her massage room, the lame jokes of her favorite clients, and most importantly, the paycheck, after an entire week of missed work.

Next she drove down Florida Street again, more peaceful at night. Most houses still didn't have electricity on, and in the dark, she could almost pretend it was all a dream.

Finally, she forced herself back to the girls' house. As she pulled up, her phone rang. One glance at the screen, and her heart tumbled, dropped, and rose again. It always did with Lark.

"Lark, hi." She tried and failed to hide her surprise.

"Wrenny! You're still alive!" Lark's voice came quick.

"I am, are you okay?"

"I'm great," she said, too peppy. "Mom told me you bought a house."

"Yeah, well … it's six feet under now."

"Sure, but we need to celebrate the house first, before we bury it," Lark said with a laugh. "I bet it's not that bad. I'm coming to see you and this infamous house."

"What? Really? I mean, you don't have to do that," Wren stammered. Either Lark was currently clean, or this was a blatant lie. Either way, it was a lie. She had promised many visits before. They both had.

Lark scoffed. "Yes, I do. I'm your big sister. You need me, and I need a change of scenery. I'm coming."

"Lark, I don't really have anywhere for you to stay. I'm on a friend's couch right now."

"Let's get a motel together, it'll be like old times. I'm sure we'll get that house livable soon."

Wren paused. It was a lifeline. But, from Lark? Sharing a place with a drug addict was a terrible idea, but it was also the only way she could afford to be on her own again while also handling the house repairs … "Are you sure? Do you have a car to get here?" The question she couldn't ask was whether Lark could actually help pay for a place.

"Hey, you're not the only fancy pants with a car. I've been working at a grocery store for a while and saved up. We can go drag our jalopies around town. Stun some boys, scare some men."

The tease in her voice embodied Lark, her childhood best friend. Wren couldn't help but smile and shake her head. "I mean, I would love to see you …" *But will you show up?*

"I'm coming. We'll fix up that little shack together."

Lark had guided Wren through school bullies, puberty, and first boyfriends. She had been Wren's hero for so long, until one day the roles changed and Lark was the one who needed saving. Now it all muddled.

"When are you coming?" Wren asked, daring to hope.

"As soon as you find us a spot to stay."

We'll call it home for however long it lasts, no commitments, no promises, no risk. "I'm on it."

Wren hung up as her mind raced. A dark ball of dread built in her chest, but she fought against it with a deep breath, and another. She had to hope. Because if she didn't believe in Lark, nobody would.

•   •   •

Wren knew how to slink through someone's house, mostly unnoticed. For breakfast the next morning, she went with a quick slice of bread and peanut butter, nothing refrigerated, only things she could keep in her bag and eat quickly. She wiped the countertop clear of any crumb and washed her knife while she ate, leaving no sign of her existence here. Though she doubted Faith or Bethany would raise their voices over a peanut butter knife, the fearful habit had become ingrained after staying in less welcoming homes as a child.

After washing her plate, Wren changed into a jumpsuit and dug her lizard necklace out of her bag for good luck. She might need it today.

Later in the morning, she would join the volunteer day at the church, but first she headed to a nature preserve outside of town to watch the birds wake up. Lark's sudden reappearance into her life—or potential reappearance—had her off-balance, and she needed the peace, the grounding. Change rode in the air around her, though she couldn't tell if it was for better or worse. It whipped in the salty air, tangling her hair around her shoulders.

The sun hung high and hot by mid-morning when Wren left for the church building. As one of the ones in need, she felt odd going, but there wasn't anything she could do for Rosa right now anyway. Maybe helping at the church would be a small way of repaying their kindness, a small step toward balancing the scales.

Gumpy rolled over the unfinished dirt parking lot beside the church. Several others had already arrived. Wren surveyed the church as she approached it. Hurricane Flynn had shown no respect for anything.

Several weeks ago, Grace Church had announced a service day planned for the church, but with entirely different intentions: rooms to paint, flowers to plant, chairs to arrange. Now, flowers were a distant thought.

The air smelled of sawdust, salt, and sweat. Wren found Ava Shields with a walkie-talkie and a checklist. She spouted off a few of the projects, and Wren opted for landscape cleanup.

More people from church arrived, and soon they had a full team making quick work of the place. Emma, Nathan, and a middle-aged couple had joined Wren, tossing smaller branches into a pile and bagging leaves.

The couple made small talk with the others. "Can you believe all the damage out there?" the husband asked.

"Right? I don't even know why some of those homes were in the flood plain to begin with," his wife answered. "I'm not sure they should be allowed to repair the ones along the channel. Just move somewhere else."

"Ah, I don't know about that," Nathan said, with a sidelong glance toward Wren. "That area had been fine for decades."

Her stomach twisted, and she said nothing.

"Anybody know where Hollis is?" Emma leaned on a rake and changed the topic. "He said he'd be here."

"I don't know, but he's about to miss it all," Nathan said. Micah had just announced an upcoming lunch break, and the place was nearly back to its former state.

"Probably paid his way out of manual labor," Wren volunteered out of habit, though the joke fell flat on her tongue. She knew him too well now.

"Speak of the devil." Nathan nodded toward a motorcycle pulling into the parking lot.

The devil wore navy shorts, a white polo, and a thousand-watt smile. He made his way to their little group, stopping for handshakes and back pats along the way like a celebrity entering the scene.

He greeted the couple by name and then the rest of them, though he kept distance between himself and Wren. The unspoken goodbye still hung between them. Last time she had seen him, she had been a wreck at the house.

Who was she kidding? She was still a wreck.

"Just here for the free lunch?" Nathan asked Hollis as Micah waved everyone in toward the building for lunch.

Hollis grinned, but it never reached his eyes. "Got held up. Work problems."

Their little group began to head to the building, but Hollis hung back and Wren stayed near him.

"Work problems?" The question slipped past her lips before she remembered her personal policy against talking about his work.

"We got hacked," he said, sticking his hands in his pockets.

"Yikes."

"Yeah. By the way, this is yours." He pulled the silver medal out of his pocket. "Left it at my place."

Wren pressed her lips down against a smile as she took it and wrapped the red ribbon around it before dropping it into her purse. "Careful saying that too loud, people might get the wrong idea."

He snickered and shook his head, looking at the ground. "I think I had the wrong idea. I almost thought we were friends there for a minute."

That stung. "Are we not?"

"Well, you left without bothering to tell me."

Wren frowned. "I didn't want to become a burden." He had obviously been busy.

She could almost see the change in him now—from the Hollis who put on a show to the real man behind the facade. The smile faded, his shields dropped, and emotions played across his face. This was the Hollis she wanted to know.

"Did I ever treat you like a burden?" he asked. "Or are you still just assuming I'm a jerk?"

"I was trying to help you out by leaving."

His jaw clenched. "That's funny, because I thought I was trying to help *you*." The way he said it rubbed like sandpaper against her soul.

"If you wanted to help so much, you could have joined the cleanup crew at my house yesterday, but you never even checked in again."

"Is that my job? To always be the one to check on everybody else? You could have invited me."

"Would you have come?"

"No, actually. Because I was already busy doing everything for everybody in this city." He waved a dismissive hand toward the grounds around them.

Is this all that existed behind Hollis's false front? Delusional self-importance? More than offended, she felt disappointed. The man she had begun to see so much in perhaps held nothing after all.

"Wow, thank God we have Hollis the hero." Wren let the sarcasm drip like honey.

His eyes narrowed, completely missing any tease in her words. "I bet Sanford is pretty glad I'm around."

That is where he wanted to go with this? Bragging about funding half the church? He took every step forward they had ever made and went running back to the starting line by proving himself to be as vain as she had once believed. "Yeah, we're all thrilled you showed up to wave some money around."

"Why are *you* here, Atwood? Why aren't you working on your own house?" *Atwood.* He turned her name into a curse.

"I don't have to explain myself to you."

His hands lifted at his sides and flopped back down again. "And I don't have the capacity to help every needy person out there. Why can't everybody do a little more of their own work for once?"

Needy? He called her needy. The word entered her heart and was pumped out, destroying everything in its path, like an oil spill. *Needy.* He tied her in with every person under a certain income level and threw them away like trash. *Needy.* Behind every hope she held, despite anything he said, she knew this would come. That he would resent her for needing his help. Knowing it would come didn't ease the pain of it though.

"I'm sorry to have wasted your time, Hollis. I won't do it again."

A frustrated sound came from the back of his throat as he ran his hands through his hair. "Wren, I didn't mean you."

She was already walking. "I've heard enough." She couldn't bear to hear any more. It was her own stupid fault for letting him get close enough to hurt her. She would never make the mistake of needing him again.

Chapter Twenty-Three

As if the nightmares while Hollis slept weren't enough, he now woke to them too. Saturday morning, after having driven back from Houston late the night before, a phone call from Quincy woke Hollis at dawn.

Perla Tech had been hacked.

A key employee had been working remotely all week, using an unsecured network—whether knowingly or not remained to be investigated. A hacker had stolen information mainly about Perla Tech employees, but they didn't know yet if client data had been compromised.

Hollis spent his morning in damage control. The media would find out any minute, and he knew they would only be satisfied with fresh blood: firing the employee—a move Hollis wanted to avoid if possible. He and Vance went to have a face-to-face conversation with him while Quincy and their information security analyst did all they could to secure their data.

By mid-morning, McCoy had texted him asking why he wasn't at the church service day. He had promised to be there. Money for the building was nothing without a face to go with it, so Hollis took a much-needed break from the incident to make an appearance—swing a hammer, pick up trash, or whatever they needed.

The thing they certainly didn't need was an explosion. And Wren didn't deserve any of it. All the people who wanted answers from him, every upset employee and parent and sibling and church member got lumped up into the one person standing in front of him, and he took it all out on her, like a monster.

Hollis stood frozen, watching Wren walk away while the rest of the church filled up plates with deli sandwiches. He could feel every word Wren had unleashed on him and, worse, the ones he had spoken as well. Hollis pressed a hand onto his chest, trying to ease the pressure that wrapped around his heart. She was right to run away from him. He had nothing to offer.

"Hollis!" Kaminski headed his way with a plate in one hand and a cup of iced tea in the other. "Glad you made it out."

Forcing himself back into the present, he forced on a friendlier mask. "Sorry I missed most of it. Work emergency."

"No problem, it's always good to see you."

That was nice. It'd be even nicer if Wren ever felt that way. Though he remembered a morning not too long ago when she had smiled at him simply because he existed. She wouldn't now, not after seeing the worst side of him. "How'd the morning go?"

"Good," Kaminski said in between bites of the sandwich. "Almost everything is done. Your sister and Joshua were out here earlier."

Hollis nodded as if he had known that, but Sophia rarely updated him. Joshua Sanford had long ago replaced Hollis as the main man in her life.

"Sophia said Maggie is having a hard time."

Hollis stiffened. Maggie was off-limits, sacred, untouchable. The doctors had discharged her from the Houston hospital this morning, with notes about a cough that had Amá riled up. "She did, huh?"

Kaminski took a long swig of tea, his eyes studying Hollis the entire time. "You know, I don't think I've ever heard you talk about her."

Hollis waited for the point, offering nothing, but Kaminski's patience for silence proved stronger. Finally, Hollis caved. "I'm not sure she likes to be talked about."

"Really? Why's that?"

"People don't really understand her. It's hard to explain." Hollis shrugged.

Kaminski nodded. "Sophia told me once that Perla Tech was founded and named for her, because Perla is Spanish for pearl?"

"And Margarita means pearl."

"Creative. I think it's funny I found out from Sophia, though, and not the founder himself."

From their space several yards away, Hollis could see the rest of the volunteers gathered around tables close to the building. This area was solely theirs, yet Hollis felt invisible listening ears all around them. "Sorry if that bothered you. Feel free to ask anything about Perla Tech. I'm happy to chat." Switching from personal conversations to business talk walked them back to safer ground.

Kaminski took another bite of his sandwich. "Nothing else about Perla Tech," he said, in between chewing. "But how are you? You look tired."

"My favorite compliment."

Kaminski laughed again. "Overworking yourself?"

"Always."

"Why?"

It was Hollis's turn to laugh because the question deserved it. Why did anyone work too much? "Because I have to. Because everybody needs me and what other option is there?"

"Well, I think we're good here, if you need a break."

Frustration rolled through Hollis, spreading from his chest to his toes like the fastest cancer that ever existed. The place he wanted to be made it clear he wasn't needed. Hollis raised his hands in mock surrender and plastered on a grin. He might be able to get away with snapping at Wren, but he couldn't snap at the associate pastor. "Okay, I can tell when there's too many cooks in the kitchen. I guess I'll head out."

"Oh, no, I mean, we want you here. I'm just not sure if *you* want to be here."

"I think so?" Surely Hollis had something more confident in him than that. "Yes, of course. Just … bad timing, I guess." Every moment here had been a mistake so far.

Kaminski studied him for another moment. "Can I be honest with you?"

"Sure." What else could go wrong?

He seemed to gather all the dad-like wisdom his fifty-odd years could offer as he stood straighter. "Sometimes, I wonder if you really want to do the things you do or if you're paying for indulgences. You know you don't have to prove anything to us, right?"

Hardball, then. Hollis widened his stance and leaned back slightly. "Believe it or not, I like to help. But if you don't want that …"

"Of course we appreciate it. But I want you helping because your hope is in Christ, not in yourself. You're not our hope, Hollis."

Hollis scoffed. "I never claimed to be."

"You don't have to claim it to believe it. What about Maggie? Are you her hope?"

Kaminski had found it—the cord that undid the rest. He pulled the one knot around the tangle of balloons that released them—flying out in a hundred directions.

Perla Tech was Maggie's hope. Except, it could never save her. Nothing could. Medical research wasn't advancing fast enough. Only God could save Maggie, and he already had. She had a pure, childlike faith.

"No, nothing is." Hollis's grip on the situation was rapidly slipping away. "But I have to do what I can, right?"

"But you aren't God, so what you do will never be enough."

Hollis wanted to scream, to hurl something into the air, to push the limits of his bike until it dissolved into pavement. No matter what he did, no matter where he was or who he helped, it would never be enough. He crossed his arms to stop the pressure that threatened to crush him. "You think I don't know that?"

"I think you keep trying to be. Tell me, is Maggie enough?"

"Of course." Hollis seethed.

"What does she do to earn it?"

"She just is."

"Maybe you're enough, too. Because you're made in God's image, not because of anything you've done."

"Then what am I supposed to do? If we're all enough, why don't we all just sit around and watch television all weekend? Why are we even out here working on the church if just being alive is enough?"

"Because we do it out of love for the God who loved us first. Not to earn it."

"I'm not sure that's enough motivation."

"Then maybe you haven't received it."

Success required knowing when you'd been beat. Hollis felt the defeat creeping across his body. "Maybe not. Maybe I'm one of the few God can't love."

Kaminski choked on his tea and muttered something under his breath. "Good grief, Hollis. That's not what I meant. His love has already been given to you. You just have to accept it."

Hollis shrugged. Kaminski was speaking in church talk, and Hollis never understood it but hated to admit it. "I'm trying."

Kaminski grinned. "Stop trying, Hollis. He loves you."

More church talk.

Chapter Twenty-Four

Sunday morning, Wren's internal alarm clock went off at six on the dot. Her heart felt heavy this morning; Hollis's words had crushed it. He had called yesterday evening, but she ignored it. She didn't want to hear him apologize for speaking his truth, no matter how much it hurt her.

Pale light streamed through Faith and Bethany's living room windows. *Needy.* She hated being here. In only a matter of hours, she would be gone. Lark was coming today, and Wren had booked a motel, though she hadn't told Faith and Bethany yet in case things changed. With Lark, things could change in an instant.

Wren showered, hoping to wash it all away. She towel-dried her hair, wishing for salty air and sandy toes. Maybe Captain Todd was operating the boat out to Kinney Island again.

She whipped her still-wet hair into a quick braid, pulled on her favorite orange maxi dress, and headed out the door in time to catch the seven o'clock boat.

A heavy layer of clouds taunted the city and hid the sunrise in a cool blue light casting dimly over the parking lot at the docks. Two gulls sat on top of the light pole and laughed at the day.

Wren nearly ran the last few steps toward the dock. She had several minutes before the boat left, but she needed to know if it was even there at all.

Warm air rushed into her chest when she caught sight of the ferry— still floating, rhythmically bumping into the dock with the smallest of waves. Wren slowed to regain her composure as she walked up to it, scanning the deck for Todd. Every step slowed further as she failed to find him. Her feet sank deeper into the cement. He wasn't here.

Losing his familiar form hit her. He should be leaning against the boat's rails, chewing a fingernail or tobacco. Had the hurricane stolen him too? Was the ferry closed? How many things did she have to lose?

"In a hurry?" The husky voice was followed by the sound of a spit.

Wren turned as the waves of relief carried her back to safer territory. Todd approached in a faded gray T-shirt with *Ridley Bay Annual Fishing Championship* across the front, barely covering his stomach.

"Are you still going out?" she asked.

"Besides one fisherman yesterday, you're the only one thinking about hanging out on Kinney right now."

"Really?"

Todd narrowed his eyes at her for a moment, probably considering her question to be rhetorical with all tourism on pause in Ridley Bay. He spit into the bay water that lapped at the dock and tossed his head toward the boat. "Come on."

As she boarded, Todd lifted the ropes around a post and pushed off. "How's your new house?"

"Trashed."

He nodded, steering slowly through the no-wake zone. "Thought you'd said Northside. Me and some buddies were up there last weekend in dinghies, pulling stubborn folks off rooftops."

"I waited it out at a friend's place." Former friend? Fake friend? She didn't know what to call Hollis.

"Glad I didn't see you there."

"Me too."

Soon they rounded the jetty and the boat burst forward, the loud motor ending their conversation. Wild wind pulled Wren's hair out of its braid and dried the last wet parts. No dolphins played in their wake today, and no sunrise met her as the morning sun hid behind clouds. All of Ridley Bay seemed to still be mourning the hurricane's devastation.

Too soon, they slowed and eased into the simple dock on Kinney Island.

"Thanks, Todd."

"What are you doin' about that house?"

"The best I can. My church helped with some, but I need professionals in there now."

"You applying for aid and all that?"

"I'm trying. It's confusing."

"Heard Perla Tech put out a bunch too."

Perla Tech. Daniel Hollis *was* Perla Tech, and as long as she lived, her name would never show up on their list. She only nodded.

"I'm not making my regular runs," he said. "What time do you want me to pick you up?"

"Nine."

"Hey kid," he called after her, and she stopped on the wooden dock. "Kinney's roughed up from the storm. Watch your step. And don't get your hopes too high."

Wren gave him her best captain's salute which Todd returned with his most disapproving shake of the head.

His warning proved helpful, though. Wren steeled herself as she crossed the dunes, preparing for the sight of her beautiful beach turned into Hurricane Flynn's angry wasteland.

Kinney Island, no-man's-land, always had a certain untamed freedom about it, a promise to escape the demands of Ridley Bay. But today, enough trash lay around to remind Wren there was no true escape. If only she could mentally filter out all the waste, the large pieces of driftwood and the washed-up shells and seaweed would have given it a wilder look.

Carefully picking her way across the sand, watching for glass and nails, Wren found remnants of humanity—a sequined purse, a child's sandal, an old toothbrush, each with their own story. She could easily imagine the woman on a cruise ship losing her purse and the family that went home with a one-shoed tot.

The earth offered its own waste as well; Hurricane Flynn left death in its wake. Several dead crabs littered the sand, along with two jellyfish and a handful of fish, half-eaten by gulls. Each a free spirit that hadn't survived the storm. Each one a painful reminder. Perhaps coming here had been a bad idea. The salt air couldn't revive her spirits if it smelled of death.

When she found a dead seagull, twisted in the sand, Wren gave up, dropping to her knees. Even the birds hadn't survived.

"Oh God, help me survive," she whispered, more to herself than a prayer. Did God hear her prayers? Anyone's? Surely hundreds, maybe thousands, of people had been praying for Kinney Island. It hadn't stopped the storm. Though she supposed it could have been worse. Maybe, in a way Wren couldn't see yet, God had spared them from something even worse.

Wren found a handful of shells. Most were crushed. She saved a few for Lark and a small horse conch for Todd.

A tiny sand dollar caught her eye amid a pile of rubbish. Wren ran her finger around the edges of it. So small. Small enough to survive where a bigger one wouldn't have.

She didn't typically bring sand dollars home. They were too fragile and rarely survived the trip. Rather than end up breaking one by accident, she preferred to stay in control, snapping them in her hands and finding the tiny doves inside.

This one didn't deserve to break though. It was a survivor. Wren tucked it into her palm; it could make the trip home.

A few steps before the crest of the dune, she stopped. *Home.* She had no home.

She looked at the sand dollar in her hand. "You have a home, little guy," she whispered. It deserved the beach, not a couch or motel. Wren carefully tucked the sand dollar back into the sand, where it belonged. She waited there until she heard the motor of the ferry.

•   •   •

When Wren arrived back at Faith and Bethany's house, they were setting up the television to live stream the church service. Wren had folded her temporary bed back into its couch form, as she did every morning, and took a seat on it now with the girls.

Micah Sanford preached from his house today—the school building where they met had extensive damage to the plumbing system and couldn't host the church. Kids would probably be out of school for another week. Wren wondered if any families would be going hungry, stretching a loaf of bread and a can of beans over the entire week.

A white fireplace mantle, lined with family photos, served as his backdrop as Micah continued his series through the book of Colossians. He brought the destruction of Ridley Bay back to the Bible as smoothly as if he had taught regarding hurricanes a dozen times. He spoke of giving thanks in all things and of prayer as gratitude and surrender.

"A lot of prayers seemed to go unanswered this last week," he said. "But prayer is not always about changing our circumstances. Sometimes, prayer is about changing our hearts. It's about communicating with a living God. You can weep with him, be frustrated with him, praise him, but don't give up on him. He hasn't given up on you."

To his credit, he ended the sermon with a prayer that included the families of the middle school where they usually met and invited the church to help in various ways. But Wren knew how many people still fell through the cracks. One of them would be here soon.

Lark had texted earlier, saying she was about to leave San Antonio. Wren had to mentally repeat Micah's promise that God hadn't given up on either Atwood. She prayed through the morning, for peace, for her sister, for middle school students, for her house. The list was long enough to last a lifetime. But regardless of how unanswered her prayers sometimes seemed to be, she still believed in this God. After years of testing every religion out there, she had found the truth. It just didn't always make sense.

•   •   •

That afternoon, Lark called and said she was an hour away. With a quick goodbye, Wren thanked the girls for their hospitality and left, packing her bags into her car and picking up groceries on her way to the motel. She had found one just outside of town. Almost every hotel and motel closer to town had been booked or closed for repairs, except for some overpriced business suites in downtown.

The place was typical in every way: exterior doors and stairs, chipped yellow paint, and an overall hourly vibe, despite offering monthly rates.

Arms filled with nearly everything she owned, she headed up to the second-floor room. She jostled the key in the door to test its strength and pushed it open. A vague scent of insecticide met her, along with stained carpet and two beds with 1990s maroon floral bedspreads.

She could almost hear Mavis's voice chirping brightly about their new home while inside she wondered how long she would be here and where she would go next.

Just as she finished unpacking the last of her things, someone knocked on the door, tapping out a musical rhythm.

Lark.

Wren lifted feet that suddenly seemed like lead. She shouldn't feel this way. Her sister—her lifelong best friend—was here. So why did it feel like a terrible thing?

"Wrenny!" Lark wrapped her into a hug and rocked her side to side. The extra inch she had on Wren served as a permanent reminder of who the bigger sister was, though her willowy frame seemed slighter than usual.

Some of the tension released, and a smile worked its way onto Wren's face and spirit as she returned the hug. This *was* her sister, her flesh and blood. They would be okay. "Lark, I can't believe you're here."

"My baby sister needs me, of course I'm here." She shrugged a duffel bag to the floor and looked around the motel room, giving it a whistle. "Nice place you got here."

Wren rolled her eyes. "If you like this, you should see my other place. Roof's sagging and all."

An effortless grin lit up Lark's face. For all of Wren's sameness of color—light brown all over—Lark was contrast: brilliant green eyes and strawberry-blonde hair. "Now that sounds nice."

A laugh built from deep inside Wren and rolled its way out of her. How did Lark make every failure, every step back seem fine? More than fine. She made it seem like life's little ironies were something to laugh at. Wren grabbed Lark in another tight hug, finding a piece of herself that had been gone too long. "Thank you for coming."

"What do we do first?"

"Mostly wait. I called an electrician and a mold company, but they're both booked until next week."

Lark moaned. "That sounds incredibly boring. Can't we go thrifting for new furniture or something?"

"And put it where? Here?"

Lark glanced around the room, a smile spreading from one side of her face to the other. "I mean, it could use an update."

Like it was a shared secret, they both burst into giggles. They had been here so many times before. Lark busted out "Hotel California" by the Eagles, and Wren joined her for a line.

"What was it with Mavis and seventies songs?" Wren asked.

Lark shrugged. "Reminded her of her parents maybe?"

"Why would she want to remember them? They kicked out their pregnant daughter."

"And yet, no matter how much our parents mess up, we're all addicted to their love and approval." Lark shifted the lamp on the small desk in the room, rearranging the space however she could. "Remember the night Mavis said we should sleep under the stars?"

"And we got so many mosquito bites—" Wren clamped a hand over her mouth.

Lark dissolved into another fit of giggles, and they were contagious. "Our teachers thought we had chicken pox."

Flopping onto the ancient bedspread that had seen better days, Wren studied the ceiling and the shapes the popcorn texture made. Lark plopped next to her. They talked all afternoon, about Lark's latest dud of a boyfriend, her grocery store job, and nothing about drugs. Wren spoke about the best thrift stores in town, her coworkers, and nothing about pompous rich men.

They made sandwiches for dinner, picnicking just outside their door, smelling the cigarette smoke, and sharing endless inside jokes, memories of childhood, and the occasional sisterly encouragement—or tease, where warranted.

This was home.

Chapter Twenty-Five

It had only been a week since the hurricane hit, but life before it seemed like a distant memory. Hollis worked out in the gym downstairs and cleaned up before flicking on the Grace Church live stream.

Sanford preached about prayer in ways Hollis didn't care for. He had grown up with Catholic prayer, with recitations and performances. As a Christian, Hollis had begun to learn about prayer as a form of communication. But Sanford took it further today, preaching about meditations, silence, and prayer as rest. Rest for whom? Sabbaths, silence, and meditation were nice ideas for people who didn't need to keep the world spinning.

All of Kaminski's claims assailed him. He couldn't remember the exact words, but he knew Kaminski had more or less accused Hollis of playing God. Maybe he wouldn't have to play God if God did a little more. Hollis turned the sermon off before it ended.

After checking in with Quincy and their staff on the latest crisis, he drove to Wong and Lehman's house. Though he was due at the Hollis home any minute, he wanted—needed—to apologize. The conversation might take minutes or it might take hours, depending on the lecture Wren had in store for him. Being hated by the women he cared about seemed to be his lot in life.

Faith Wong answered the door. "Hollis," she said with a wide smile. "This is a surprise, come on in."

Hollis stuck one hand in his pocket. "Sorry, I don't really have much time. I was just dropping by to see if Atwood is around."

Wong frowned. "No, she left."

Only now did Hollis realize her car hadn't been in the driveway or on the street. He glanced over his shoulder. "Do you know when she'll be back?"

"No, I mean, she's not staying here anymore."

"Where is she?"

Wong shrugged. "She said she was going to stay with her sister."

"Her sister?" Hollis's voice rose an octave. Unless there was another sister Wren hadn't mentioned, this was the drug-addicted sister. "She lives in San Antonio."

"I don't know, I guess she came into town or something, and they're getting a hotel. Why don't you call her?"

Because she ignored his calls and he didn't blame her. Pressure revealed a side of himself that he hated too. He took a step back. "I'll try. Thanks."

"Of course. Really, you can come in. I can make some coffee or something, you look kind of tired."

Apparently he needed to do something about his look. "I have to go, thanks though."

As he walked back toward his car, it all seemed wrong. The Wren Atwood he'd spoken with only days ago would surely not be staying with her sister.

During the drive to his mother's house, he called her again. To his surprise, her voice came through the line after only two rings. She didn't even bother to say hello. "Hollis, please drop it." She sounded more tired than angry.

"Wren, I need to apologize."

"Not if what you said was true."

"It wasn't. I was stressed out and blamed you for stuff that had nothing to do with you. I'm sorry."

Silence.

"We're too different, Hollis."

"Too different for what?"

"To do this … to keep trying." She huffed a sigh. "Never mind."

Trying what? To be friends? He wasn't sure they had ever even broached anything more. "Faith said you're staying with your sister," he said. "Are you sure that's a good idea?"

"No, not really. But that's how this works. You decide who counts as a person, and my sister and I don't make the cut."

"That's not true." He knew what it felt like to have someone judge his sister as a lesser person, and he had never done that to anyone. But living with a drug addict was dangerous, plain and simple.

Silence again. This time, she was gone.

Hollis lowered the phone, a silent cry of frustration balled in his chest.

How much time had he wasted apologizing to her? She had only ever been a waste of time. Sure, they had spent a few days together during the hurricane, but it was a relationship of crisis, nothing real. She had made it clear a thousand times exactly what she thought of him, so he didn't know why this latest argument even mattered. He had proven her right, and now they were back to their petty disagreements. That's all they would ever have. Anything else had been imagined—a woman he had built in his mind, nothing like the real one who hung up on him now.

Hollis had to force it out of his head. He had no time for this. He needed to refocus on the countless other issues at hand. Shoving it all down, further and further until he could tread on it, he pulled on a smile for Maggie.

•   •   •

Renew Wellness welcomed Wren back to work with a breath of fresh air—particularly in comparison to the motel. The spa had not been damaged, and its vitality shone through now. A soft floral scent drifted from the stack of freshly laundered towels piled on the front desk. Bright yellow lemon slices floated in a large pitcher of ice water nearby. Soft music played over the speakers, piano notes interspersed with nature sounds.

Indie walked into the front room, carrying a basket of robes. "Hey girl, welcome back."

Wren wanted to grab her in a hug. Indie and this spa were the most normal things she had seen in over a week. Together they folded robes and chatted about the past week. Wren could relax here. She had more in common with the girl with purple hair, a tattooed boyfriend, and a slacklining hobby than she did with most of the church. Or Daniel Hollis.

"Dang, you're one of the ones who got screwed," Indie said, after Wren had explained the house situation.

"Yep. Story of my life."

Indie laughed and carried the robes to the other room.

Wren's soul soaked it all in—this reminder that the life she had built *would* go on. A break from thinking about the house, the endless to-do list, her sister, and the man who had called her needy. Their argument had left a little splinter she carried with her now, reminding her at random moments that it existed, that she would never be enough for someone like Hollis.

But here, she needed nothing; in fact, here, she was the one needed. Her clients needed her for pain relief. Her room waited for her to bring it to life with scents, sounds, and warmth. At work, Wren could be present: no shadows of the past, no overwhelming future, just work.

The day moved slowly, but she didn't mind. Clientele varied, many still scattered or displaced as the city recovered. Some of her regulars missed or canceled appointments while new faces took their place, looking for a break from the stress outside.

Wren was tempted to schedule a massage for herself. A week of house work had left a knot behind her left shoulder that she couldn't reach. But she waited. Rosa needed that money for now.

Nick only came in for two clients. He didn't want to talk much—the storm had hurt his forecasting pride. But he offered to come help with Wren's house however he could. And he passed his third client of the day on to Wren: a man known for giving exorbitant tips. Wren gave Nick a silent thanks; he supported her in his own way.

The day lulled her into a sense of normality again. It wasn't until she started Gumpy and drove toward the Northside that she remembered life wasn't back to normal. Pulling into a fast-food parking lot, Wren rested her forehead against the steering wheel before turning the car west and heading out of town toward the motel.

•   •   •

Back at the motel, Lark was sitting on the bed, a cooking channel on the TV and a bowl of cereal in her lap. "Hey, workin' lady," she called to Wren, without looking up.

"Hey, lookin' lady," Wren replied, tossing her purse onto the bed and digging into the mini fridge for a salad. "Do any job hunting?"

"Sheesh, in a rush?"

Well, yes. She didn't entirely trust Lark's intentions, though she constantly tried to correct her line of thinking.

Lark didn't wait for her to answer. "Actually, I did a lot of research on home repair. I'm ready to go rip up some carpet and walls now."

"That sounds good. My church can send some volunteers over next weekend to help."

Lark grunted. "You want to wait around all week?"

"I'm not sure I know how to do that stuff without my friend Levi."

"Lucky for you, your big sister knows everything now." Lark took her bowl to the bathroom sink and rinsed it out. "Can we go see this dream house?"

"Now?"

"Burning daylight, Wrenny."

Wren looked at the salad bowl in her hands that she hadn't even taken a bite of yet. "Give me ten minutes."

"Five."

Wren wolfed down the salad and stretched tired muscles before grabbing her purse and heading out again.

Soon they turned onto Florida Street. The houses surrounding hers stood in various stages of disrepair—or repair, depending on how you looked at it. Some neighbors had yet to return. Perhaps they never would.

They parked in front of Rosa, and God bless Lark, she loved it.

"Oh, Wrenny, the blue one? Look how cute it is! Those perfect windows on each side, like it's got a little face, oh my gosh."

Wren couldn't help but catch the energy. They admired all its features from the outside before braving the inside. With a warning to watch out for falling ceiling pieces, frayed wires, and fatal mold, they entered.

A dank, musty smell assaulted their senses, and Wren pulled her shirt over her mouth and nose. Lark followed suit. Wren hadn't been to the house in a day, and apparently it only took one day with the windows closed and no fan or electricity for it to become a haven for mold.

With her shirt serving as a mask, Lark started a muffled version of ABBA's "S.O.S."

Wren finished it with a mix of laughter and coughing.

"Show me around, Wrenny," Lark said.

Wren gave the miniature tour through the home, and they ended in the backyard for a breath of fresh air.

"It's really not that bad." Lark lowered her shirt from her mouth. "You could have a good party here."

"Are you serious? We can't even breathe in there."

"Once you get the carpet out of there and sanitize it, it'll be livable."

"Lark, I don't think you grasp how much there is to do. It doesn't even have electricity right now."

"Do you really need that? I mean, at least you won't get eaten alive by mosquitoes in there."

"Yes, I need air conditioning. I love my house, but I'm not trying to die in it."

"Not trying to live in it either," Lark mumbled.

"I am too, it's just going to take time."

"Agree to disagree," Lark said. "At least your tree's still standing."

"Thank God. I love that tree."

"Like any good bird." Lark patted her back patronizingly. "Come on, let's tear up some carpet. We'll make it a party."

"Now? We don't even have the tools. And I just worked a full day," Wren said, stretching the muscles already tired from a long day.

"You want to let that carpet sit and grow mold all week?"

"I'm pretty sure it's already moldy, we probably need professionals."

"Honey, we have YouTube," Lark said. "I am a professional."

Wren searched her for sarcasm, but instead she found genuine confidence, along with a sheen of sweat. "Mold is toxic, I don't have any masks or cleaners or anything."

"To the store then." Lark raised an invisible banner like they were heading into war.

Minutes later, bare shelves welcomed them into the hardware store. Only a few stragglers remained, scattered through the aisles. They finally hunted down gloves, a couple of box cutters, and a pry bar that Lark claimed were all essential to carpet removal. Wren insisted on protection from the mold, but only a few cheap masks and small bottles of cleaners remained. Lark reached for one, swearing it would be best.

"It just says all-purpose cleaner, how do you know this kills mold?" Wren asked.

"It has bleach, that kills anything."

"Won't that just stain everything white?"

Lark turned it over and read the back. "If we're using it under the carpet, it won't matter anyway."

Wren sighed and reached for another cleaner as they both scanned tiny print for mold information. "Too bad Mavis never taught us anything," she grumbled.

"What did you just say?" Lark asked.

Wren gestured to the aisle around them. "We don't know anything about houses or housework."

"Maybe not, but Mavis taught us plenty."

"Like what?"

"Like what?" Lark repeated, a bit too loud. "Like how to cook a meal for a buck, how to sew a patch on clothes, how to find a job anywhere doing almost anything. If Mavis didn't teach you anything, it's because you weren't paying attention."

"I know all that, but I don't see what good it is."

"Because you're blind," Lark snapped.

Wren wanted to argue, but Lark's tone made it clear the conversation had ended.

Sure, Mavis taught them to identify bird calls and constellations. Wren would have much preferred a mother who taught her how to care for a home, how to stay, and how to fight for her place and not drown. Quite simply, Wren wished she'd had a mother, but God had given her Mavis.

Chapter Twenty-Six

After the fourth night in the motel, Wren woke with the strange urge to carve the days onto the wall like a prisoner. Familiar fears arose—what if she ran out of money? She had slept in a car before and could again. But she would rather move back to San Antonio and live with Mavis than do that. People could always tell when you slept in a car, middle school classmates most of all.

Wren had enough money to cover the motel, but when her mortgage payment came due, they would feel the squeeze. And it would cut into her repair fund.

Covering her face with her hands, she breathed in the scent of her own skin and oils rather than the musty mattress. *It's not that bad*, she promised herself. Emergency funding would come through once Wren finished the application. Lark would find a job soon and help pay for the motel. They would be fine.

Mostly, Lark had been researching home repair instead of jobs. But it was helpful. Every evening they visited Rosa and took another step toward recovery. They stopped by the city's recycling center for free materials and watched videos on how to tear out carpet, cut into walls, and test wood for moisture.

The motel bedspread seemed to creep up to Wren's throat of its own accord. She fought the sense of overwhelm every day, and she was getting tired of fighting. Giving massages all day, only to go work on the house afterward, wore on her muscles.

Finally, she threw the bedspread back. While she had a working shower, she wanted to use it.

As she stood in the yellowed tub, hot water ran over Wren's shoulders and into her hair. It soothed the stress of sleeping on an old mattress. She lifted her shampoo, inhaling the sweet jasmine and citrus scent before squeezing it into her palm and lathering it slowly, savoring the experience.

Lark thrived at blowing with life's winds and enjoying whatever pleasures came her way. At times, Wren found it shortsighted, but perhaps she could benefit from trying to be more present. Tomorrow wasn't a given.

She lifted the body wash, turning it over to pour silky white soap into her hand. Instead, a watery, bubbly mess spilled out of the bottle. "Ugh." Wren popped the top off and looked inside. It was half-full of the watery mess. "Seriously …" she muttered. So much for her creamy, moisturizing lather. Wren finished up her shower with the soapy mix.

Wrapped in a towel, she stepped out of the shower to find Lark awake, with the TV on.

"Did you pour water in my body wash?"

"Yep." Lark bit into an apple without looking away from the TV. "It was almost empty. Had to get the last bit out."

"I can buy more."

Lark laughed. "Who cares? That's the good stuff, you can't waste it."

"I care. It's not the good stuff anymore if it's watered down."

Lark's eyebrows shot halfway up her forehead as she swung her gaze to Wren. "Wow, really? Your precious skin can't handle watered down soap?"

"It doesn't matter, I'm not going to live like that."

"*Like that?* I'm sorry, your highness, but adding water is not below you, and you better get off your high horse."

"It's not a high horse to ask you not to mess with my stuff."

"Since when is it yours or mine?"

Since I'm the one paying for it all, Wren wanted to scream. "Could you just not water it down?"

Lark took another bite of the apple. "Please, princess, tell me more about how the wealthy live."

"Whatever. I work full-time at a good job. I'm allowed to have a few simple pleasures, okay?"

Lark snorted.

"What?" Wren demanded.

"A few simple pleasures? The phone, the car, the name-brand soap, the clothes you care way too much about. Maybe if you didn't have so many simple pleasures, you wouldn't be so stressed."

"My clothes are all thrifted."

"Congratulations. You still own more clothes than the two of us combined in all of high school."

"Fine. Please, let the unemployed tell me more about money management." Wren instantly regretted the comment.

Lark shot her a look. "When did you decide you were better than everyone else?"

Wren huffed. "Have you seen my house? I know I'm not better than anyone."

"Your house is a perfect example. You think you're a martyr, a hero for the underdog, because your house got flooded. If you would get over yourself, you'd be applying for more aid instead of crying about what you can't do."

"I'm trying—"

"Look, this one is the easiest thing," Lark said, pointing at the TV. "You could literally have it in a week …"

Blood rushed to Wren's head, drowning out Lark's words. She had followed Lark's finger to the television and found Daniel Hollis there on the screen. Hot and cold washed through her, wrapping around her chest, drying out her mouth.

The volume was too low to hear what he was saying, but a gray suit jacket covered a crisp white button-up, and a black tie perfectly accented his dark features. A single dimple showed at the edge of his mouth as he spoke to the newscaster with a slight smile permanently in place. Even the interviewer seemed charmed.

Silence reigned in the room. "Seen a ghost?" Lark finally asked, looking from the TV to Wren and back again.

"I know him."

"Perfect! He's in charge of some big local fund. Ask him for the money."

Needy, needy, needy. "I would rather go bankrupt."

"You just might." Lark scoffed. "What's wrong with you?"

"Nothing. I don't want anything to do with him." She wanted it to be true. He would only hurt her. So why did that statement leave a gaping hole in her chest?

"Okay, this just got juicy. Spill, Wrenny. What's wrong with the pretty boy in the suit?"

Suits. She knew him as so much more than a suit now. Mental images of Hollis in rumpled clothes and with a five o'clock shadow filled her mind—the man who saved turtles, loved his sisters, and repeated first grade.

"Nothing. Everything. I don't know, Lark." She didn't. She knew he could hurt her, and she hated that. He also knew too much about her past and judged her for it. Wren needed to rebuild the wall against Hollis, and fast. "He's rich and charming and thinks he can get whatever he wants, and he has no idea what it was like to grow up like we did."

"So?"

"So, why would I want to be around him?"

"Oh, I don't know, because you don't want to repeat your childhood forever?"

"I'm not trying to repeat it, I'm trying to learn from it."

"And what did you learn?"

"To avoid people like that." Wren jabbed a finger toward the screen just as they finished the interview with Hollis.

Lark laughed. "You can't just hate anybody and everybody who got Christmas gifts as a kid."

"Our lives were totally different. I can't ignore that."

Lark groaned and gave her an exaggerated eye roll. "Would you stop with the drama? Sure, a little more money might have been nice, but Mavis was a good mom. There are plenty of kids who had it worse."

"Worse than homeless?" Wren asked.

"We weren't always."

"A six-month apartment lease here and there doesn't count."

Lark stood, her volume rapidly increasing. "Who are you to say my home doesn't count?"

"I'm not! I'm just saying, she could have applied for funding or something. There's help out there."

"You're one to talk." Lark swept a hand toward the television, though Hollis's face had been replaced by the weather forecast. "You won't even apply when it's right in front of you."

"That's different."

"Really?" Lark crossed her arms. "You know what I think?"

"I don't care."

Lark's eyes widened and anger flashed across them. "I think you're the most hateful, judgmental, materialistic person I know."

Wren's blood boiled to the surface. "You don't know what you're talking about."

"Right, because I didn't finish my last semester of high school, I must be stupid."

"I never called you stupid."

"You don't have to, Wren. It's written all over your face. In one look, you decide exactly how much someone is worth in your screwed up little system. Too much and they're a snob; too little and they're everything you're running away from."

Wren wanted to argue, but Lark had verbally punched her in the gut and she struggled to find the words.

In the second grade, Wren had tried to skip two monkey bars to prove she was better than the boys. She believed herself to be a great trapeze artist swinging through the air. In reality, she missed and smacked down, flat on her back on the hard, packed earth below, knocking the air straight out of her lungs. The boys had laughed as she looked up from the dirt and wondered if she was dead, or perhaps wished she was.

Once Wren caught her breath, she would be ready to fight.

It wasn't true. What Lark said was a lie. She would never judge someone like that.

But it was true. And Wren hated that it was true.

"Kids like that were jerks to us," she muttered.

"Is that who the pretty boy is? Is he a jerk?"

It would be easy to say yes, to disparage him, to fall into old patterns. But the truth was she knew him now. And he didn't mean what he had said. "No," she whispered.

"Then you can't lump him in with every junior high brat you ever met."

Wren nodded, her voice stuck in her throat.

Truth was truth, whether it came from the mouth of a preacher or a drug addict. And Hollis wasn't a jerk. His apology had been sincere. Her walls were the only lie.

Chapter Twenty-Seven

Lark got a job at a smoothie shop the next day and worked late. When she got back to the motel, she claimed to be too tired to talk, which was fine with Wren. They zoned out to a home repair show that offered very little in the way of practical advice.

Saturday, Lark slept in too late. Wren watched the clock tick away all the good hours for home repair, tempted to leave and get started by herself. But she knew Lark would lose it on her if she did that, and no one with a brain would wake a sleeping sister.

By the time Lark was ready to go, the humidity and sun reminded Wren of the spa's sauna. Holding back her comments, they climbed into Gumpy's seats, rolled the windows down, and headed to the house.

Trash lined the street—more piles of pulled floorboards, rolled carpets, destroyed dressers and kitchen cabinets—like one big, ugly yard sale. Rosa greeted them with a nearly lifeless sigh. The front door still sagged, requiring both sisters to push on it. Wren had no idea what to do about that—another phone call for Levi.

The girls stood in the doorway, surveying the house for a moment. The job seemed insurmountable. Where did one start to climb Mount Everest?

Lark handed a mask and a box cutter to Wren. "Walls?"

"Walls," she repeated, latching onto any sense of direction.

Wren walked to the living room. They had already ripped up the carpet earlier in the week and scrubbed the exposed concrete with disinfectants to help treat the mold, and the house now smelled of Pine-

Sol. Though no doubt still a toxic wasteland, at least it was an improvement over the smell of mildew.

They took turns slicing into the drywall a few inches above the waterline. It should have been easy digging a knife into soggy walls, but nothing ever came easily. Their cuts never looked straight, and it took multiple passes to get the knife all the way through the wall in some areas. They snagged on beams and caught nails.

Wren began to deeply regret turning down Levi's offer to bring volunteers by today. But she hadn't wanted her church friends and Lark mixing. Nothing good could come of it.

Lark talked about her new job while they worked, and the people she had met. "I thought San Antonio could get wild," she said, stabbing at the wall. "But Ridley Bay can hold its own."

"What do you mean?"

"Just the stuff they talk about."

After finally clearing the lower half of the wall in the living room and hearing more about Lark's new coworkers, Wren cut into the insulation. The fiberglass pads rubbed against Wren's arms and legs, and microscopic cuts began to make her itch and burn.

Lark pulled a piece and dropped it to the floor with a grunt. "This is freaking ridiculous." She tossed the box cutter on the ground, and it skidded across the floor. She pulled her hair off her neck and headed for the back door. "This is a kid's game, Wrenny. You're on your own."

Wren pulled off her gloves and took a long swig of water to calm her nerves. The heat was getting to them. Surveying the little progress they had made, anybody could see they were drastically under-prepared. With a sigh, she headed out the back door after Lark, who sat on the bottom step, head bent over her lap.

Wren joined her. "I don't think your two years of advanced age are enough to get you out of work."

"Let me sit down for a minute!" Lark's eyes popped open, bright and fierce.

Wren scooted back. "Okay, geez, sorry."

After a silent moment, she stood and got Lark's water bottle from inside. She held it out like a peace offering.

Lark took it without looking at her. "It's already better than some places we've lived. You should just move back in."

"I don't even have a working front door, Lark."

"All you can ever see is what you don't have."

Wren had nothing to say to that. She didn't think asking for walls, floors, and doors in her house seemed like too much.

The old oak tree waved in the breeze, tossing the shade erratically around them. A few doves called from nearby trees. Despite the heat, the air held a certain crispness that hinted at autumn's return. Wren struggled to hang on to it, grasping at the hope of change. She stood after a few minutes. "Ready to get back to it?"

Lark stared out into the yard. "I have to work this afternoon."

"At the smoothie shop? What time?"

"Evening shift. Drive me back to the motel so I can get ready. Then you can come back and do whatever else you want."

Alone.

Not even Lark could handle the situation here, and Lark was one of the toughest people she knew. Nobody wanted to be here. Sometimes not even Wren.

•   •   •

Careful not to wake Lark, Wren dressed in silence on Sunday. She should invite Lark to church, but her sister hadn't spoken to her the rest of the day yesterday, and she had a feeling today would be the same. Rather than risk a confrontation, Wren left early for the first service, to hopefully leave and return unnoticed.

The church returned to their meetings at the middle school this week, and Wren drove into town, ready for the familiarity in a life currently on the fringe.

But would the church be split into two now, between those who needed help and those who survived on their own? The *needy* and the self-reliant? The thought sent hives down her legs, still sliced by fiberglass. A gauze maxi dress covered the marks in a pink floral pattern, and she wore a breezy kimono in a yellow floral, nearly bursting into a field of wildflowers.

When Wren arrived at the church, Micah Sanford's wife, Rebecca, and his daughter, Ava, greeted her at the door with hugs and mercifully short questions about her week and her house. Wren found Faith and Nathan inside and joined them in the auditorium.

Micah preached through Colossians, speaking of new life, of peace and forgiveness. Promises that had drawn Wren to this church from the very beginning.

She didn't deserve forgiveness, yet she had received it. And then took it for granted, refusing to pass that forgiveness and grace along to anyone else. She had held on to so much bitterness, doling out judgment on others as if she were a god herself.

Much like both Lark and Hollis had accused her of doing.

Even now, this morning, she wanted to blame Lark for sleeping too late for church, but the truth was that she was embarrassed to invite her sister. Wren feared letting the church know about her family and her past, afraid to let her two worlds mix. The fact that Wren put her own pride above Lark's eternity sent conviction wrapping around her heart.

Then there was Hollis. She had assumed he needed to be humbled and assigned herself to the job. All because she was angry at her past, not at Hollis. He didn't deserve any of it.

Like her very own hurricane, Wren left a path of destruction behind her. And she was tired of it all—the walls and the fears, the hurtful words she hid behind. She had more to mend than just a house.

After the service, Wren waited in the front hall, visiting with Faith and Nathan and searching for Hollis. Apologizing for two years of harsh quips, rude rejections, and prejudice seemed a daunting task, but she would figure out how. She had to.

Levi found her first. He gave her a hug like the pretend big brother he was. "How's it going?"

"I think I went through a cheese grater yesterday trying to tear out insulation." Wren flipped the lower part of her dress up to reveal the evidence on her calf.

He chuckled and patted his pant leg. "Jeans, Wren. Get some."

She grinned and held her flowing, tiered dress out at the sides. "I prefer breathability."

Levi raised an eyebrow at her in utter disappointment.

"Oh, actually, instead of fashion advice, I could use some tips on doors."

They went over the logistics of repairing the door, but Levi stopped her on the second question. "Why don't you let me send a couple guys over to help? I don't understand why you backed out yesterday, it sounds like you could use the extra hands."

Wren hesitated. "I just want to get as much done as possible on my own first. I don't want to waste the … goodwill." She gestured lamely toward the church. It was true, too. Hollis had been right: she was needy. She needed a lot, and she didn't want everybody to resent her for it.

"I think we have plenty to spare," Levi said. "And we really need to get that roof repaired before you do too much inside, or else the next good rain will ruin your work."

"I know, I'm just waiting on some FEMA funds to come through. Or insurance. I don't know, really."

Worship music filtered into the hallway as the second service started up, and Levi glanced at the doors leading to the auditorium. "I better get in there, but let me know when you want us to come and help out. I might even have someone who can help with the roof."

"Sure," Wren said, without much sincerity. She peered around him. "Hey, have you seen Hollis come in, by any chance?"

Levi glanced at the ceiling in feigned annoyance. "By any chance," he mumbled, shaking his head.

"Just answer me."

"No, I haven't. Didn't see his car out there either."

A car that would be hard to miss. Wren brushed off the thought. "Any idea where he is?"

"No, but I'm pretty sure you have his number. Or condo key?" He quirked an eyebrow.

Wren scoffed and gestured toward the auditorium doors. "Get in there. You obviously need some church-ing."

He muttered something about who exactly needed church and headed for the doors. Wren waited around in the hallway a few more minutes, grabbing a coffee and making small talk with the hospitality team. He wasn't coming.

She wouldn't be making any flailing apologies today. At least not to Hollis. Maybe she and Lark could get together tonight after Lark got off work. They needed a reconnect. Something touristy and fun, instead of house work for once. The wetlands would be perfect.

Chapter Twenty-Eight

Hollis showed up at his mother's house Sunday evening with enough food for everyone, and the twins weren't even there this time, of course. Amá excused herself from the dinner with other plans and left in her own car.

Sitting down to his Thai meal for four, with Maggie slouched in her wheelchair next to him, Hollis picked at the fried rice.

"How are you feeling, Mags?"

No response.

Hollis adjusted her tablet and made sure it was working properly. Everything was in order.

"Done any paintings lately?"

Her usually jumpy vision fixated on a spot on the ceiling.

Amá had said Maggie had been lethargic since the trip to Houston. She blamed Hollis for abandoning them. But lethargy could come from anything. Sickness, bad mood, poor sleep, seizures … Hollis grabbed Maggie's hand—staring could be an absence seizure. She jerked her hand away and groaned an unintelligible complaint. He was being as jumpy and paranoid as Amá.

"Do you want to go outside?" he asked Maggie.

Other than an increase in hand fidgeting, she didn't respond. Maggie wasn't quite herself. It could be stress from the storm and Amá, or physical stress from the trip to Houston and tube procedure. Either way, a little fresh air would help.

Without asking for permission from Amá, he wheeled Maggie toward the van in the garage. He didn't want to stay in that house.

Soon they pulled into the wetlands' parking lot. Hollis unloaded Maggie and headed for the south side of the looping trail. The early September weather was still hot, but the evenings were beginning to cool just a bit earlier, and the breeze held a fresh crisp. It made being outside easier for them both.

Hollis was silent as they walked, his mind wandering. As a child, he had imagined life without Maggie. But as he grew, he realized it wasn't Maggie he wanted gone, it was the disease.

He liked to imagine their life without Rett Syndrome. Would they all be closer, without the crushing weight of caregiving spreading them out? Would all four of the Hollis siblings be out here, right now, walking and talking and laughing at the antics of their parents? Would their dad still be around if he hadn't been pushed away by the pressure?

It was easy to picture life as perfect, but maybe it wouldn't be. Maybe they would have all gone their own ways—possibly even further than they were now. Maybe Maggie was the only thing holding them together.

When his thoughts carried him away, he found it even harder to talk to Maggie, to find something brotherly to say. Because he felt nothing like a brother.

They made it to the halfway point at a slow, quiet pace when he heard a voice ahead of them, hidden by the curving path and shrubs.

Hollis's heart rate picked up. This park was typically abandoned, and he counted on that. He knew half the city and preferred to keep his private life, and his sister, away from them.

The voice was … singing? A woman's rendition of Billy Joel's "Only the Good Die Young" floated toward him. Probably not someone he knew. While he debated whether to turn Maggie around, a startled green heron flew from between the branches when someone rounded the curve.

The woman paused singing when she came into view and spotted Hollis, and then she started singing again. Strawberry-blonde hair flew out around her face like a lion's mane, topping off a lithe frame. Thankfully he didn't know her.

Hollis gave a polite nod and turned his head down toward Maggie as they passed her.

"Hey, I think I saw you on TV," the woman said.

Hollis stifled an internal groan. That was the point of the interviews, right? Publicity? But it was supposed to be publicity for Perla Tech. Not Daniel and Maggie. Even if Maggie was the reason for Perla. Such a familiar twist, a push and a pull.

He tugged on a smile fit for Hollis, Perla Tech Founder and CEO. "I bet you did. I'm Hollis," he reached out for a handshake.

She returned it with a wolfish grin. "Small world. I think I like it."

Suddenly she seemed familiar. Hollis's mind raced. He was usually good with names and faces. Why couldn't he place her? He recognized the cadence in her voice. Had they talked on the phone before? "I'm sorry, you seem familiar, have we met?"

"Not yet. I'm Lark."

The name of a bird. He knew of only one Lark. Her coloring was different, and her features were gaunt, but the cut of her nose, the melodic tone of her voice—Wren's sister was standing before him in the flesh. Did she know who he was, besides the news spot? "Nice to meet you."

Another voice came around the corner singing the next line of the same song.

· · ·

Singing along with Lark and studying the feather she had found, Wren suddenly realized there were more feet—and wheels—on the ground in front of her than just Lark's. Her head snapped up, and she found Daniel Hollis, with eyes as dark as night.

"Hollis," she said, slack-jawed and out of air.

"You two know each other?" Lark asked, a poorly veiled attempt to sound innocent.

"Yeah, we do." Hollis's voice sounded tight, brisk.

Wren could see the guard drop over his face. Like a painting with every line set into place on purpose, nothing moved of its own accord. Hers, on the other hand, was moving entirely of its own will. Wren's gaze ran down from his face to his arms and to the wheelchair he gripped and the woman who sat in it. Her hands bowed at her mouth, she slouched to the side in her chair, a tablet positioned in front of her on a metal arm. The woman had the same heart-shaped face as Daniel, but with blue eyes.

"This is your sister?" Wren tried to sound friendly as she smiled at the woman.

"Yes." His tone was so tense that Wren glanced back up at him.

His eyes gave it away. Despite whatever shields he tried to use, she saw the emotional scars. He had told her once that kids could be cruel, but she hadn't realized the depth of his understanding. In front of her now stood a former child who wanted to stand and fight as badly as he wanted to turn and run. Wren recognized the emotion.

The mountainous apology she had prepared this morning seemed miles away from her. In this unexpected place, words fled from her. Her mind scrambled to find them, to pull them back together.

Instead, she lifted the feather in her hand. "I just found this." She knelt in front of the wheelchair to get on eye level with his sister, though the woman didn't look at her. "Maggie, right? I'm Wren. Do you like birds?"

"Yes." A robotic woman's voice sounded from the tablet next to her, and Wren nearly jumped out of her skin with surprise.

Forcing herself to appear cool, she held the feather for Maggie to see and waited for her eyes to cast around it. "I think it's from a Great Blue Heron. It looks gray, but in the sunlight you can see the blue." She wasn't sure how much Maggie could understand, as she chewed on one hand. Wren hadn't been familiar with the syndrome Daniel had named, and she didn't know what it meant.

Unsure of herself, she stood, eyes darting between the brother and sister. "You two have the same hair." It didn't lighten Daniel's mood in the least. If anything, he tensed even more. The kid inside of him locked down, and Wren wanted to reach him and set him free.

Her hand extended out of its own will, its own need to touch him. She quickly swept the wayward hand toward Lark. "I guess you met my sister, Lark."

"Yes," Lark answered for him. "He was just about to tell me about the emergency fund his company set up."

Oh, no you don't. Lark was not going to swindle him in the middle of the boardwalk. Before Wren could derail Lark, Daniel did it for her.

"Sorry, that's for business hours only," he said, with a suave Hollis smile. In one swift move, he pulled a wallet from his back pocket and produced a business card. "The main line can direct you to the Perla Foundation."

"Perfect, thanks." Lark took it with an air of smugness, as if she had somehow made progress rather than deepening the canyon between them. A canyon that tore away at Wren's walls as fast as Hollis built his.

Without a goodbye, Hollis gripped Maggie's wheelchair and began to navigate around them.

"Hollis, wait." Wren scrambled for the state of mind she'd had this morning. "Can we talk?" She took his brief pause for concession. "Lark, do you mind giving us a minute?"

"What?" Every sour emotion crossed Lark's face. But Wren held her ground with an eyebrow raised. Lark finally shook her head with an amused huff and turned to continue her walk, belting out the next line of their song.

"I've got to get Maggie out of the heat," Hollis said with more than a little agitation in his voice.

Time was not on her side. Yet her mind wandered—dancing between the man who played guessing games with her in the middle of a hurricane and the one who called her nothing more than another needy waif.

"I wanted to apologize," she finally spouted.

No change in Hollis. Maggie began to moan.

"I'm sorry. For throwing away the coffee last Christmas, and everything I said about your car, and assuming you were like people from my past. I've been wrong." She should have planned a better speech than this, but words tumbled out, making up for lost time.

Hollis's hands on Maggie's wheelchair loosened, and he took a step toward Wren. Hope for restoration fluttered through her heart. He closed the gap between them, his eyes boring into hers. He leaned close and Wren inhaled him, holding onto the breath.

His voice came as a whisper. "Do not apologize to me just because you feel sorry for me, or Maggie."

"Daniel—" Wren drew back in surprise and met his eyes. "I'm not. I was planning to tell you …"

"Right." The hurt showed so clearly in his eyes, and she desperately wanted to heal it. He turned his back on her, gripped Maggie's wheelchair, adjusted the girl's head that was tilting to the side, and kept his gaze forward, past Wren, as he navigated around her without a word.

A fist squeezed around her chest as she watched him leave. Wren struggled to force a deep breath into tight lungs. Another breath. The salty, fishy scent of the marsh met her nose, along with slight decay in the air. Wren glanced at the feather in her hands, matted by the sweat of her palms. Did everything beautiful have to die?

Hurricane Wren had hit. The fact that her name rhymed with the real storm had to be a bad sign.

She could remember the very first time Hollis had asked her out to his company's Christmas party. At the time, she resented all he seemed to stand for, but she had been wrong. Even at his most pompous, it was only a carefully designed front to hide an injured kid and a good heart. She saw through it now—she knew him now. And it shocked her with immediacy and familiarity, like their souls had walked together before.

But in his eyes, she could only go down. Now, he knew she was judgmental, homeless, and living with her drug-addicted sister. Now he knew her past, and her future, and he wanted nothing to do with her.

Wren willed her feet forward to catch up with Lark, but her feet wouldn't move from this spot—this middle ground between the man who would never ask her out again and the sister who no doubt had choice words ready for her.

This was where she always landed: stuck. Stuck in no-man's-land. Unable to move forward—or backward. Since the day she was born.

Chapter Twenty-Nine

Maggie started coughing on Monday.

On Wednesday, a fever joined the cough.

Amá grilled Hollis about why he had taken her out of the house on Sunday in her "already fragile" condition. Objectively, Hollis knew a walk couldn't have made her sick, but the thought struck a chord that wouldn't stop playing in his head.

Friday, Amá called to say that Maggie had been admitted to the hospital. Invisible hands wrapped around Hollis's throat. The visit to the park never should have happened. If they had stayed at the house, Amá wouldn't be mad at him, Maggie might not be sick, and he wouldn't have thrown Wren's words back in her face.

The shock on her face, clear as day, when he accused her of a pity apology told him he had been wrong. But his defenses flared when Maggie came into the picture, and he had been on the receiving end of too many pitying glances and words to hear anything else.

He had picked up his phone a dozen times in the last few days to call her, only to set it back down again. Once again, he had proven himself to be an irredeemable jerk. What words could he possibly offer that hadn't already been spoken between them?

His insufficiency seemed to build its own billboard, complete with flashing lights and an arrow that pointed to the man who would never be enough.

And he couldn't even be at the hospital that Friday. Perla Tech needed him. He couldn't miss out on another day of work for Maggie's latest hospital stay.

Hollis called in the recruits instead: Lilia and Sophia. The twins promised to go to the hospital as soon as cheer practice ended. They all knew the real reason was more about calming down Amá than visiting with Maggie.

Once they had promised to go, Hollis tried to focus on work again. But if he wasn't at the hospital with Maggie, what was the point of Perla Tech? Guilt rose throughout the day, along with the need to do—and be—everything. Hollis forced his focus on the company as much as possible.

The money Perla Tech had pumped into Ridley Bay was beginning to come back—their name had splattered national news stories, and new inquiries came in daily. New clients, new requests, new partnerships. Quincy and Hollis discussed plans to manage the influx, assessing the company's current and projected capacity.

He worked through the day, silencing updates from Amá, spreading out increased workloads as evenly as possible, and forecasting company growth based on the latest developments.

In his element, the hands around his throat began to loosen. He could run a company; he could breathe.

Until his phone rang.

Wren.

Had he ever seen her name on an incoming call? He had always been the one to call. Of course he should answer and tell her he was sorry for the rude words at the wetlands. He should tell her he accepted her apology. Yet the apology was unwarranted because she had been correct in all her assumptions. He *was* selfish; he only did what benefited himself.

The invisible hands tightened again as he watched the call end in voicemail.

He had to let someone down, always. *Never enough* repeated like a chant in his mind.

•   •   •

A phone call at four in the morning woke Hollis with a start.

Amá.

The twins had taken turns at the hospital Friday afternoon and evening, which meant Hollis had the Saturday shift. But surely it didn't have to start at four.

He answered with nothing more than a grunt.

Amá didn't bother with niceties. She spoke rapidly, in a jumbled mix of Spanish and English. Hollis forced himself to sit up in bed, waking his brain up enough to detangle her words. Maggie had pneumonia, that much Hollis had suspected, but now something was wrong with her heartbeat.

"Cardia arrhythmia is a normal part of Rett," Hollis said, aiming to sound as awake and calm as possible. An investment of effort now might buy him another couple of hours of sleep before she demanded he go to the hospital.

"*¡No!* You are not listening, Daniel! Her heart is not keeping up."

"Amá, she has had pneumonia before. She will be fine."

"She has not had it like this before, *hijo*. And if you came to see her, you would understand."

She won soon after that, and Hollis wandered through the condo, slowly flipping on the lights. He stood in front of his pantry, motionless, willing it to open into some other world.

Once he went into that hospital, it would be even harder to leave. Hospitals held on tightly. He had learned that as a child, spending countless hours on cold linoleum floors with homework in his lap. His dad had often kept the twins during those visits, but Daniel had always been old enough to handle himself.

Grabbing a protein bar and a banana for breakfast, Hollis packed a messenger bag for the day—snacks, his laptop, a fleece pullover. As much as he hated hospitals, he at least knew how to deal with them.

As familiar as family, and as welcoming as a shark tank, the hospital doors opened to Hollis and swallowed him whole before the sun had even risen.

When he reached Maggie's room, all was quiet. Amá lifted a solitary hand in weary greeting from her spot on the sofa, which left … cold linoleum. Hollis settled onto the floor at the end of the sofa, out of the way of any medical staff potentially hurrying into the room. He leaned his head back against the tweed, listening to the beeping of Maggie's machines, the irregular cadence of her heart, and the occasional cough.

His mind drifted through potential product development, the faces of women with bird names, and times when he had babysat rambunctious twins while his mother took Maggie to the hospital. Finally he landed on a specific memory. A day when his dad had taken him out for ice cream. He couldn't remember what they had been celebrating.

Daniel had asked if he could stay there forever.

His dad had laughed. "I'd like that. Tell you what, you and I should open an ice cream shop together one day. And we'll live in an apartment above it."

It would be theirs, and theirs alone. An escape, together. They had named it—something like Daniel and David's Delicious Desserts.

His dad drew an architectural sketch on a napkin. "This is where all great businesses begin." He handed the napkin to Daniel.

Hollis still had it, somewhere in his desk drawers. Back in his condo, he began searching, searching, searching—

A nurse burst into the room, and Hollis pulled in a deep breath as if surfacing from underwater. The sun shone through the cracks of the curtains, and he realized he'd been drifting between reality and dreams.

Amá was already up and talking to the nurse. They were both too loud. Hollis stretched and took a seat on the end of the sofa with his laptop, as a silent bystander.

Maggie woke in a sour mood, though he didn't blame her.

A doctor entered next and spoke with Amá about diagnoses and treatment plans. Hollis tried not to eavesdrop, but he couldn't help it in the small space. Amá asked for various tests, and the doctor dismissed her. Meanwhile, the nurse next to Maggie tried to take her vitals, but Maggie thrashed away from her, groaning wordless protests.

Hollis lifted his eyes from his laptop, flicking between Amá, the doctor, and the spectacle with Maggie.

The frustrated nurse slammed her penlight back into her pocket. "Can I get a hand with this, Dr. Shah?"

Instead of moving, the doctor began to jot down an order on a notepad. She mumbled, "Let's get her on sedative—"

"No, thank you," Hollis said, loud enough to be heard over Maggie's grunts. "She doesn't need any further respiratory depression."

The doctor seemed to just now see him.

He walked to Maggie's side. "She doesn't need to be sedated. She needs to not be manhandled." He directed that comment at the nurse.

Hollis squatted next to Maggie, who looked everywhere but at him. A maze of oxygen lines ran against her pale cheeks. Even in her bad mood, she didn't have the strength to rip them off. He held her hand, unreasonably cold, and brushed back wild black hair. He had learned to calm her moods as a child, and it made him feel important.

"Is your lab running behind today, Dr. Shah?" he asked.

She leveled a look back at him. "It's working just fine, thank you."

"Then why can't you get those blood culture results my mother has asked for?"

"Pneumonia is an infection in the lungs, sir," she answered in the tone of someone speaking to a child. "We can use chest x-rays to diagnose that, not blood cultures. Those results are a low priority right now."

He could speak to children too. "And what do you use to identify sepsis?"

"It's not sepsis." The doctor busied herself looking at Maggie's chart unnecessarily. "But if you really need to see it …"

"We do," Hollis said.

The doctor didn't bother looking up again. "We'll be back to check vitals in a few minutes. If she isn't calm by then, we'll need to discuss medication."

When they left, Amá launched into her complaints, railing against the medical system that had failed her and Maggie since day one. While Hollis didn't mind taking on medical staff, his mother's rants were harder to handle.

"She'll be fine, Amá. She's had pneumonia before."

His mother stopped pacing to face him fully. "Look at her, Daniel."

Calmer now, Maggie let her head loll to the side, and she stared at the level of his stomach. Her cheekbones were more pronounced than usual, and her hands had fallen to her sides. A grayish hue ran under her skin, though he attributed that to the harsh hospital lights. "I see her."

Amá only shook her head and let out a cry. She grabbed her phone and left the room.

•   •   •

What Hollis had expected to be a long, boring day of watching Maggie sleep turned out to be much more. The more tests they ran, the more doctors came in and out of the room. Her arrhythmia worsened, her cough deepened, and her white blood cell counts came back too low. The infection in her lungs was rapidly overtaking her system.

Hollis kept the twins updated, and his dad called after hearing about it from the twins. Hollis soon realized he had forgotten his phone charger. His phone died by noon.

Sophia came by in the afternoon, with Joshua Sanford in tow. Seeing the boyfriend here irked Hollis for no good reason. He excused himself from the crowded room to purchase an overpriced charger in the gift shop.

Taking the longest route back to Maggie's room, through the hospital he had memorized years ago, Hollis offered silent prayers as he went. His thoughts flitted through them. Prayers that he would be able to calm Amá. Prayers that the doctors would be able to help Maggie. Prayers for strength to face what might happen next.

When he got back, the young Sanford stood outside the room, texting someone. "Hey." The best talking point Hollis could come up with at the moment.

Sanford looked up. He had to be close to Sophia's age, maybe seven years younger than Hollis, but he looked so young. Had Hollis been that young once? Should twenty-eight feel as old as it did today?

"Hey," he replied, putting his phone away. *One point.* Not that Hollis was keeping score; nobody could be good enough for his sisters.

"How's it going?" Hollis asked.

"In there?" Sanford tossed his head toward the door. "Soph's pretty worried."

Hearing a nickname for his sister, coming from a boy, stiffened Hollis's spine. "Nice of you to come with her."

He shrugged. "I hope it's okay. I know this is a family thing, but I wanted to be here for her."

Hollis wanted to claim he wasn't needed, but it was probably best for Sophia. Nobody in their own family really knew how to support one another. "Of course. You're welcome anywhere Sophia is."

The kid's face lit up. "Thanks, I appreciate it."

After a little more awkward small talk, Sophia stepped into the hall. With a quick smile for Sanford, her eyes landed on Hollis, concern etched into them.

"Daniel—" Her words clogged up.

Hollis beat Sanford on the move, wrapping his baby sister into a hug. "She's going to be fine," he said. "She always is."

Sophia shook her head against his arms. "This feels different."

He pulled her back to look her in the eyes. "Sophia, there's nothing wrong with Mags. It's no worse than pneumonia for anyone else."

"You know that's not true," she whispered, barely audible.

It wasn't entirely true. "She'll be fine." The more he said it, they more they could all believe it. And they had to believe it. Every time.

Chapter Thirty

Lark worked evenings all week, and Wren faced the house alone. On Saturday, she found a few neighbors to help her cut out the rest of the drywall, turning down Levi's offer yet again. She didn't fully know why she did it, but something about allowing Grace Church to work on her home seemed wrong. She didn't like the pity or feeling her worlds collide.

Insurance had approved some of her claim related to the roof and water damage from above, though she now had to find a way to get the funds for the deductible. FEMA had denied her request for funds, which nearly broke Wren down, but they provided a list of things she had missed in her initial application. Once she provided more information, she could try again.

Between the emotional and physical toll of it all, her muscles and soul ached by the end of the day. A hot shower and a motel mattress did nothing to help.

Sunday brought with it a weight that pressed onto her chest, heavy in the predawn gloom, squeezing air out of her lungs. It came from more than just tired muscles. The walls started to close in, and Wren jumped out of the bed. She had to escape.

As out of breath as if she were running a marathon, Wren hurried to dress, and shimmied out the door silently. The stale air of the motel's parking lot met her, and she took the stairs two at a time to escape it. She needed fresh air and knew exactly where to find it.

Her car practically drove itself to the dock. Other than Gumpy's rumblings, she drove in silence. The quiet of the morning asked not to be broken by music.

When she stepped out and smelled the salty air, the weight began to lift. Finally free enough to sense it, she needed more than fresh air—she craved a moment with God. Supposedly, God could be found anywhere, even in a motel room, but she preferred to seek him in the wild.

A group of middle-aged fishermen waited for the ferry ahead of her. Todd pulled back the chain barring the boat and took tickets as professionally as a man who smelled like dead fish could.

He huffed when he saw her. "Could you at least pretend to have a ticket so you don't make me look bad?"

Wren grinned. "My apologies, Captain, I didn't realize you had an appearance to keep up."

He snorted as he turned his back to her and took over the wheel. "Give a kid a free ride once …"

Wren took a seat closer to Todd and farther from the fishermen, tucking her bag and towel into her lap. The burst of speed outside of the wake zone always reached into her veins. Nothing could compare to the feeling of salty spray and wind in her hair. If she could be a bird, she would choose an albatross—to feel this way for years at a time, never landing.

Todd reached the Kinney Island dock all too soon. Wren took her time at the dock, letting the fishermen off first.

"How's the house?" Todd asked, spitting into the ocean as he held the boat in place with a single hand on a dock rail.

"Making progress, but it's slow."

"Where you staying while you wait?"

"A motel."

Todd spit again with a hocking sound. "Is that through the temp housing program?"

"No, just on my own."

"You got any idea how long it's gonna take to get that house fixed up?"

Wren fidgeted with her bag strap. "Not really."

"Too long. You better get in something through the city or FEMA."

"Maybe. My sister's staying with me."

A storm crossed over Todd's already harsh features. "That druggie?"

Wren flinched. She and Todd knew each other too well. "She's clean right now."

"Let her go, kid. She's poison."

Indignation rose in her chest, and they stared each other down, the boat rocking underfoot. "She's family."

"Sure. But the drugs ain't."

Wren took a step off the boat to gather her thoughts that swayed wildly in the waves. "I'm all she has."

"She needs more than you," Todd said, pointing a finger upward. "You better introduce her to the big guy." Then, with a push from the dock, the captain-turned-preacher took his gruff self out onto the water.

Speechless, Wren watched him longer than necessary. Even Todd was onto her.

Turning with feet that felt like lead, Wren plodded past the fishermen setting up camp on the pier and began her solitary walk along the beach.

Crossing over the dunes and into the solitary wilderness, Wren lifted her arms, letting wind lift her spirit like the albatross she longed to be. God was here, in this wind, these waves. Lark would probably love this place, yet, for some reason, Wren struggled to share it, much like the church. As if sharing it with Lark would somehow taint these best things in her life.

Todd's words added to the conviction that Micah's sermon had brought last week. Breathing out a long sigh, Wren mentally threw the worries to the waves. Worry belonged to Ridley Bay, not Kinney Island.

With a silent prayer, she continued her walk, hunting for any shells she might bring back to Lark, like a peace offering. That was all she could offer for now.

Half an hour in, she had only come across a few simple and broken shells. Nothing worth bringing home. Turning to walk back empty-handed, she spotted a large, creamy white sand dollar.

She lifted it gently, running a finger over the razor edge. This one was large and strong, and it might survive the trip back, for Lark. Some said the sand dollar, perfectly round with a lily-like outline and five small holes, represented the four nail holes and the spear wound on Christ.

Wren snapped it in two.

Guilt heated her chest as five small pieces fell out—the five doves of peace.

She cracked each piece in half again. Because if she didn't break it now, someone else would. Every sand dollar ended up broken. At least this way, she was in control.

When the last piece fell, Wren sank to her knees. "What am I doing?"

A dry sob escaped her lips. Despite all her talk about authenticity and simplicity, she always fought for control. Yet everything ended up broken in her hands.

She bucked against the church helping her. She had pushed Hollis away endlessly. All for control. Because of fear. She held Kinney Island and Grace Church back from Lark for nothing but sheer selfishness. Was she hoarding God? What a fool.

"Oh God, I'm sorry," she whispered, tears swimming in her eyes, blurring her vision as she stooped down to gather the broken pieces of the sand dollar.

In her fear of brokenness, she forced it upon herself. She had lived in this pain for too long—always wanting more in life, yet breaking away before she could depend on it. She relied more on the brokenness of the world than the goodness of God.

Wren held the broken sand dollar in her palm. Was she too late? Would God give up on her now? This couldn't be fixed.

She wiped the back of her hand against her eyes, and something white beneath a foamy wave caught her eye. She took a step toward it as the wave washed out. In its wake, an enormous, perfect sand dollar sat, larger than the last.

Her breath caught in her chest as she reached for it. Maybe God gave second chances.

The moment she touched it, another appeared to her left. The wave pulled farther out as the tide shrank, and a third sand dollar sat just beyond the second. Each larger than the one she had broken.

Her hand lifted to cover her mouth when she spotted a fourth—and a fifth.

Not only did God have more for her, he had enough.

Wren scooped up the three sand dollars closest to her.

She needed to trust God for once. Whether he wanted to give her more or take away what she had worked so hard for, she could trust him. He had enough. And there was enough God to share with Lark too.

"I don't know how to do this," she whispered, half in prayer. She didn't know how to keep a sand dollar intact, and she certainly didn't know how to begin to fix the brokenness in her life. But all she had to do right now was get three sand dollars safely back to Ridley Bay.

Head raised in purpose, Wren cradled the sand dollars and made her way back to the boat. She needed to see her sister.

•   •   •

Lark needed God, and Wren might be the only person in her life to tell her about him. With fresh determination, she caught the next boat back to the mainland and drove to the motel in time to invite Lark to join her at Grace's second service.

The likelihood of Lark accepting was remarkably low, of course, and Wren couldn't blame her. She hadn't exactly been a role model of Christianity. But she had God on her side.

She burst through the motel door, and an angry groan greeted her from the bed.

"What are you doing?" Lark's muffled voice asked. She rolled over and away from the light at the door.

Wren plopped onto Lark's bed. She held out a sand dollar. "Look what I found."

Another groan. "I don't really care about your little seashell collection."

Wren tugged at Lark's arm over her eyes. "It's beautiful. I never find any this perfect."

With a sound of disgust, Lark hauled herself up slowly, huffing and groaning as if she were eighty years old. "What do you want? Congratulations?"

"No, it's …" Wren tucked the disappointment away. The shell was meant to be her starting point. She would have to jump straight into it. "Never mind. Hey, would you go to church with me this morning?"

"Are you serious?" Lark barked, sending Wren back several inches. "You woke me up for a freaking seashell and church? What is wrong with you?"

Wren pulled back a little farther, to the edge of the bed. "I just … I think you might like it."

"I'm not going to *church*." Lark spoke as if Wren had invited her to hold a rattlesnake.

Mavis had raised them in pantheism, seeing all things as God and God in all things. As adults, both girls had strayed from it. Wren had tested every God and tried every religion on like an outfit before finding the truth. Lark, however, had walked away from it all.

"You might like it," Wren said.

"Are we done here?" Lark asked. Without waiting for an answer, she threw off the covers and stumbled toward the bathroom, holding on to the wall along the way and taking with her all of Wren's newfound hope and energy.

She had to fix this. Surely she could do more than just break things. Wren looked around the room for something she could offer.

"Can I make you some breakfast?" Wren asked through the bathroom door.

Lark yanked the door open, pants around her ankles. "What is wrong with you? I said leave me alone. Go to your stupid church and get out of my face."

The rejection burned like bile in Wren's throat. There were two Larks. The best friend who talked late into the night about everything and the big sister who viewed Wren as nothing more than a petulant child.

"Okay." Wren stepped away and picked up her keys. "I'm going."

Whatever she thought God wanted her to share with Lark, she must have misunderstood. The lines between heaven and earth must have crossed. She couldn't fix what was already broken.

.   .   .

Winding through town slowly, Wren stalled before arriving at church, too early. In the parking lot, she pulled her windblown hair into a tousled braid and shook sand from the hem of her red skirt. She double-checked her appearance in the rearview mirror. No makeup, no accessories save for a pair of hoop earrings she had in her purse. She felt bare—emotionally and physically exposed. She touched the sand dollar on the dashboard, as if for luck.

Though things hadn't gone well with Lark or Hollis, she wanted to try again. Surely she wasn't too far gone. God seemed to be offering some promise of a future to her. She just had to find her way to it.

Scanning the parking lot as she entered, she saw neither his motorcycle nor The Car. Her heart rate increased. Did he skip church again? He almost never missed church. Why would he avoid it now? Surely not because of her, or any fight. Maybe he was just running late.

Inside the doors, she spotted one of Hollis's twin sisters walk in. If only she knew which one. Wren put on a friendly smile and waved at her. "Hey, do you know if Hollis is going to make it in today?"

The girl smiled back, though it didn't quite reach her eyes, certainly not the way Hollis's smile did. "I don't think so. He's with Maggie right now."

"Oh, okay. By the way, I'm Wren. I think we've met, but could you remind me of your name?"

This time a laugh danced in her eyes. "It's okay, I'm Sophia. My sister Lilia hasn't been at church in a while. But if you get us mixed up, you can call any of us Hollis. We share the name. Daniel doesn't get to claim it."

Wren instantly liked the girl. "Sophia. Got it. And you're right, he doesn't."

Sophia caught Joshua Sanford's eye, and together they headed into the auditorium with a quick, polite goodbye to Wren.

Waiting in the lobby for another moment, she pulled out her phone and studied it, willing some notification to appear—something from Hollis, as if they had that sort of relationship.

"Hey, Wren."

Her head popped back up to find Emma near her. "Hey."

"How's the house doing?"

Everybody asked her that, every time. "It's coming along." Her go-to reply.

"Is there anything we can do to help?"

She started to say no but stopped herself. Then, searching her mind, she came up empty anyway. "Sadly, it mostly needs professionals now. Thanks though. Once we have walls and everything, maybe we can have a painting party."

"Oh, I'd love that."

Wren had never thought of Emma as the most genuine person, but she saw nothing hidden in her eyes now. "I'll keep you updated." Maybe some of the past judgment she perceived had been her own.

When Faith and Bethany entered, they both checked on Wren as well and reminded her that their sofa was always open if she needed it. She thanked them and finally gave up on Hollis, heading inside the auditorium as the last worship song played before Micah preached.

Everything felt off today. The sand dollar waiting on Gumpy's dashboard had seemed like such a promise only hours ago, but maybe she had misinterpreted it. Restoring anything around her appeared impossible. Wings clipped, nose diving to the sea, she was an albatross with nowhere to go.

Chapter Thirty-One

Hands coated in oil, Wren pressed the outer edges of her palms down the mole-speckled back of an elderly woman. The woman usually fell asleep halfway through the massage and always apologized, quite needlessly. Sleep was a compliment to Wren. Today, though, the woman remained awake, feeling quite chatty.

Early in her career, Wren had been pleasantly surprised to find that massage therapists could play shrink as well as any counselor, bartender, or hairdresser out there. While many clients enjoyed the quiet, just as many preferred to release emotional tension alongside the physical.

The woman off-loaded the stress of watching the hurricane, the fear of seeing her street fill with water, the shock of seeing what had happened to "other" parts of Ridley Bay. A small initial frustration in Wren's soul passed quickly, putting her own experience aside. Like any good therapist, she played the part of neutral listener and occasional empathizer, offering only guided questions as needed.

Wren moved down the woman's legs, eliciting a heavy sigh. The woman had poor circulation, and her weekly massage provided the relief her body craved.

In this place, Wren could repair brokenness. More than that, she could create beauty. She could soothe aching bodies and reinvigorate weary spirits. Here, she could heal.

The morning filled with back-to-back clients as Ridley Bay returned to its usual pace. At least, for most of the residents. The wounded few slipped out of the news stories and into the slow toil of rebuilding. Here at the spa, Wren lived between those two groups. Here, she bridged them.

At her lunch break, Wren stopped by the front desk, peering over Indie's shoulder to the computer. "When's my next appointment?"

Indie hummed around a sucker in her mouth as she scrolled through the schedule. Electric blue now colored the ends of her hair, replacing the former purple. "Nothing until two."

The stretch of time sounded glorious, and Wren suddenly craved a break. "I think I might take a long lunch."

"No prob. Tessa and Nick are here to take any walk-ins."

"Thanks, Indie." Wren pushed away from the desk and grabbed her purse from her room, unsure why she suddenly needed to escape the place she loved. Healing could take its own toll, but today it seemed more to inspire her—solidifying her determination to create beauty in the other spaces of her life. Remembering she could heal here fueled the desire to do it elsewhere.

Gumpy sputtered and trembled as he fired up. Wren patted the wheel. "It'll have to wait, sir." The electrician was visiting today, and a roofing company later this week. And Lark had yet to pay for any of the motel cost. Sputtering cars were low on the list.

Wren dialed Lark as she pulled out of the parking lot. "Hey, I've got a long lunch break. Do you want to get something together?"

"Thanks, Wrenny," she said, her voice tired, quiet. "I'm about to head to work though, so I can't."

Tucking away any disappointment, Wren reminded herself to be happy Lark was working. "No problem, maybe dinner."

"Maybe so."

"Proud of you, Lark. Go sling those smoothies."

Lark snorted. "Livin' the dream."

Ending the call, Wren wound through the streets along the bay mindlessly. She hadn't brought anything for lunch—preparing meals in a motel with a mini fridge and microwave proved nearly impossible.

She was unsure of where she was heading, and Gumpy seemed to drive himself straight into the heart of downtown. Wren cruised the streets slowly, craning her neck to look up at the block of towers that made up

Ridley Bay's business district. It wasn't much compared to San Antonio, but it had never been her scene. Too much concrete.

She pulled into a fast-food restaurant just a block over from the main street. Inside, Wren ordered a small burger and fries from the dollar menu. It was an old habit from days when her mom had worked at a burger joint and Wren had hung out there after school.

As she sat down to her favorite comfort food, Wren glanced around the place, foolishly hoping to see a familiar face before reminding herself that Hollis was vegetarian.

Instead of his grin, she found a woman sitting in a booth on the opposite wall. The woman had thinning gray hair, three layers of ill-fitting clothes, and a large tote bag that clearly held most of her belongings. She sat next to the wall, with her phone plugged in to charge, sipping on a cup of water and snacking on a granola bar. None of the employees seemed to mind. They probably knew her name.

The burger turned to rocks in Wren's mouth as she forced herself to chew. That could be her mother. It could be her sister. At times it had been Wren.

I should buy her food.

Of course she should. Even Hollis had once asked Wren who she was feeding.

She glanced at her own dollar menu meal. Truthfully, Wren had a few extra dollars for another meal. Why didn't she feed anyone?

Her mind waged a battled. What if it humiliated the woman? What if she didn't want pity? What would Wren say?

It doesn't matter.

Internally roaring over her self-consciousness and fears, Wren stood and crossed the linoleum floor to the woman's table before she could overthink it. She knelt next to the woman and let words tumble out. "Hi. I was just about to order a shake. Can I get you something?"

"Sure." The woman nodded slowly. "You sure can."

"What would you like?"

"Just a burger is fine."

Wren stood to go place the order but stopped and squatted again. "Could I pray for you too?"

"Sure," she said again.

"What's your name?"

"Flora."

Wren said a prayer for Flora's health and safety, and for God to show her his love. "Can I give you a hug?" Wren asked, when she finished the prayer.

"Oh, honey, I'm all dirty."

Her words stabbed Wren in the chest, and she dipped her head, clearing her throat. "We all are."

Flora lifted an arm up, and Wren wrapped her into a hug. Unwashed clothes, greasy hair, smoke, and a thousand emotions enveloped Wren.

"Thank you," Flora said, her voice weak. "People give money, but money never bought anyone's time before. So thank you."

"Of course, Flora. God sees you." With one last quick hug, Wren stepped away. She placed an order for a large meal for the woman, and a shake, all to be sent to her table. Then she gathered the last of her fries and left. She didn't need to wait around; she deserved no special thanks. Her own pride, not the other woman's, had nearly gotten in the way once again.

And she was sick of her pride.

As Wren drove away from downtown, the heaviness in her heart doubled. She had been so sure God wanted her to restore things with the people in her life, with Hollis and Lark, yet she couldn't seem to reach them. Was God calling her on to new people and places? Maybe God meant for her to heal elsewhere. Instead of staying stuck between two worlds, perhaps God was calling her into a new one.

•   •   •

When she clocked out for the day, Wren drove to the edge of town, unwilling to let a couple of disappointments ruin her day.

Pulling into the gravelly parking lot of Madre Tierra, the plant nursery Hollis's aunt owned, she subconsciously scanned the parking lot and felt a minor and very irrational disappointment that his car wasn't there.

But she was here for Lark anyway. Perhaps, if Lark didn't want a sand dollar, she would enjoy a potted plant, a sign of life in the decaying motel.

Wren entered the iron gates of the garden center's outdoor section, wandering through the rows as she snuck glances at the woman at the cash register. She was short, barely reaching five feet tall, with black hair cut just below her ears. This had to be Hollis's mother's sister. Wren searched for signs of Daniel in her face. The moment the woman greeted another customer, Wren saw it: a wide smile that sparked in her eyes, wrinkling them into slits and illuminating dimples in her plump cheeks. It had Daniel Hollis written all over it.

After closing out with another customer, the woman came over to greet Wren. Between the woman's bits of English and Wren's pieces of Spanish, they discussed plant options, soon navigating to a small section of ivies that could survive the low sunlight in the motel. After choosing one, Wren meandered through the row of pots, stalling for no good reason.

When she could stall no longer, she grabbed a bag of potting soil and completed her purchases.

As she drove, Wren felt words bubbling up. She needed to ask Lark for forgiveness. Though it would be an even more awkward apology than the one she offered Hollis. Because this time, she had to apologize for years of judging her own sister, her own family. Wren had never voiced it, but Lark claimed it was written all over her face, and she was right.

Though she couldn't endorse some of Lark's lifestyle choices, the least she could do was love her sister, regardless. And keep pointing her back to God.

Wren pulled into the motel parking lot with the sunlight fading and a bright moon rising above the building. Taking a deep breath of parking lot grease and cigarettes, Wren adjusted the potted ivy in her arms and headed inside.

The room was empty. "Lark?" she called out anyway, as if her sister could find a way to hide in this tiny space.

Disappointment was beginning to take up residence in her chest. Wren set the ivy down on the little desk and pulled out her phone to call her sister.

No answer. The smoothie shop should be closed by now. Wren sent off a text before reaching into the fridge for a microwave dinner.

She ate, watching television and waiting. Still nothing from Lark.

She called again and got the voicemail.

After a shower and changing clothes, she tried one more call.

This time, Lark's voice came through. "What?" she answered, though she sounded distant, like she spoke several inches away from her phone.

"Hey, are you coming back soon? I brought you something."

"Okaaay, I'll see it later." Her words slurred. Other voices sounded around her.

The hairs on the back of Wren's neck began to rise. "Where are you?"

"With a friend."

A friend, here in Ridley Bay? Nothing good could be happening right now. Wren's internal alarms began to sound. "Lark, where are you? How about I come get you?"

"I'd rather if … you join me." Lark laughed, a sound as disjointed as her words.

"Lark, just tell me where you are."

"Home."

San Antonio? "You … left? You didn't say bye."

"Bye, Wrenny. Better?"

The line clicked dead.

Wren dropped her phone and buried her face in her hands. "Oh God …" That was as far as her prayer made it. The rest was a simple chant that matched her heartbeat. *God save Lark. Save Lark from herself.*

Pacing the hotel room, Wren finally decided to call Mavis, but Mavis hadn't heard from Lark at all. She had no idea where to find her.

"She's probably still in Ridley," Mavis said. "There's no telling. But Wrenny, sometimes she gets her hands on different things and … it's different. It's best to just wait it out."

"Wait it out! I can't do that. What do you mean by 'different things'?" Wren's mind raced. Lark hadn't started taking drugs until after Wren left San Antonio. She had never experienced this helplessness firsthand.

"You know, not her usual. Sometimes coke. It makes her more aggressive."

"Cocaine?" Wren nearly shrieked. "We can't just let this happen. She's been doing so well here."

Mavis huffed. "Because Ridley Bay is so much better, isn't it? Are you trying to steal Lark away from me too?"

"Drugs are stealing her, Mavis, not me."

"You think you know what's best for everyone, don't you? You think because you made it out of here, that makes you better."

"No, but you have to agree drugs aren't best for Lark."

Mavis wasn't listening anymore. "It all goes around, you know. You think you're different from me, but you're the exact same. I escaped my parents and my hometown, and now you're running away from yours. But you can't outrun being an Atwood."

"I'm just trying to help."

"Maybe we don't want your help." Mavis hung up.

Wren wanted to scream, to throw something, to be more than all she had been born into. She paced the floor, fighting tears, digging her keys into the palm of her hand. "What do I do, God? What do I do?" She wrapped her arms around herself, holding tightly.

Finally, she couldn't take the confinement of the space anymore. Grabbing her purse, Wren rushed back to her car and began driving around. She had no idea if Lark had gone back to San Antonio or not. All she could do was look around Ridley Bay.

She drove around the motel, looking for Lark's beat-up sedan without success. Then she drove around the smoothie shop and all the nearest blocks. She drove to the seediest parts of town she could imagine.

Nothing, nowhere.

It was well past midnight when Wren returned to the motel, with tear-stained cheeks. She rested her head against Gumpy's steering wheel and prayed. It was all she could do.

Chapter Thirty-Two

Her heart pounded from the moment she woke. Every fear she had about Lark seemed to have doubled, tripled in the night. Wren tore back the curtains of the motel and scanned the parking lot for Lark's car, but it still wasn't there. She had a couple of hours before work and knew she couldn't go in without looking one more time.

Wren rushed through her morning routine, panic rising in her throat. Her sister was out there, somewhere, on cocaine probably mixed with God only knew what opioids and other drugs. She could be dead.

Pressing the panic down, Wren hurried out of the motel and to her car. She had no idea where else to look, but she drove on instinct. Lark likely hadn't gone to San Antonio without telling Wren. She would have to be in her right mind to make that drive. So she must have caved somewhere here in Ridley Bay. Or maybe she had made it a little ways out. Wren headed out of town, to the last few motels and mobile homes scattered across the plains.

Home.

Wren hit the brakes and pulled off to the shoulder of the road. Lark had said she was home. *No, no, no, no.* Whipping the car around, Wren ignored Gumpy's bucking protests as she pressed the gas and pushed back into town.

The drive to Florida Street took years. It took so long, Wren felt at least three hairs turn gray by the time she hooked a hard turn onto the street and swerved just in time to avoid hitting an ambulance that came flying up the road with horns honking and sirens blaring.

Four police cars lined the street, halfway down, and she knew exactly whose house they were at. Panic drove her heart rate upward, drowning out conscious thought.

She slammed the car into park behind a police car and jumped out. Lark's car was parked haphazardly in the front yard. Had Lark been in that ambulance?

Her neighbor Paula stood on the sidewalk and rounded the front of the car to meet Wren. "I'm sorry, I thought you got robbed. I didn't know it was your sister," she said.

Robbed? There was hardly anything worth taking. "What happened?"

Before Paula could answer, Wren caught sight of her sister walking with an officer at her side toward a police car.

"Hang on." She ran toward them.

Another officer in the yard turned toward Wren. "Stop! Don't move!" His hand reached for his hip.

Wren jerked to a halt, hands automatically lifting. Her heart beat in her throat. Only now did she see a strange man sitting on the curb, hands cuffed behind his back.

"That's my house," she said, her voice trembling.

Her house, where the front porch rail leaned haphazardly over the patio and the window on the left was broken. *What on earth?*

The officer walked toward her, hand still resting on his gun. "Are you the owner?"

"Y-yes." She struggled to focus, her eyes darting between the cop and the house.

Another officer joined the first, walking up behind him and patting his shoulder. "Wren?" he asked, in a familiar tone.

Her mind had to scramble out of its panic to recognize Grace Church's security guy. "Isaac?"

"This is your house?"

She nodded, taking in the scene. The officer who had stopped her turned to join two others standing over the man on the curb. "Is my sister okay? Is she in trouble?"

"What's your sister's name?" Isaac asked.

"Lark." Wren couldn't even muster any self-consciousness to worry about how this all looked to him.

Isaac gave her a grim look, still not answering her questions. "She said she lives with you."

"Well, sort of. Right now, at least."

"Were you here last night?"

"What? No. We're staying in a motel right now."

"Was Lark with you last night?"

"No. She wasn't."

"Was she allowed in the house?"

Wren only now realized the front door was missing ... entirely gone. "Yes, I mean, she's been helping me with it. But ..."

"Did you know about the party?"

He was grilling her. The usually friendly face on Sunday mornings was questioning her, as a suspect for something? Wren's stomach twisted as awareness of the situation overtook the panic.

"Party? No. I had no idea. What happened?"

He waved her toward the house. "Looks like they had a pretty wild time."

She followed him, heart still in her throat, trying to take it all in, from the broken window to the tilting rail and the missing door. She followed Isaac up the steps, and with one look inside, her heart fell to her toes.

Bottles of beer and liquor dotted the living room, some smashed against the exposed concrete floor. Someone had pulled off some of the upper drywall—the part of the wall that had survived the storm. A kitchen cabinet door dangled on one hinge. The smell of weed and urine overtook any moldy scent.

Wren stood, frozen in place, taking it all in with a hand over her mouth. The personal violation upset her more than any of the damage.

"Let's clarify again," Isaac said. "Was she allowed in the house? Last night? Because if not, we could be looking at criminal trespass. It's kind of up to you right now."

She shook her head. Condemn her sister? "Lark was, but not whoever else was here."

"If your sister was allowed in, her guests are too. We can't charge them for it."

"Who's outside? Who was in the ambulance?" *Who attacked my home?*

"That guy had cocaine on him. The ambulance was for an overdose, but she'll be okay. I think there were others, but they cleared out before we got here."

"Is my sister okay?"

"Maybe still a little high. We can have her removed, but that's about it."

"No, no, I want to talk to her."

He hooked a thumb into a loop on his vest. "Insurance should cover some of this. Get some photos. You can request the official report from the department in a couple of days."

"Thanks." Finally, the embarrassment settled in. "I had no idea, Isaac, I really didn't. Is this … Will this stay between us?"

He gave her a serious look. "Of course. And we'll be out of here in a few minutes. Your sister is outside. I'm going to go talk to her." Isaac strolled out the door, leaving Wren to walk through the house and examine the damage further, trying to figure out what to say to Lark.

As if there were words for this.

She found the front door. It sat at the bottom of the back porch stairs, cracked, like someone had used it to surf down the stairs.

True to his word, Isaac and the other officers loaded up the cocaine guy and cleared out of the area in a few minutes. Wren stood in the empty doorway, watching the police cars pull away, along with several neighbors peeking at the spectacle. Wren Atwood had been the one to host a crack party in the neighborhood. It burned in her stomach, fueling a steely determination.

Freed from her own interrogation, Lark strutted toward her, head held high. "Told you it was a great place for a party. You should've been here."

"Guess you should have invited me."

"Aw, don't be sad. I told you where I was."

"Mm."

Lark grabbed her purse from the other room and started to walk right past Wren, as if they weren't going to talk about it.

"Where are you going?" Wren asked.

"Back to the motel."

"No, you're not." Wren finally knew what she had to do. She wouldn't be caught in Mavis's trap, providing for Lark while feeding her addictions. As much as she loved her sister, she would have to love her from afar.

Lark turned slowly, so slowly it became creepy. "Why not?"

"Because we're not living together anymore."

Lark studied her for a long moment. "This wasn't my fault, you prick." She pointed at the empty doorway. "I invited some coworkers to kick back after work. I didn't know they'd go friggin' wild."

"You knew drugs and alcohol would be involved. And this isn't your house to invite anyone to."

"Fine, no more parties."

"Lark, no more drugs. You have to stop. This isn't you."

Lark's jaw tightened as a cold wrath crossed her features. "How do you know who I am? You never come see us."

Wren took a deep breath of the reeking house and felt it stiffen her spine. "You're right. I should visit you and Mavis in San Antonio. But you're not allowed to stay with me anymore."

"Perfect, I'll go stay with the coke guy." She waved a hand in the direction the police cars had gone. "Is that what you want?"

"No. I want you to go back to San Antonio and check into rehab. I don't want to lose you."

"You don't care."

"I do. I care a lot. That's why you can't stay with me."

Lark let out a string of curses directed at Wren. If Wren had a front door, she would close it. Instead, she waited, forcing her face to remain neutral while listening to her flesh and blood curse her.

"You think you're better than me, but you're nothing," Lark said, pulling her keys from her purse. She stepped right up to Wren's face, nearly nose to nose. "Don't waste your time driving to San Antonio. I don't want to see you."

Wren stared right back into those bright green eyes, her heart thudding in her chest, the pain of losing her sister seeping through. "I love you."

Lark laughed and spat at Wren's feet. She stalked to her car and pulled out of the grass, thumping over the curb and nearly grazing the side of Wren's car on her way out.

Across the street, Paula's face disappeared behind a curtain.

Wren sank to the top step, only now realizing she had completely missed her first two clients at work today. Her life was ripping apart at the seams.

•   •   •

She sat on that step for a long time before embarrassment sent her inside. Wandering through the house, she knew she should start cleaning, gathering bottles, and mopping up urine that missed the toilet. But she couldn't. It was too much. So she wandered to the back steps instead and sat down again.

Her own sister. Her own house. Mavis was right. Wren couldn't outrun being an Atwood.

With no hope of pulling herself together for work, Wren called and apologized profusely, citing a family emergency.

It was nearly lunchtime before she could move again. Wren forced herself into motion and tidied as she walked through the house, whispering apologies to Rosa. This poor girl had been through too much.

With no front door, it was completely open to theft. She carried the last remaining items from the kitchen and bedroom to her car. She would practically be living out of it, just like she had sworn not to.

A series of croaks from her phone shook her trance, and she found a text group exploding with messages.

<u>Levi</u>
Y'all pray for Hollis and his family, his sister is in the hospital
<u>Emma</u>
What?! What's wrong? Which sister?

<u>Levi</u>

Maggie, pneumonia, and it's pretty bad

<u>Faith</u>

What can we do? Should we send a gift or something?

<u>Levi</u>

I'll ask

<u>Bethany</u>

Praying!

Who's Maggie?

<u>Emma</u>

Middle sister, she has a genetic disorder

<u>Nathan</u>

Paying

**Paving*

***PRAYING*

<u>Levi</u>

Said no flowers, probably could do food or something. Emma?

<u>Emma</u>

Oatmeal cookies coming right up

Everything about the house faded away in an instant. Hollis's sister was in the hospital. Without stopping to think twice about whether Hollis would want her there, Wren grabbed her keys, propped the front door in place as well as possible, and left. She was tired of her own brokenness taking her focus; she wanted to do more. She wanted to help.

Chapter Thirty-Three

The nurse mumbled the date and Maggie's latest vitals to the doctor. Distantly, Hollis registered her saying Tuesday. He had lost track of time. Days and nights blurred inside the hospital room where artificial lights and dark curtains created an eternal purgatory.

His phone had been uncharacteristically quiet for days now. Quincy and Vance were on strict gatekeeping duty and doing too well at it. Without work to keep up with, Hollis had lost track of the outside world.

If today was Tuesday, his dad should be flying into town tomorrow morning. That's how bad Maggie looked.

She had worsened over the weekend and every moment since. Her body didn't seem to be responding to antibiotics. They had her on a ventilator and so many other lines and cords that Hollis had lost track of what they were each for. The sight of her twisted like a knife in his gut.

They talked to her throughout the day, taking turns by her side, whispering things to her. She didn't respond to any of it, but they had spent their entire lives believing she understood more than she acknowledged. Always believing in her.

When his mother's friends arrived, he excused himself from the claustrophobic room, taking up a post in the hallway. He didn't want to be around the dramatic scene. They had to believe Maggie would be fine. And the more people that poured in with premature condolences, the harder it became to believe.

Hearing footsteps and voices approach down the hall, Hollis straightened his shirt, trying to tuck the wrinkles away. He re-rolled the cuffs above his wrist. The nights in the hospital showed.

Hollis glanced up to see familiar faces. Micah and Rebecca Sanford, hand in hand. He knew they were coming sometime today. Sophia and Joshua had let them know the situation, along with a few others at Grace Church. His phone had pinged with their prayers this morning.

"Hollis," Micah called out, a few feet away.

Hollis smiled. Then erased it. Was smiling weird in a hospital? He felt out of body. Sleep deprivation did that. "Sanford." He gave them each a handshake. "Thanks for coming, you really didn't have to."

"Of course we did," Rebecca said, with eyes full of concern. "I'm so sorry she's sick."

They didn't even know Maggie. They were sorry for Sophia's sake, maybe Lilia's, maybe his. He wasn't used to letting people in on his problems. "Me too." Hollis pressed his back into the wall.

They visited briefly in the hallway, letting his mother's friends finish their visit inside the room. The Sanfords knew more about Hollis's family than he expected—no doubt because of Sophia. It only served to remind Hollis that his sister had practically chosen a new family.

A voice overhead called a code to some room, and two nurses went running past. A ball of dread built in Hollis's core—Maggie's room could be the next one coded.

Amá and her friends exited the room just as Sophia and Joshua walked up. Taking over the new shift, Hollis, his sister, and the Sanfords entered the room. Mostly to stand around, to talk and pray, to look at Maggie, and to try not to.

•   •   •

Maggie's door was a turnstile of guests—church friends, nurses, doctors, family—her room never emptied. After the Sanfords left, Sophia and Joshua volunteered to stay in the room and give Hollis a break, and he couldn't even pretend to pass up the offer. Giving Maggie a quick kiss on the cheek and whispered promises, Hollis stepped out of the room.

Once in the hall, he realized he didn't know how to spend the break. He smelled of Lysol and sticky sweet medication. Head home and shower?

Call Quincy and work through the latest at Perla? Go to his condo's gym and run until he stopped thinking?

Spinning on his heel, Hollis headed toward the elevator. He could figure out where exactly he was going once he reached his car.

The elevator button lit up, and Hollis waited, running through his options, wishing he had brought his motorcycle here. He could go get it. The open air on the roads outside of town, going fast enough that the mental image of Maggie unresponsive and pale would finally give way to the focus required at that speed—

"Hollis," a surprised voice spoke.

Wren Atwood stood in front of him, on the elevator, one hand holding it open. Dressed in a yellow tank top and a billowing orange skirt, she looked like the sun, especially in contrast to their dismal surroundings, and for a moment, Hollis found it hard to think of her as anything else.

"Atwood."

A small frown crossed her face as she stepped into the hallway next to him. "Levi texted. I'm so sorry Maggie's sick. How are you doing?"

The fight slipped out of him, the need to burn rubber into the highway replaced by the need to bury his head in his hands and let it all out. He struggled to find the drive that held him up. "Not great."

"Hollis …" Wren reached for his hand, and he was more than willing to take hold of the anchor she offered. "Do you want to get some air?"

"More than anything."

He followed the sunlight into the elevator, down four flights, and through the sliding hospital doors.

"How about a walk on the bay?" she asked. "Sand between your toes helps a lot of things."

"Sure." He would do just about anything. "But we're taking my car."

A look of distress flashed across Wren's face before she pressed her lips together and drew them into a smile. "Okay."

Hollis stared at her for a second, only now realizing it had been a test, a subconscious push to see if she would push back. A challenge, to see if she would stay when he had no charisma to offer.

Her head tilted. "So, did you want to go now, or …"

With a slight shake of his head, Hollis led the way to the parking garage, unsure what to do with the sun once it was within his reach.

.   .   .

Wren wasn't sure if Hollis remembered the plan to head to the bay. He went all the wrong ways, hitting the highway first with an ear-splitting roar from the car's engine as it burst forward. Why did such a fast car have to be so loud about it? Wren kept it to herself.

Hollis remained quiet throughout the drive, never speaking a word, either lost in thought or perhaps imprisoned in it.

Eventually, he began to wind back through town, until they reached the southernmost point of the Ridley Bay beach. A small park led to the beginning of the boardwalk, though here it was nothing more than cracked concrete on a retaining wall rising several feet above the sand. Only a few houses lined the boulevard on the opposite side. He obviously knew where to escape the crowds.

Unbuckling from the most expensive seat she'd ever sat in, Wren followed Hollis to the seawall, where he hopped down onto the large, uneven steps leading to the sand. He reached a hand back to help her, and she took it—jumping in a skirt rarely ended well for her. At the last step, he pulled his shoes off and left them there, joining her barefoot on the warm sand.

Only the sound of the waves surrounded them. Wren wanted to break the ice around him bottling him up so tightly she worried he might burst. But she couldn't think of any words they hadn't tried before. And based on Hollis's demeanor, she couldn't offer many promises for Maggie either.

Wren reached into her purse and tugged out the second-place medal she'd been holding on to for too long. "This thing is getting pretty heavy. Thought I better give it back."

Hollis huffed out something just short of a laugh as he took the medal. Weighing it in his hand, he slowly wrapped the red ribbon around the silver circle.

Then, before she realized what he was doing, Hollis lifted his arm and, with full force, launched it past the waves, into the ocean.

"Hollis!" Wren watched it sail and splash down past the wave break. Turning to him, she watched for any sign of anger, remorse, perhaps humor. None.

He stared straight ahead. "I hate second place."

The weight pulling that medal to the ocean floor seemed to press onto them both. "You would tell anyone else it's okay to be third, fourth, last. Not everyone can be first in everything."

"I can be."

It was such an arrogant, prideful thing to say, yet it didn't bother her. Wren only felt sorrow for him, for the impossible expectations he carried and the satisfaction he would never find.

As suddenly as he'd thrown the medal, Hollis doubled over, hands on his knees, the weight he carried finally driving him down, breathing as if he'd just finished the 10K race again. His voice was strangled. "I can't save her. I can't."

The raw pain in his voice cracked her heart wide open. "I'm sorry." *For all of it.* The pain he had carried for so long, every unkind word she'd spoken, Maggie's sickness, all of it.

"She needs me." He gasped for a breath he couldn't catch. "But I'm running away from her. I shouldn't even be here, I should be with her."

"It's okay to take a break."

"No, it's not. I'm not enough. I never will be." The admission forced him down, and he dropped into the sand. He knelt in defeat, though no one was the victor.

With a heavy sigh, she sank down by him. "You don't have to be enough. God is."

He said nothing. If any words could change his mind, make him see his own worth, his security in Christ, she would offer them, but he would never believe her. He had to discover it for himself.

So for now, she did the only thing she could. She took his hand in hers and stayed there, watching the sky turn orange, holding on until he could breathe again.

Chapter Thirty-Four

Life ended in an instant. Even when he knew it was coming, for years, for decades, it took him by surprise.

The monitor in Maggie's room skipped. And never picked up again.

Daniel didn't notice the first missed beat, so used to its arrhythmic sound, but he noticed the second and third. The skip lasted, and lasted, straight through eternity.

Amá acknowledged it first, with a wail. And a flurry of doctors and nurses hurried into the room.

Hollis was helpless, a child again, flooded by every emotion that had ever surrounded Maggie—every bitterness, every envy, every sorrow. It threatened to wash him away.

There would be no second chances. No time to get it right. Every time he had been frustrated at her, every moment he had wanted to hide her away—now his to carry forever.

The wall pressed against his back, and Hollis leaned against it, needing it to hold him up. A small version of himself was trapped inside his ribs, pounding his fists against their cage, screaming at the world. But on the outside, a calm stillness settled over his features, locking down the wild creature inside.

He could have stayed trapped there forever with the pain pulling him down with Maggie, but the twins came over and hid their faces in his chest. Wrapping an arm around each one, he pulled them away from the bed, the commotion, and the sounds of their mother's grief.

His father, here now, moved from his stoic position in the corner of the room and took their mother in his arms, helping to muffle the cry.

The medical team declared the time of death and, one by one, silenced the beeping machines and pumping lines. A nurse slipped out last, giving them a chance to say a final goodbye.

Lilia stepped forward first, tiptoeing until she could stroke Maggie's hair. "I'm sorry we got so busy … I should have made time …" she whispered. The rest came out in choked tears.

Sophia whispered all the things she had ever loved about Maggie.

Hollis knew his turn came next, but he had no idea what to say. He sat on the stool next to her bed, still. Then, slowly, he lifted her hand in his and rested his forehead against it. He dropped his voice as low as possible so his parents wouldn't hear. "It was never your fault, Mags." None of it. None of the pain. It was Rett's fault, not Maggie's. "I'll see you again, and you'll be able to walk, and talk, and tell me everything you ever wanted to say. We'll be up there together, thanks to you."

He propped his chin on their hands and sat in silence with her for a moment, memorizing her.

Amá had quieted, and he knew it was her turn, so he brushed Maggie's hair back and kissed her forehead. "Goodbye."

The doctors had lied. They had said girls with Rett Syndrome could live well into middle age. Maggie was only twenty-three.

•　　•　　•

Hollis

She's gone.

That was all Hollis's text said, two days after they had sat in the sand together. Wren knew what it meant, and she knew what he needed but didn't ask for. She left work early and drove straight to the hospital.

She arrived to find his twin sisters standing in the hallway. By the looks on their faces, she knew it had happened.

"Hollis told me," she said to both twins, trying to figure out which was Sophia and which was Lilia. "I'm so sorry."

One stepped forward and hugged her. Sophia. "This is Wren," she said quietly to her sister.

"Lilia," the girl replied, with a simple lift of her hand in return.

Maybe the girls didn't want a stranger here with them at this moment, but they looked so lost and alone here in the hallway, Wren couldn't leave them. Soon a nurse led them all to a waiting room down the hall.

They sat on the two couches in the room. Sophia ducked her head into her hands, crying silent tears. Despite only a few short years between them, Wren wanted to gather them to her like a mother hen. She rubbed Sophia's back.

Lilia gave her a few short glances before speaking up. "Are you the girl who got flowers?"

"What?" Wren and Sophia both asked.

"The flowers. Maggie told me Daniel gave a girl apology flowers."

Now Sophia shot Wren a look too.

The morning glories. "Yes, I am."

Lilia sighed and studied her hands. "Then you should know he's good. Like, really good. Daniel, Hollis, whatever. I hope you forgave him."

"I know. And I did."

"He gave Maggie a voice."

Wren thought about it for a second but had clearly missed some message. "A voice?"

"The app," Lilia said.

"What app?"

She squinted her eyes at Wren, like it was a trick question. "The one that started Perla Tech."

"Okay …" She still didn't understand.

Lilia spoke in short sentences, like surely one of them would make Wren remember something she should have known. "The eye-gaze software. The one that turns tablets into custom communication devices. How do you not know about this?"

"To be honest, I don't know much about what your brother does."

Her mouth dropped open slightly, and she stared at Wren. Because everybody knew what Daniel Hollis did. Except for Wren.

"You know about the healthcare app he sold, right?"

Wren shook her head, knowing she was failing the test here.

Lilia narrowed her eyes again, but before she could deem Wren worthy of any further discussion, the man himself entered the room, holding immeasurable pain in his eyes.

Wren wanted to stand, to go to his side, but she froze, feeling out of place in the family affair. What if she had misinterpreted his text? Did he not mean for her to come?

He sat beside Lilia and pulled her into his chest. She buried her face in his shirt.

Wren found a box of tissues in the room and passed a few to Sophia before offering them to Lilia, still feeling awkward and unsure. But when she held the box out to Hollis, he reached for her wrist with a gentle tug. She sat down next to him and leaned into his other side, willing to carry whatever part of it she could, to hold him up, as he did for everyone else. An invisible line seemed to string between his heart and hers, as the pain slowly built in her chest.

Soon, Joshua Sanford arrived and joined Sophia. No longer the only non-family member in the room, Wren relaxed more deeply into Hollis's side. Though she had never considered herself much of an anchor, she would weather this with him.

Chapter Thirty-Five

A week later, the Saint Mary Cathedral filled in with families of other students with special needs, families Amá knew from therapy or support groups, extended family from both sides, friends of the twins, and friends from Grace Church. A few random connections showed up too: Maggie's hair dresser, some of her previous assisting caregivers, and a journalist who had once interviewed Hollis. Regardless of her intentions, Hollis had her removed from the building.

The priest spoke briefly about death and heaven. One of Maggie's teachers gave a beautiful speech about how bright and loving Maggie was. They showed a slideshow the twins had pulled together. The Grace Church band performed her favorite hymn, Blessed Assurance.

"Perfect submission, all is at rest, I in my Savior am happy and blest."

The words promised a peace he couldn't find. Hollis's survival depended on Wren, who sat next to him, per his request. She made it easier to breathe. They hadn't talked about their last argument or whatever words had been carelessly spoken, but it seemed forgiven by both.

The service was short, and the family wore light colors—the Colombian tradition for a child's service, for someone without sin, for Maggie.

When the family left for the burial, Wren stayed behind to help clean up, and he immediately missed her warmth.

Hours later, family filled the Hollis home, cousins and aunts and uncles filling the empty spaces where Maggie should have been. Despite the heaviness of the day, Amá played hostess well, pouring all the energy she usually gave to Maggie out onto their extended family.

After playing translator between Flores and Hollis family members for as long as he could, he snuck away to Maggie's room and found his dad hiding there as well. They acknowledged each other with a nod.

Someone had moved many of Maggie's things into the room, crowding it. A stack of paintings lay on her dresser. Hollis riffled through it until he found the red rainbow. He rolled it carefully while his dad watched. "Don't tell Mom."

"I won't. Daniel, you can have whatever you want." He lifted his hand from his lap, revealing a necklace chain that ended in a daisy. "I gave her this, for her tenth birthday."

Hollis joined him at the foot of the bed. They sat in silence for a moment before his dad spoke again. "I should have been around more. I'm sorry."

Hollis nodded slowly. It was true. "We knew you loved us."

"It's not past tense, Daniel. I love you. And I want to be around more. Now."

Now? He had needed his dad when he was six and failed first grade, but he had worked too much. He had needed him at fourteen, when his parents split up, but his dad had decided to go live like a bachelor. Did he need a dad now, at twenty-eight?

"Remember the ice cream shop?" Hollis asked, studying the carpet.

"We can still open it."

"I'm not sure we need to anymore."

His dad didn't answer for a long time.

"I guess not."

•   •   •

The haunting hymns, rapturous photos, and shared tears lingered in the high ceilings of the cathedral long after the family had left for the burial. It captured the sorrow of the Hollis family's loss, but it also seemed to provide closure for Wren as she prayerfully surrendered her own sister.

When Hollis invited her to the burial, she almost agreed but decided that she needed a small break from the weight of it all. The last week had been full of working overtime, cleaning up the house, and staying in touch with Hollis and his sisters. After helping tidy the cathedral, she planned to collapse on a motel mattress for a much-needed nap.

Several other members of Grace Church stayed behind to clean up—clearing rows, wrapping framed photos on a display table, and tidying cookie crumbs in the foyer. Wren volunteered for cleaning up the flowers, joined by Ava.

"I think we can preserve some of these for Ms. Hollis," Wren said, carrying two vases to the foyer. Though the Hollis family had taken several bouquets to the graveside, there were still dozens remaining, thanks to Daniel's aunt.

"Oh, I love that idea," Ava said. "What do you have in mind? A dried bouquet?"

"I'm thinking pressed and arranged into a clear frame."

"Sounds pretty, especially with these anemones. Do you know how to do it? Any time I've tried to press flowers, they always fall apart."

Wren nodded, remembering the frames and collages that had decorated their walls at various times through her childhood. "My mother loved to make art with wildflowers."

"So she taught you?"

"I guess so." Another thing Lark had been right about. Mavis had taught them a thing or two, but Wren had been so wrapped up in the shortcomings, she hadn't been able to see the good. "She always shared her love of beauty with us."

They worked together, going through the many vases lining the foyer and pulling the best flowers from each. Ava gave her own input based on her knack for floral arrangements, while Wren knew which would press best.

"I'd hate to see the rest of these thrown out," Wren said, looking over the several bouquets remaining.

"Should we take them to the Hollises?" Ava asked.

"Sophia said no. She said her mother doesn't want to watch them die. What about the hospital?"

"That's a great idea."

Working together, they rearranged the bouquets to look less like funeral flowers and loaded them into Wren's car. Rebecca Sanford, Ava's mother, joined them in loading the last few.

"Any updates on the house?" Ava asked.

Wren sighed. She hated lies, and she was tired of hiding her past. It had caught up to her present. Wren pulled in a breath and leaned her back against the car, the parking lot asphalt warm under her feet. The lacy hem of her charcoal dress whipped against her ankles in the wind. "It's worse. My sister came into town and ended up trashing it. I'm still trying to get a front door."

Rebecca didn't hide her surprise. "I didn't know you had a sister."

"What happened to the house?" Ava asked, genuine worry etched on her face. "Why would she trash it?"

Wrung dry from the last several days, Wren felt bare. "I don't know." A lie. But the two women in front of her were whitewashed and clean; what would they think of Wren and Lark, the broken and the addicted? "Actually, I do know." Wren caved. She told them all about Lark, the drugs, the party, the house, and the fallout.

Rebecca moved to bring Wren under her arm. "Oh, honey, what can we do?"

Wren stayed in Rebecca's arms without answering. What if Mavis was like this? What if her mother cared? What if Wren and Lark hadn't been fending for themselves since they were children?

Wren finally straightened, drew a level breath, and pushed back, plastering a weak smile on. "The church has already helped with hurricane recovery so much, I can't ask for any more."

"Of course you can," Ava said. "That's what we're here for."

Wren sniffled and laughed, a weird snorting sound. "To help with drug addicts?"

"Jesus came for the sick," Rebecca said. "And addiction is a sickness, more than a choice."

"That's a gracious way to put it," Wren said.

Ava tilted her head. "We all need grace. Where would you be without it?"

Her tone implied the question was rhetorical, but Wren disagreed. "I'm not sure grace has done much for me. My house is destroyed, I'm broke, my sister is addicted to drugs, and my mom won't talk to me. I think *this* is where I'd be without grace."

"Oh honey, that is hard," Rebecca said. "But I see where you are, and I see the grace of God there too. Without grace, you wouldn't have any hope beyond your circumstances. But you do. You have hope and grace to pull you through the day."

"Without it, we're all just a few wrong steps away from being in Lark's place," Ava said.

Wren wanted to argue, to claim she would never be like Lark. She had fought that destiny with everything in her, for years. But it hadn't all been on her own strength. Hope and grace, things that sounded so far away right now, held her fast. Things Lark didn't have.

Twisting her keys in her hand, Wren finally admitted a truth she had told no one in the last week. In light of Hollis's loss, she didn't want pity. But she had losses of her own. Hope would have to carry her through losing her house. "I got denied FEMA funds a second time." She choked on the words. Her tear ducts were primed and ready after the funeral, and they sprang to action yet again. "I'm going to have to give up on the house."

Rebecca grabbed her hand. "Sweetie, you are not giving up your home," she said with a fierceness that surprised Wren. "We have a benevolence fund. We're not letting you go down."

Wren stared at their hands. "It's too much. I don't want to drag the church down with me."

"That's not how it works," Ava said with a laugh. "I know it's more blessed to give than receive, but sometimes you need to let others have the blessing of giving to you."

"We'll cover what we can and find people to fill in the rest," Rebecca said. "The finance team will help you find more too. I'll have to run it by Micah and the elders, of course, but I'm very convincing. So do *not* sell your house." She gave Wren a pointed look.

How much time had Wren wasted in stubbornness and fear, when this love was waiting for her? She might be an Atwood, but she was also one of the redeemed. And she wasn't stuck. God had made a way. "Thank you," she croaked out, and wrapped her arms around the women.

•   •   •

"You have a guest," Indie said, with a quick rap on Wren's open doorframe.

"A guest?" Wren frowned as she finished putting a new sheet on the massage table. She had clients at work, not guests. "Who is it?"

Indie shrugged. "A cute guy."

Her pulse spiked as only one face filled her mind. It had been five days since she had seen Hollis last, at the funeral. She followed Indie toward the reception area to find him.

He leaned against the front desk, dressed in a navy polo and salmon shorts. Hollis straightened when he saw her, fidgeting with the keys in his hands. "Hey, can we talk for a second?"

Confusion wrinkled Wren's forehead as her mind raced through every possible disaster that could bring him here. Something with his family, maybe. Wren glanced at her next client, already waiting on a seat.

"Can you get Mrs. Wright checked in?" she whispered to Indie. "I'll be right back." She turned to Hollis and waved him outside.

"What's wrong?" she asked as soon as the door closed behind them. Possibly a stupid question, given his circumstances, but this didn't look like grief. Nervous energy radiated from him as he shifted his stance.

"I'm leaving."

The words settled into a silence between them, weighted and sinking.

"What?" Wren's voice came out dry.

"I'm going to Houston, for work." His eyes darted toward the parking lot. "I don't know when I'll be back."

A hollow spot formed around his words. She recognized a runaway, and she had plenty of arguments for him to stay—his family here, his friends, his company. Whatever drove him, he couldn't outrun. But if she had learned anything about Hollis, it was that he didn't need an argument. He needed someone on his side.

"If that's what you need," she said, ignoring the pulse in her ears. She forced herself to focus on the fact that he had come to tell her. That had to mean something.

He lifted the key fob in his hand. "I know you hate it, but this is the condo key. I'll be gone a few weeks, maybe months, so if you need somewhere to stay—" He took her hand and placed the key in her palm. "Just leave it at the front office when you're done with it."

For a second, Wren had to remind herself to breathe. She didn't want this goodbye. "It won't be the same."

"You'll be okay."

Wren held one arm across her core, grabbing onto the other arm that hung lamely at her side. "Will you?"

His eyes came back to hers, dark as the void his words created. He shrugged, and the motion tore at her heart.

This was her last chance. "Before you leave. Please know I didn't apologize because of Maggie. Lark made me realize what a snob I had been. You did too. Getting to know you showed me how many stupid assumptions I had made."

"You might have been right about some of them."

"Hmm. So you do secretly star in toothpaste commercials?"

That earned a grin from him. He ducked his head. "No, and there's not much else good about me either."

"That's not true."

His smile disappeared. "Then I'd better go while you still think that."

"Daniel … you don't have to."

"I do." It was final.

Wren couldn't stop herself. She stepped closer, weaving her arms through his, wrapping around him. When his arms came around her, she felt every ounce of the loss—his, that drove him away, and hers, at seeing him leave.

He stepped back first. Giving her nothing more than a nod, he turned and walked away.

And she knew without a doubt it would be the last she heard from him. Whatever they were meant to be for each other had run its course.

Chapter Thirty-Six

Hollis went to Houston to oversee a clinical trial, leaving Quincy in charge of headquarters. When the trial ended, he couldn't bring himself to go back to Ridley Bay, so he flew northeast to connect with potential investors. In between meetings, he worked remotely from coffee shops, in towns where he knew no one and never had to smile. Maybe it was atonement, maybe it was coping.

Far from home, no one knew he was a failure on the inside. He could focus on business wins and even convince himself he was worth something again.

Benefiting from his undivided attention, Perla Tech grew at an unprecedented rate. It had been ready for this; they had a scalable structure, a large hiring pool, and a long list of goals.

The Perla team doubled down on the eye-gaze app, improving the machine learning response; Hollis wanted it automatically customizing to user preferences.

Their smart glasses entered production, and they finished funding the first trial of their brain-computer interface. Soon they would bypass the tablets and even the glasses and move straight into converting electrical activity in the brain into movement and communication. One day, they would finally understand what these minds trapped inside of broken bodies really wanted.

While he traveled, he met with families and individuals who used Perla Tech software and hardware. People with ALS, cerebral palsy, autism, and more. They worked together, identifying gaps in assistive technology and brainstorming ways to fill them.

It had all gone well until he flew to Seattle for a charity event Vance added to his calendar. That was when he met Chloe Baker.

Hollis showed up to the event just hours after landing, in a suit he hastily ironed in the hotel. He greeted the organizers and began swapping handshakes and business cards when the girl entered the room, conspicuous, like a beacon of light in the dark.

Everything about her was so familiar. Her wheelchair, the hands that bowed at her mouth, the dark hair falling at her shoulders, her deceptively small frame. Maggie, ten years ago.

When her mother caught Hollis staring, he instantly looked away, hiding a stare like so many others had done to his sister.

Pushing out the double doors on the side of the room, Hollis escaped into the hallway. He pulled at his tie and undid the top button of his dress shirt in an effort to regain his breath. Nothing could loosen the noose around his neck.

Was it because of Vance's planning that Hollis had somehow avoided families with Rett so far?

Hollis bent over, pressing his hands onto his knees to support himself as he tried to wipe away the mental image of Maggie in her wheelchair at the table when he kissed her goodbye and moved to Houston. He had been so desperate to get away. She had been thirteen, with all the time in the world ahead of them. Hollis blew out a breath slowly, steadily.

If he did this all for Maggie, what did he do now that she was gone?

"You can do this," he whispered to himself. He loved his work. He loved connecting with these families. He understood them, and he never hid his own experiences from them. He could face Rett.

With another deep breath, he turned on his heels and walked back into the conference room.

The family stood just off to the side, and while Hollis circled toward other parts of the room, he couldn't take his eyes off the girl and her parents. When his eyes caught with her parents' yet again, Hollis headed toward them. He looked like a creeper and owed them an introduction.

"Hi, how are y'all?" he asked, with a wide smile, playing up a friendly, southern side. He introduced himself as the founder of Perla Tech.

Steve and Melissa Baker introduced themselves and their daughter, Chloe. Mr. Baker owned a local law firm. Mrs. Baker gushed a few praises for Perla Tech—they used their seizure-tracking software. Hollis chatted for a moment, but his gaze kept returning to Chloe.

Finally, he dropped down into a squat to get just below Chloe's eye level, as her head tilted downward. He gave her the brightest, friendliest smile he could. "Hi, Chloe, my name's Hollis. It's nice to meet you. How old are you?" She didn't have an eye-gaze device, only a set of communication cards hooked around the back of the wheelchair. He knew he wouldn't receive an answer.

"She's twelve," Mr. Baker said.

Hollis kept talking to Chloe. "Twelve is a great age, Chloe. My sister Maggie had Rett Syndrome. She really liked to paint. Do you ever paint?"

Mrs. Baker had made a surprised sound when Hollis mentioned Margarita's Rett. "Oh," she breathed, placing a hand on her husband. "Had."

"Chloe has painted before," Mr. Baker answered. "But it's a bit messy for my taste."

"It is pretty messy." Hollis absorbed every direction that Chloe's eyes darted. He already loved her, and he knew this was his calling. "That's the fun of it, right?" he asked, with a wink that she didn't even see. "Do you have any brothers or sisters?"

"She has one brother," Mrs. Baker answered. "But he lives with his biological parents, so she doesn't see him much."

That stole Hollis's attention. His eyes flicked up to the Bakers. "What?"

"We're a family by love and law, just not blood," Mrs. Baker said, running a hand affectionately over the girl's hair.

Hollis's brain short-circuited. "Did you know …?"

"Of course," Mr. Baker said. "God allowed Chloe into our lives. And he has shown us his goodness again and again since then."

They … *chose* Rett? Hollis stood on joints that felt old. Goodness? Hollis loved Maggie, and even Chloe, but to see God's goodness in Rett

… He hadn't learned that yet. And it must have shown on his face because the Bakers kept talking.

"You know, we do our best, but there's so much we can't control or fix. So we've learned to lean on God," Mr. Baker said. "And that's the best thing I've ever learned."

"But it's … hard," Hollis said, careful not to say anything that could offend Chloe.

"Most good lessons are," Mrs. Baker said. "This might sound pushy, but I'd love to share how Jesus has shown up for us, if you're interested."

Hollis shook his head slowly. "Actually, I'm a Christian too. But …" He didn't know how to voice his rebuttal. But what? But his God had never been enough?

"So you understand," Mrs. Baker said.

A silent sigh escaped Hollis's chest. "Yeah. Sure."

"Once you can lean on God, you can handle just about anything," Mr. Baker said with a wide grin.

Hollis asked them about eye-gaze technology for Chloe, but her mother said she hadn't been able to use it, despite several tries. He promised new options within the next year and discussed including them in early trials. After swapping business cards with the family, he said goodbye to Chloe and continued working his way around the room. A question buzzed at the back of his mind, though, like a mosquito. *Why is my God not enough?*

•   •   •

Shucking off his coat, Hollis tried to shake off the chill of December in the Northwest when he returned to his hotel room late that evening. The wet clung to him, and he had just upped the thermostat in the hotel room when his phone rang. Sophia, again.

The twins kept him updated on life at home. They told him about their dad buying a condo in Ridley Bay, to live there part-time. Hollis was glad for it. The twins didn't need him as much now with two parents around again. They still called him regularly, a fact he deeply appreciated, though since Thanksgiving, their calls had become even more frequent. At least one twin called every single day, usually with nothing to say other than to ask him to come home for Christmas.

"Hey," he said, grabbing a hand towel to rub over his hair and neck, moist from the drizzle outside.

"I'm engaged!" Sophia shouted.

The towel fell from his hands. "What?"

"Wow, Hollis, don't sound so happy for me."

"I—"

Giggles erupted over the phone, and a second twin's voice sounded in the background. "Give me that," she said, snatching the phone.

"Sorry, that was Lilia," the real Sophia said. "And I am *not* engaged."

"Thank God."

"Hey!"

"I didn't mean it like that," he said.

"It's a good reminder of why you should come home though, isn't it?" she asked in a singsong tone.

"I think it's the opposite. You guys are a mess."

"Yes, we are," Lilia said. Now that he knew they were both there, he could make out the slight differences in their voices. "But so are you, so come back and make it a party."

"I'm sure you're busy enough with real parties, you won't even notice if I'm not there," he said.

"We're trying to get better about that," Lilia said.

"Life's too short to be too busy," Sophia added. "We're prioritizing."

"And I made the cut?"

"Of course," she said. "That's why we want you here for Christmas. We're already missing one sibling."

His eyes darted from the gray clouds outside the windows to the geometric-patterned chair in the sitting area of the hotel suite. It might have been wrong to leave them all in the middle of grieving, but he'd had nothing to offer. He couldn't fix it. In Maggie's absence, he felt worthless. "I'm not enough to make up for that," he said.

"Maybe if we get a Ouija board, we could have all four of us," Lilia shouted from the background. "Or a medium!"

A laugh slipped out before Hollis could stop himself. "You weirdo. Sounds like the worst Christmas ever."

"Exactly, and it wouldn't be fair for you to skip it," Sophia said.

"You guys are really selling this."

"Come on, we just miss you," one of them said.

"Is this for Christmas gifts? I can send something." Now he sounded like his dad.

"It's for you, tonto." Definitely Lilia speaking. "You need us."

Hollis sighed. He probably did need them even more than they needed him. "I'll think about it."

The twins cheered and gave hasty goodbyes before rushing off to some study group.

They weren't the only ones asking. His dad had called a few days ago to ask if Hollis would come back, if only for the holidays. Amá had called too, not even to guilt Hollis about it, but just to say she missed him. Even Vance had reached out, suggesting that Quincy wasn't the person to host the company's annual Christmas party.

He never heard from Wren, but that was his own fault. She had sent him a text six weeks after he left, thanking him for the condo stay and saying she had found housing. Unsure of how to reconnect, what to say, how to apologize and thank her all at once, he didn't reply. Then time stretched on until it was too late to reply. He thought about it far too often.

Anything he had outrun had caught up to him today, in the form of Chloe. Despite missing home, his own bed, and the warmth of the Texas sun, he wasn't sure he could return. Though he'd started to think it had less to do with Maggie, or even himself, and more to do with God.

"The Bakers said you show up," Hollis said, speaking aloud to the empty hotel room—probably a sign he needed to return home. "So where are you?"

As if on cue, his phone started ringing again. The associate pastor at Grace.

"I was asking God, not Grace Church," Hollis mumbled. He answered the phone with a tone brighter than he felt. "Kaminski."

"Hollis, it's been a while," Kaminski said. "How are you doing?"

"Good, staying busy."

"It sounds like it, I've seen a few updates from Perla." Kaminski kept up with Perla, which earned him some points in Hollis's book. "I'm guessing you got the newsletter, but we're hosting the first service in the new building on Christmas Eve and a ribbon cutting the week before that. I wanted to reach out and invite you. We'd love to see you at both."

Hollis almost had to laugh. How many invitations did it take? He finally resigned to his fate. "I can try to be there for the Christmas Eve service."

"Not the ribbon cutting?"

"I don't think so." Not because he had any plans. For some reason, he just didn't feel like it. "And please don't mention my name, either."

"Really? I mean, I can appreciate that, but it's also just a chance for us to publicly thank you."

"Yeah, you can skip that. I'm not sure it's anything worth recognition."

"That's fine. But between you and me, generosity is a biblical virtue and you're a great example of it."

Then why did it never seem like enough? "It's not like I give everything. Have you seen my car?"

Kaminski chuckled. "Well, you're allowed a little fun, just don't let it take over your heart."

Hollis let out a cross between a laugh and a snort. "It doesn't." He hadn't even thought of it in all the time he'd been gone. The keys were in the condo. Maybe Wren drove it into the ocean. The thought brought a grin.

"Listen, I'll let you go," Kaminski said. "But can I say a prayer for you first?"

Hollis never asked for prayers and rarely received them. He preferred to be on the giving side. But for once, even he could admit his own need. "Sure."

"Father God, thank you for the holidays, to remember your ultimate gift, and for all Hollis gives through his work, talent, and donations. I pray for comfort for him and his family. And I pray that they would take everything to you, coming before you again and again, because that's where we find rest. In Jesus's name, amen."

When they hung up, Hollis stared at the wall. Did he take anything to God?

That's where we find rest.

Hollis blamed God for not being enough, for not making Hollis enough, but maybe God didn't want to join Hollis's race. Had he ever really tried to simply rest? Was God enough for that? He dropped his head into his hands. He wanted to be like the Bakers, like Kaminski, like Maggie, to know God's goodness personally, not as an abstract idea.

"God, I give up. I can't figure it out, I can't find that peace." He knelt to the floor, so tired of carrying it all, desperate for peace. "Help me."

Nothing happened. Should something happen?

"I don't even know what rest looks like if I'm still working and everything. But everybody else seems to know some secret to doing it with joy."

Silence.

His shoulders dropped. What if God would not let him in on the secret? What did he have to do?

"I can't do anything," he whispered. He could do absolutely nothing to earn God's love, to create peace, to absolve guilt.

Admitting defeat released him. The vise around his chest loosened, and in its place a warmth lifted his breath higher and higher until he laughed. God loved him anyway. For no good reason whatsoever, he loved this weird, laughing-alone-in-a-hotel-room guy.

Hollis rubbed his hands over his face and leaned back against the bed. No tangible proof existed, no medal he could hold that proved it, no knitted blanket of peace, but he knew he had something. Because he finally saw his own powerlessness, and he was completely and totally fine with it.

Chapter Thirty-Seven

The week before Christmas, Hollis flew back to Houston and drove to Ridley Bay, arriving late on a Thursday night. After retrieving his key from the lock box, he entered the condo for the first time in months.

After months of being a stranger in a hotel room, the familiarity of home greeted him with warmth and comfort. Though it wasn't exactly the same as he had left it. A hint of femininity rested on it, in a slightly floral scent that lingered in the otherwise spotless condo. The ghost of Wren's presence here made the place both more homey and more alone.

The only thing out of place was a woven piece of artwork hanging on the wall in the kitchen. White rope braided and knotted decoratively around a sand dollar delicately suspended in the middle.

A note was pinned up with the piece, and Hollis reached for it, running a finger over the twisted ropes.

"Let us approach the throne of grace with boldness, so that we may receive mercy and find grace to help us in time of need." Hebrews 4:16

Her *s*'s swirled, and she dotted her *i*'s with spirals. Hollis read it three times, tracing his thumb over the letters before pinning it back at the top of the decoration.

When he headed to bed, his room looked untouched, and he suddenly wanted to text Wren and make sure she hadn't slept on the couch. One look at the clock stilled his hands on his phone. He couldn't text her at this hour.

Despite the comfort of his own bed that night, sleep escaped him. Minutes ticked by, second by second, until they seemed to freeze entirely. He prayed for the rest he had begun to discover a week before. Though he felt it in his heart, a peace that slowed his striving, his body didn't get the memo. Forcing his eyes shut and counting sheep did nothing to stop his wandering mind, remembering days with Maggie, days with the twins, the day his dad sketched that ice cream shop.

Finally, he sat up and flipped on the lamp. He had that ice cream shop napkin somewhere. And if he wasn't going to sleep, he might as well do something.

Hollis reached into the drawer of his nightstand and combed through the papers and oddities that filled it, finding nothing. Giving up on sleep entirely, he moved to the desk in his room. There was more to go through, and it took longer, but he still found nothing personal. Did he have nothing besides work?

Arms crossed, he surveyed the room, eyes landing on the closet. He kept a box on the top shelf for mementos. It had to be in there.

Hauling down the plastic bin, he popped off the blue lid and settled in for a trip down memory lane. There were birthday cards, trading cards, a small Catholic Bible his grandparents had given him, a picture of his dad and him standing next to a car they had fixed up, both looking too proud.

His hand froze when he reached in again, hovering above the next item in the box. A Christmas ornament. A popsicle stick frame lined with fingerprints in red and green holding a photo of Maggie as a young child, as clear in the photo as in his memory, dressed in a green sweater, head lolled to the side.

Pain clenched around his heart, and Hollis pressed a fist against the spot.

He remembered everything about it: the simple gifts they exchanged as kids, the way Maggie's therapist made sure to create something for everyone in the family. He remembered opening it on Christmas Day and telling her how perfect the fingerprint lines were. He had given her a pinch pot from a school project and for once felt like their gifts had been a good match. He hadn't undersold himself, and he hadn't outshone her. It had gotten harder over the years, as he had grown and she had regressed.

When he finally set the photo down, he tore through the remaining items in the box, desperate to find more of her gifts. A hand-printed

Christmas tree on a tea towel, a photo pasted into a clear ornament, and a snowy ripped-paper collage appeared.

That's it?

He hadn't kept them all. What was he missing?

The pain spread from his chest through every part of his body. His stomach ached. There would be no gift from Maggie this year. None, ever again.

Why hadn't he kept more?

His vision blurred, his breath failed him, and the tears came. The mixed emotions surrounding Maggie fled, and only grief remained. Grief for the sister he lost to a diagnosis. Grief for the sister he lost to death. Grief for himself, the kid who had struggled for so long.

This time he didn't fight the flood. He let it wash him away. Yet it didn't pull him under. With every tear, the confusion and fear began to release, the guilt loosened its grip, and peace met him once again.

He loved Maggie—he always had. She had caused some of his hardest moments, created some of his best memories, and inspired some of his greatest accomplishments. With each minute that passed, Hollis found himself able to accept each truth.

Their family had never quite found the right way through Rett, but that was Rett's fault. It was the fault of a broken world, not a broken family. It didn't mean anyone had failed, not even Amá.

No, he couldn't save Maggie. But it wasn't up to him. God alone could, and he had saved Maggie's soul, if not her body. He saved Hollis too.

The flood passed, the tears spent, leaving only a pounding headache behind his eyes. But he hadn't drowned. With a steadying breath, Hollis stood and set the Christmas picture frame on the edge of his desk. He never wanted to hide Maggie again. Rather, he wanted to learn from her. To be honest, to find little bits of joy, to always believe in God's goodness, like his sister did.

This was his story. Woven together, knotted, and twisted, creating the person he was today. God had his life mapped and charted, and even if Hollis couldn't see it all, he could at least trust it.

•   •   •

The next day, Hollis worked through sleep deprivation and a tear-induced headache, operating on four cups of coffee and new peace. Quincy had managed well enough in Hollis's absence but seemed more than willing to pass the reins back. Employee relations and meetings weren't exactly his forte.

The Perla Tech Christmas party waited for him at the end of the day, and Hollis changed into a black suit with a pink dress shirt and a gaudy tropical tie before heading to the hotel ballroom they rented.

Last year's party had been a classic Winter Wonderland, and this year HR went the other way with a Happy Hula-days theme. Neon colors greeted him, along with a Santa on a surfboard and a snowman in a lei, waiting as photo ops. Beach balls drifted around the room, caught in random games of keep-it-up.

The energy of the space drummed up his own, as Hollis forced himself into the middle of it all. Honestly, Maggie would have loved it. He should have brought her to one of their parties. But the past only held his flaws, and while he couldn't outrun them, he could learn from them. So he would bring Maggie into the party today as best he could, during the speech.

Hollis greeted new hires he had previously met over video calls and chatted with remote employees he rarely saw.

After the Hawaiian dinner, Hollis took the stage, thanking and congratulating everyone for the year's work and reminding them of the company's vision. A photo of himself and Maggie lit up the screen behind him, for all to see, as Hollis introduced his sister. The earliest founding team members knew her, but many here tonight did not.

He spoke of his loss earlier in the year to a silent room, then lifted his cocktail. "To my sister, Margarita, the pearl behind Perla." Unsure if the applause was for his speech or the bonuses that had been sent out earlier that week, he exited the stage.

Quincy had recently accused Hollis of working like a madman. Maybe he had been crazed, but he wasn't anymore. Now, nothing drove him. No need to impress anyone or atone for any guilt. He didn't need the money or the growth. For once, Perla Tech existed simply because it was the gift and passion he wanted to share. Because Hollis knew how hard it was to love someone with severe disabilities, and he wanted to help. He wanted anyone struggling with disabilities to find a little joy and light in their day. If that's what their company did, to any degree, it would be a success. Honestly, if that's what he could do for himself, he would be a success too.

As the main events wrapped up, Hollis made a quiet exit. The employees would stay and party for another hour or two. Most years, he joined them. But tomorrow he had an early morning planned.

Arriving back at the condo, Hollis double-checked the details his dad had texted him about the boat and meeting time. He had asked if Hollis would go fishing with him—as casually as if they did it every Saturday morning. They had gone before, years ago, when Hollis was still in college. But getting covered in fish blood wasn't Hollis's idea of a good time anymore.

<u>Hollis</u>

I'm a vegetarian

<u>Dad</u>

I thought you were pescatarian?

<u>Hollis</u>

Nope

Hollis shook his head at how little his dad knew about him. But when his dad had pivoted to sailing, Hollis had no excuse to get out of that one.

Chapter Thirty-Eight

Hollis woke before the sun and dressed in layers, pulling on waterproof pants, a Henley, a fleece pullover, a forest-green anorak, and a beanie. It felt stuffier than a suit. The winters in Ridley Bay were mild, and he rarely wore all this, but the wind on the water held a bite at this time of year.

They met at the docks, as a cold sun rose over the bay. His dad led him to the small sailboat he had chartered, and soon they were drifting through the marina, along with a handful of other boats.

After navigating out through the channel, they reached open water, where his dad cut the motor and let the winter wind pick up the sails. Only the sounds of flapping sails and a quiet breeze accompanied them here.

Hollis missed the noise of last night's party and wished they'd brought the twins or some other conversational buffer. For some reason, he could carry a conversation with anyone about anything, but not with his dad.

Cutting through the silence, his dad spoke first. "Been a while."

"Didn't do much sailing in Boston?"

"Ah, well, I meant a while since doing this with you."

Right, because his dad had lived a second life without any of them. Hollis nodded. "I hear you're splitting your time between Boston and Ridley now."

"I am. I have a lot more flexibility these days, so I wanted to be here more." In his job as a corporate lawyer, flexibility had never been the issue.

"Why now?"

His dad studied the wheel in front of him before answering. "I always thought there'd be a right time. But the longer I waited, the harder it got to own up." He cleared his throat and lifted his sunglasses, wiping his arm across his forehead. "And then I was too late."

"That's why I moved back four years ago," Hollis said, aware of his own tone. He had run off for a few years after graduating, only talking to his sisters and Amá on the holidays, rather like his father. But he had come back much sooner, his recent detour not counted.

"You always were smarter than me."

He didn't think smarts had anything to do with it. Maybe guilt. Maybe the need to connect with his family in a way he never had growing up, to find the places and rhythms they never had quite worked out. Maybe simply because he loved them and wanted to be near them.

"I hope I'm not too late for the rest of you," his dad said.

"The rest of us never mattered as much."

The look that crossed his dad's face, dragging it downward, almost made Hollis regret the statement. "That's not true. Why do you think we're out here this morning?"

Hollis shrugged. "I'm the only one who would go with you?"

"You're not my last resort, Daniel. You're my son."

"Really? Because I've been doing your job for the last fourteen years. Am I supposed to just hand it off now?"

"I think the job is nearly done, as you pointed out. None of you need me anymore, but I'd like to at least be on the same team, if you'll give me a chance."

"I can't have a team with players who leave when it gets hard." Not only did Hollis have to protect himself, he had to protect the twins. Who knew when his dad would leave again?

His dad scoffed and crossed his arms. "Spoken like a true businessman."

Blowing out a sigh, Hollis pulled against the edge of the boat, stretching his arms. He should be more forgiving. Had he learned nothing about how short their time could be? He ran a hand over his hair and turned to his dad.

Before he could apologize, his dad spoke first. "You know, if you want to talk about quitters, I seem to remember a certain five-year-old walking off his dad's T-ball team."

Hollis chuckled. "The coach sucked."

His dad's laugh came full and whole. "Hey, you coach a dozen preschoolers to victory, then we'll talk."

"Is that when we switched to motocross?"

"Yeah, vehicles seem to work better for Hollises."

Conversation flowed more easily around memories—as long as they avoided anything too sensitive. His dad talked about work too, and Hollis returned the favor.

The higher the sun rose, the easier the quiet spaces became. The ocean seemed to buffet it, offering a peace of its own that allowed them to just be. The sun warmed the cool air, and its warmth reflected from the water, casting onto Hollis's face.

Wispy clouds from the morning built slowly into larger puffy masses. Keeping a close eye on them, his dad decided to call it and head back. They didn't mess with bad weather out here.

Hollis savored the last hour at sea. The wind now whipped a little harder at his face, and he had forgotten how much he enjoyed this feeling.

"Look," his dad said, pointing upward. A large cloud covered the sun, but rays shot out of it, casting one directly onto their boat.

A memory slipped into Hollis's mind, unbidden but welcome. "I have a friend who calls that a heavenly hello." Wren would love it out here, and Hollis suddenly wanted to take her sailing.

"Sounds about right. I took a long route here, but I'm starting to think God might really love us, to give us beauty like that."

Only a few weeks ago, Hollis might have disagreed, based on the life and death of his sister. But he never would have known the love of God without her. Without being brought to his knees, he never would have looked up and found Christ. "We don't even have to earn it," Hollis said, leaning his forearms over the railing. "He just loves us."

•   •   •

They made it back to shore with plenty of time for Hollis to switch out of sailing clothes and into chinos and a dark green sweater before dinner. Amá had invited him to the house that evening, along with the twins. Hollis offered to bring something, but she declined—probably not trusting his cooking or choice of takeout.

Like a kid sneaking back past curfew, Hollis ditched his bike and helmet a block away from the house. Amá would know he had brought it, but she didn't have to see it. One less scolding would make the reunion a little easier.

At the front door, the scent of spices and tomatoes greeted him. Hollis walked into the kitchen. "Smells good," he said, setting down the bottle of wine he had brought, refusing to show up empty-handed.

Amá wiped her hands on a kitchen towel and came to give him a hug. "*Hijo*, you are finally home." She held his face and reached up to give him a kiss on each cheek. "I hope you still like enchiladas."

Enchiladas had always been his favorite meal. "Of course."

"Every Wednesday night," she said with a smile, wagging a finger in his direction.

When he was growing up, she had cooked enchiladas every Wednesday night, and Hollis had made sure to be home for dinner. Did she know his favorite food? "Was that for me?"

Amá laughed. "Did you think it was for Margarita?" Maggie rarely ate more than two bites of anything. His mother opened the oven door and pulled two large pans from the oven. "I have cheese for you and beef for the rest of us."

Watching her in confusion, Hollis stepped out of the way. She'd always had a motherly side, but it had been consumed by her second child. He assumed it would die with Maggie. The warmth could melt away any moment with his mother, but he appreciated this brief appearance.

Amá set out plates, refusing to let Hollis help.

"Be a good guest. Stop trying to help."

"I'm not a guest, I'm your son."

"And I'm your mother, and I said to sit down. You've done more than enough for this family."

That surprised Hollis into obedience. He poured a glass of wine and took a seat on a barstool, watching as his mother set the table for five—Maggie's spot remained empty. "Who else is coming?" Hollis asked.

"The twins are bringing a friend."

Unreasonable disappointment hit Hollis. They begged him to come home but didn't want to see just him after all. He tempered it with logic—it was probably Joshua. And he did want him to be around their family more. Although describing Sophia's longtime boyfriend as a friend seemed weird. Hollis decided to dig into it.

"Amá, what do you think of Joshua?"

Before she could answer, voices entered through the front doors. "The girls are here," she said.

Chapter Thirty-Nine

As if they were looking for a third sister, Sophia and Lilia had practically adopted Wren. It started when Wren tried to give Sophia the framed flowers from the funeral and Sophia insisted Wren deliver them straight to their mother's house. She ended up staying for dinner. A week later, Lilia showed up at the spa for a massage, and they talked the entire time.

When Wren accepted Daniel's offer to stay at his place, she asked the twins to help her bring stuff over. It made it feel less invasive if his sisters were there. Their jokes at their brother's expense helped Wren relax. Though the more she learned about him, the more acutely she felt his absence.

After that, there were church events, cheer meets, and the night Wren had helped the Hollis women clean up Maggie's room. She ended up crying right alongside them, and it solidified their friendship.

Though she never asked, the twins kept her updated on Daniel—she blamed them for the fact that she could only think of him by his first name now. If he didn't contact her, perhaps he didn't want her to know about his life, which hurt, regardless of how deserved it might be.

Having pushed him away for so long, she had finally succeeded, just in time to realize her mistake. Wren had kept every good thing at arm's length for most of her life, for fear, for control. But she was done living that way. And if Daniel ever gave her a second chance, well, a hundredth chance, she would prove it.

In late December, she pulled up to the Hollis household with Sophia and Lilia in tow. The Spanish mansion with its terra-cotta roof welcomed them. It used to make Wren uncomfortable, but now she saw it as a friend, along with the mother who welcomed her into it.

Daniel hadn't exaggerated his mother's games. She played favorites, often switching between the twins, based on their actions. Wren wasn't in the contest and could ignore it for the most part, except when she had to console a frustrated sister.

Grabbing bags from their Christmas shopping trip, the twins carried their haul into the house while Wren left hers in her car.

She held the door open for the girls, and the air that drifted out was flavored with melted cheese, toasty tortillas, and salsa, causing her mouth to water. Whatever unfair games she played on her children, Ms. Hollis was a wonderful cook. Now Wren knew where Daniel got it.

"I still think you should have gotten that blue shirt for Joshua," Lilia said as they entered the front hall. "It would help the stench."

"He has multiples of it," Sophia said. "He doesn't wear the exact same shirt every day."

"He's like a cartoon character," Lilia said, laughing.

"Okay, yes," Sophia's facade cracked, and she started to giggle too. "And at least now I know where he buys them."

Their laughs were contagious, and Wren loved listening to the sisterly ribbing.

They broke past the wall of the hallway, stepping into the light of the kitchen and—

Daniel Hollis.

The air was punched right out of her, and he looked equally surprised. Wren shot a quick look to Sophia. The sisters didn't look one bit surprised as they launched themselves at him, squeezing in for a double hug. They had to have known he would be here, and they hadn't told her, a move both offensive and suspicious.

Daniel sent her a confused look above his sisters' heads. He might not want her here. Wren backed up a step and set her purse down on the entryway table. Should she leave? It suddenly felt less like dinner with friends and more like she had invaded his family, his space. She slipped back into the kitchen, prepared to say goodbyes.

"I hope you don't mind," Lilia said to her brother. "We sort of stole your friend, and she's ours now."

"I don't mind." His eyes didn't leave Wren's. "It's good to see you."

With words so simple, a heart could fly. "You too."

"She's our shopping buddy," Sophia added, looping an arm through Wren's and tugging her farther into the kitchen. "Honestly, it's for the best, she keeps us a little more balanced."

Half a grin built on his face, and his eyebrows rose. "Shopping buddy? For my sisters?"

Wren felt like she had been caught doing something she shouldn't. "They made me."

"Right, because you were sooo reluctant when *you* suggested going to the Salt and Sea Market," Lilia said.

"Well, you wanted to go to the mall, and I do have standards," Wren countered.

Daniel's smile burst out like sunbeams, warming the entire room, almost too much. She couldn't even lie to herself about the effect it had on her. "Give it up, Atwood. You've been caught shopping with the mini Hollises."

"I am an adult—"

"We are not mini yous—"

Both twins jumped in to protest the nickname. Their mother quieted them all, shooing everyone toward the dinner table, never giving Wren another chance to consider leaving.

The head of the table remained empty, as usual, while the twins took over one side of the table and their mother took a spot opposite them. Wren sat next to her, near where Daniel sat at the foot of the table.

After not seeing him for three months, the longest stretch of time since he had first come to Grace Church, Wren couldn't keep her eyes off him. He had grown his hair a little longer on top, and a slight shadow grew on his jawline. But it was his eyes that held her attention. Here, in his home, his guard was down, and the pain she had last seen in him had dissipated, the weight lightened.

They all listened to the latest developments with his company. Wren knew the whole history of it now. How he had created a medical records software right out of college and sold it for several million dollars. The profits helped start up Perla Tech, which he soon moved to Ridley Bay. No ivory tusks or sweatshops.

Their mother reached a hand across the table and squeezed Daniel's. "We're very proud of you."

Daniel looked unsure of what to do with the attention, or with being the current favorite. He reached for a second serving of enchiladas. "Enough nerd updates, I'm boring myself to sleep. Tell me about sophomore year."

The twins took turns with their rants and raves, all things Wren had heard about for the last few months.

"And we just finished up Christmas shopping," Sophia said. "Which, by the way, buying gifts for your brother who has literally everything is impossible."

"You're in college, and you don't even know what literally means," Daniel muttered, shaking his head.

Sophia made a face at him.

"We checked out the Ouija boards, but Wren wouldn't let us buy one," Lilia said.

"Thank you," Daniel said, with a pointed look at Wren. He turned back to the twins. "What do you two want? I'm sure you have a list."

Lilia propped her chin on her hands and put on her best puppy dog eyes. "Just you, big brother."

"Shut up."

"Honestly, we are just glad you're here," Sophia said.

"Thanks, but unless you want coding classes, I suggest you speak up."

The twins spouted suggestions with triple-digit price tags while Wren forked down another bite of rice and listened with amusement.

"What about you?" Daniel asked Wren. "Are you coming over for Christmas?"

She nearly choked on her food. Was she invited? She cleared her throat. "I'm going to San Antonio, actually. A quick visit to see Lark." Did she imagine that slight look of disappointment that crossed his face?

"How is Lark?" he asked, with a hidden look in his eyes, like they were speaking in code. But his family knew all about her sister.

Neither Lark nor Mavis had spoken to Wren for several weeks after Lark left Ridley Bay. Then, Lark called last month to say she had lost a friend to fentanyl. It scared her into checking into a nonprofit rehabilitation facility. *They talk about Jesus a lot,* Lark had said with a laugh.

"Recovering," Wren said. She prayed for Lark daily.

"Will you see your mom too?" Daniel asked.

Sophia cleared her throat distinctly, raising her eyebrows at Daniel.

"Sorry." He looked between his sister and Wren. "I guess that's not … never mind."

"It's okay." Wren smiled at Sophia's protectiveness. Mavis had not forgiven Wren yet. Maybe she never would. "I'm hoping to see her, but we haven't talked in a while."

Daniel's face dropped. "I'm sorry."

Wren shrugged. "Me too." That's how Mavis handled life, though. She ran away. It hurt Wren, more than she cared to admit, but she was learning to accept it. She waved her fork at the twins. "I have these two for late night talks now anyway."

Daniel faked a frown. "Not sure I want your gossip buddies to share my DNA."

"Daniel, we have *only* good things to say about you," Lilia said, in a tone far too sugary sweet.

"Right …"

"Especially about times like when you donated blood and then passed out cold in front of that girl you liked—"

"Yeah. That's exactly what I thought."

Sophia and Lilia dissolved into giggles, their mother only shook her head, and Wren shot Daniel a sympathetic look.

"You're not allowed to be friends with them anymore," he said to her, dryly.

"I'm afraid they're very persistent. Kind of like another Hollis I know."

With that single-dimpled smile in place, he held her eyes just long enough to give her hope. Maybe he hadn't completely given up on her. And if he offered just one more date, no matter how bad it was, she would go in a heartbeat … Then again, maybe it was her turn.

•   •   •

Once they had dinner cleaned up, the twins settled in to show off their shopping loot to Amá, and Wren excused herself, heading toward the door. Hollis hopped up to walk her out and stepped into the dark yard with her, the porch lights illuminating their steps.

The minute he saw her this evening, he remembered why he had gotten so stuck on this girl. She seemed to carry fresh air itself. Even her clothes reminded him of the wind—wide, flowing pants and a cropped cream sweater. Like a fool, he wanted to catch the wind, and he would do anything to keep her here a little longer. Somehow, having her here made it feel more like home than this house ever had before.

"How's your house coming along?" Hollis forced himself to ignore the way the breeze cast her hair around her face. "Are you back in it?"

"Getting close. I should be able to move in just after the new year. The twins want to help me shop for new furniture, but I don't think they understand budgets or thrifting."

"I understand budgets." Hollis said, before realizing he sounded like a dork.

"And thrifting?" Wren raised her eyebrows at him.

"I like to learn new things."

"Hmm. I'm a pretty good teacher. And I will need some extra hands for moving stuff in."

Hollis spread his hands. "Oh, well, I charge for that."

Her smile grew, wide and bright. "And I charge for house sitting."

Hollis breathed out a laugh. "Guess we're even then. Did the condo corrupt your morals?"

"Ah, they were pretty corrupt to begin with. I think I'll miss the view, though, which is what I was afraid of."

"You can come by anytime."

Bright as lightning, her smile flashed as she dipped her head. "I'd say same to you, but I'm not sure there's any reason you'd want to see my house."

He could think of a few, though they had more to do with Wren than the house. "You've got me beat on outdoor space, that's for sure."

Wren tilted her head toward him. "Then you're welcome anytime."

"Where are you staying now?"

Her smile slipped away, and Hollis regretted the question. "I got an aid placement in an extended stay hotel. I kind of hate it, but I'm also grateful for it, if that makes any sense."

"It does."

"It's definitely better than staying with Lark."

"How is she?"

Wren updated him on Lark's party and subsequent absence. Hollis was speechless. He'd had no idea. She hadn't spoken a word of it while he'd been grieving Maggie.

"I can't believe you had to deal with that on top of the hurricane damage," he said.

"Eh, what's a little bankruptcy?"

Hollis winced and Wren laughed.

"I'm kidding," she said. "Turns out, God really does provide. Insurance covered a good bit, and the church helped a lot, along with a few charity funds."

"I would have too," Hollis said. "I'm sorry I wasn't here. You could have reached out …"

"Thanks, but I didn't need to."

And she wouldn't, after the way he had talked to her. "Wren, I'm sorry for the things I said, before Maggie … I let stress take over. I didn't mean what I said."

"I know. And it's okay, I'm pretty sure I've said even worse."

"Sheesh, it's not a contest." Hollis grinned.

Wren laughed. "Thank goodness. I don't want to know who would win."

Hollis watched the shadows dance across her face as an easy quiet settled in the wind around them. "So, San Antonio for Christmas?"

Wren nodded. "I haven't been back in years. I was always afraid to go, like I would somehow end up trapped there."

"But you're not anymore?"

"No. It's better if I visit on my own terms. I'm not letting my family come here anymore, not until they're healthy." She stared out at the yard, rubbing her arms as a cool breeze wrapped around them. "You know, I thought I had climbed out of that pit all by myself, when I never actually could have made it out without God's grace. And I love my family, but they're not my identity—Christ is."

"There's a peace about that, isn't there? When you know he's on your side."

"Definitely."

"I just have to keep reminding myself of it," Hollis said, with a chuckle under his breath.

"Well, we're both works in progress."

"That might never end."

"True." She rubbed her arms again.

She was getting cold, and he should let her go before he did anything really stupid like offer a jacket. Instead, he let the magnetic pull take over. Hollis reached an arm out, and without missing a beat, Wren stepped into it, their arms wrapping around each other easily, warm and close, familiar and foreign.

"I'm glad you're back," she said, softer than the weave of her sweater. "You're staying, right?"

A grin tugged at his lips, and he let it grow. "If I didn't know any better, Atwood, I would think you want me to."

She moved back and lifted her chin. "Then it's a good thing you know better," she said, her smile belying her words.

Chapter Forty

Grace Church opened its new building on Christmas Eve. Tucked into the middle of the city, the white stone building shone like a beacon, with strings of twinkling lights lining the roof and decorating the oaks scattered around the property.

As part of the new creative team, Wren had worked with Ava to help decorate for the holidays. Not wanting to waste time and money on a Christmas display that would only last two days, they had chosen a wintry theme that could stay up for at least a month or two.

Rather than use Christmas trees, they foraged branches and sticks, painted them white, and stood them in tall planters. Thrifted white ornaments filled clear glass vases on the welcome tables, with boughs of evergreen as backdrops. Snowy cotton ball garlands hung in front of the children's rooms for a bit of whimsy.

Wren paced through the church on bare feet, having arrived early to breathe in the newness and expectancy of the place. She loved how it all turned out, though the feeling wasn't quite pride. It was more grateful. Grateful to be part of this church and to be creating something beautiful.

The only thing she would change was adding more color, but Wren brought her own, wearing a deep-red cable-knit sweater over a forest-green skirt. Golden half-moons hung from her ears, and the top half of her hair was wrapped into a braid crown. She had spent more time on her appearance today than she wanted to admit. But today she planned to put herself on the line, and she needed every bit of confidence she could gather.

Visitors began to stream into the church, both familiar faces and seasonal seekers. The Hollis family arrived together: Daniel, his sisters, and his mother, who had lost out on the vote for a Catholic service this evening.

She greeted them each with a hug. An electrical sense of expectancy built in Wren until it was hard to breathe. Focusing on an inhale, she picked up the slightly woodsy scent on Daniel's brown fleece jacket and the new paint in the church.

"I thought you were going to San Antonio," Daniel said, letting go of their quick hug.

"In the morning, only for the day."

"So you don't get trapped?"

Wren's mouth twisted to the side. "Just for the best."

Though visiting Lark in the rehab center seemed like a safe bet for Christmas, family time needed to happen in small doses, at least for now. The look in Daniel's eyes said he understood.

"I heard I missed a big announcement at the ribbon cutting last week," Daniel said. "Something about a backpack program?"

Though the church had left the middle school behind, they had started something new there, supplying students in need with enough food to get them through the school breaks. Wren was only a small part of the larger group spearheading the program. "Yep. No more hungry kids on Christmas break."

"Good." His grin matched hers.

"Oh, and you missed a shout out to some 'special donors,'" she said, with finger air quotes. "I'm surprised they didn't want to be there."

"Mm. Maybe they needed rest more than acknowledgment." Daniel stuck one hand into a jacket pocket.

She eyed him for a second before reminding herself not to linger. "Maybe so. We're pretty grateful to them though."

"They're blessed to be part of it," he said, looking around the foyer.

Sophia and Lilia joined them before she could reply, with hot chocolates from the welcome table, passing one off to each of them. People were shuffling into the new auditorium, and the twins invited Wren to sit with them, but she could hardly handle being that close to Daniel right now. Her nerves were wired too tightly, so she excused herself to sit with a few other holiday loners—Nathan, Faith, and some of the college kids that had stayed in Ridley Bay for the holidays.

Micah Sanford preached about Christmas as the ultimate expression of grace.

"It's a gift, but not the kind saddled with expectation of something in return," he said. "This grace was given to us when we were broken, lost, stuck in our own sin. That grace, so perfect, is what motivates us now to give it freely to others."

Wren cried easily and blamed it on the holidays. The beauty and promise of Christmas brought out her emotional side.

When the service ended, groups hung around the foyer, and some drifted outside, standing under the lights strung between trees. She found Daniel out there, surrounded by their friends, just as she had hoped. Her heart raced like a hummingbird's wings as she attempted to casually join in the conversation. Thankfully, she was learning to let go of her pride, because she was about to make a fool of herself.

Emma, Faith, and Levi described the Bible study group's latest gift exchange—the battle for the basket of desserts Emma had baked and the best gag gifts, including a toilet-shaped coffee mug.

Her cue was coming. Her heart rate doubled.

"Sounds like I really missed out this year," Daniel said, with a laugh.

Now or never.

"Actually, I have something for you." Wren reached into her purse for a small gift bag. She passed it to Daniel, and confusion flickered across his face.

Her heart thundered in her chest as he reached inside the bag. She could have easily done this in private, but she wanted to take the risk he once had, in front of their friends.

He pulled out the bag of coffee—the same Colombian brand he had given last year. She had tracked it down thanks to the twins and their aunt, who kept some on hand. But Daniel wasn't looking at the coffee; he was reading the note stapled to the top.

Do you believe in second chances?

His eyes met hers. "Yes."

Pulling a breath, Wren took the leap. "Then will you go out with me?"

From the group around them, she heard a gasp, but she wasn't sure who it came from, maybe Emma. Wren was too focused on Daniel. A low whistle sounded, likely from Levi.

Wren added the rest hastily—the worst date she could find. "Somewhere terrible, of course. There's a middle school opera next week."

Daniel's confusion melted away, replaced by eyes that scrunched, a single dimple that quirked into place, and a smile, brighter than any Christmas tree, that lit up the night sky. "Wren, I'd go anywhere with you."

He laughed as he caught her in his arms.

•   •   •

With ease that defied her lack of experience, Wren welcomed friends to her home on New Year's Eve. Thanks to help from Levi, thrifted strings of lights cast the backyard in a soft, warm glow. A fire crackled in the pit Wren had dug out and lined with stones. Smoke drifted through the lights and past the tree branches, disappearing into the dark sky above.

Several people gathered around a small patio table, loading marshmallows onto skewers or dipping crackers into a cheese ball. Paper cups sat on the railing, with more inside on the kitchen countertop, names scrawled on each one, proof of a house full of people.

Most of their Bible study group showed up, along with a few of Wren's coworkers, Lilia, Sophia, Joshua, and a few neighbors. Wren carried a large bowl of popcorn outside, hoping she had bought enough snacks. One deep breath of fresh, cold air, tinged with the warmth of the fire, helped hold off any worries. Even if they ran out of snacks, they'd be okay.

Her neighbor Paula came up to Wren, one little boy wrapped around her leg while the other ran wild in the yard, shouting in pretend battle with another kid from down the block. "This is nice," she said, biting into a stringy, melty marshmallow. "I don't think I've ever been to a housewarming party."

"Me neither," Wren admitted.

Paula wiped her hands on a napkin and picked up the toddler, settling him on her hip. "I guess I should have brought something. But, with the holidays and everything, you know …"

"I know. I really do. I'm just thankful to have our homes back."

Many neighbors still had work to do on their homes. Some of them had slowed or stalled on progress. A couple might never make it back. Wren's side of the street sat a little lower than Paula's and their homes had received more damage. Mr. Ortiz lived with his son for now.

"Me too," Paula said, before turning her attention to the yard. "Oh, he turned that stick into a sword again, I swear …" She left their conversation to chase down the little warriors.

Just then, Lilia went bounding past Wren, toward the house. "Daniel!"

Wren turned in time to see him catching his sister in a hug. His eyes met Wren's and crinkled. Before he had released Lilia, Sophia was there. Wren waited her turn. The man was not short on love.

After greeting his sisters, he crossed the porch to her, wearing black jeans and a dark gray sweater over a white button-up. "Sorry I'm late. I stopped by my mom's first."

She stepped right into his arms like it was the most natural thing in the world, the slight scent of woodsy aftershave tickling her nose. "It's okay, I'm glad you saw her." Wren had invited Ms. Hollis, of course, but she declined.

"You look radiant," he whispered.

"Trying to keep up with you," she said, brushing a finger over the neckline of his sweater.

They had managed to squeeze in two dates already: the middle school opera and a sunset dinner cruise. As it turned out, there was no such thing as a bad date with Daniel Hollis.

"I brought you a housewarming gift," he said. "It's on the front porch."

Wren tilted her head. "Lead the way."

He held her hand as they crossed through the mostly empty house. She had moved many of her smaller items back in but still needed to replace the living room furniture. The Sanfords were giving her an entire bedroom set they no longer needed.

Daniel opened the front door and gave a grand sweeping gesture toward the front porch. A mat sat in front of the door, and Wren stepped outside to read the swirling print on it.

Live, Laugh, Love

The very thing she had once made him promise not to give. She dropped her head back in a laugh. "Are you serious?"

"You're welcome." A mischievous grin danced across his face.

She wrapped her arms around his neck. "I love it." The mat was awful, but she loved that he listened and remembered and knew exactly how to tease her.

He pulled her back slightly and frowned at her. "That was a sanity check, and you just failed."

She pressed a hand to one side of his face and kissed the opposite cheek. "I'll be crazy for you."

A smile as bright as any firework lit up his face, more contagious than ever. There was no cure for the Daniel Hollis virus, and she didn't mind in the least.

He kept one hand on her back as they returned to the backyard to join the others at the fire pit. She probably shouldn't be in love with him after only two dates, but she was. Based on his goal-oriented, family-loving self, and what the twins had divulged about his dating history, she knew her love wouldn't go to waste.

"You guys are too cute," Sophia said, handing Daniel a skewer with a marshmallow.

"The nerd actually got a girl." Lilia shook her head.

"She did just admit to being crazy," Daniel said, as Wren laughed.

He wrapped his free hand around her waist, bringing her closer. They had earned this. After a year of missed dates, they weren't wasting any more time.

Before long, the warmth of the fire couldn't overcome the chill outside, and they moved the party indoors. Wren was suddenly glad she hadn't moved in furniture because they wouldn't have been able to fit this many people inside. Empty as the house was, they had enough space to all move around easily.

The crowd thinned a bit as midnight approached. Paula took her boys home for bedtime, and the twins and Joshua headed off to another party they had been invited to.

"You were absolutely right about the sage green in here," Emma said, studying the living room walls.

Wren gave her a side hug. "Thanks again for helping me paint it."

"It was kind of fun. I can see why Levi likes working on houses."

Daniel and Levi were talking near enough to overhear, and Levi bumped Emma's arm. "You did okay, but I think you should stick with baking." He lifted a forkful of her chocolate cake from his plate to show his appreciation.

Several of them had also helped lay wood flooring to replace the carpet and overhauled the kitchen cabinets with a dark teal and white color scheme. A frame in the living room featured a swatch of the rose-printed bedsheet curtains, a nod to Rosa's former namesake.

God had given her home back to her even better than before and filled it with friends and neighbors. Rebecca Sanford was right. His grace had been holding her the entire time. And though Christmas with Lark hadn't gone as well as she had hoped, she knew his grace was there too. God would either redeem the Atwoods or give her a new family with the Hollises. Maybe even both.

"Five minutes until midnight," Faith called out, raising a handful of sparklers she had brought. "Are we doing this?"

Bundling back into jackets and hats, they all headed outside for the final countdown. Soon, sparklers flared and gold flames illuminated her yard, casting a warm glow on everyone as smoke drifted to the sky.

Signature dimple in place, Daniel lit two sparklers and passed one to Wren. "Let's make some sparks fly."

Acknowledgments

I owe many thanks to Reagan Rothe and the Black Rose Writing team for taking my dreams and turning them into reality. Thank you also to Katy Schlomach for your wonderful edits, you made the story stronger than ever. Thank you to my husband, Scott, for your unending support. Thank you to my family for being my first readers and biggest cheerleaders. Special thanks to my sister Lydia Dobbins for the valuable feedback, and to my dad, Michael Dobbins, for the legal advice.

It takes so many people for a book to reach readers. From the Black Rose Writing authors who offer encouragement and advice, to the babysitters and teachers who help with my children, thank you all. Above all else, I thank God for planting these stories in my heart and giving me the opportunity to share them.

About the Author

Anna Daugherty is the award-winning author of *Outside of Grace*. A native Texan, she holds a journalism degree from the University of Texas at Austin. After several years of writing and editing for magazines and newspapers, she rediscovered a passion for fiction. Now, she writes with unflinching honesty, bringing the light of grace to some of the darkest issues facing believers today. Anna lives in the hill country with her husband and their three young daughters. When she isn't writing or chasing a toddler, she can usually be found enjoying the outdoors or hiding away with her Kindle in hand.

For updates and bonus materials, visit her website at annadwrites.com.

Other Titles by Anna Daugherty

Note from Anna Daugherty

Word-of-mouth is crucial for any author to succeed. If you enjoyed *Reaching for Grace*, please leave a review online—anywhere you are able. Even if it's just a sentence or two. It would make all the difference and would be very much appreciated.

Thanks!
Anna Daugherty

We hope you enjoyed reading this title from:

www.blackrosewriting.com

Subscribe to our mailing list – *The Rosevine* – and receive **FREE** books, daily deals, and stay current with news about upcoming
releases and our hottest authors.
Scan the QR code below to sign up.

Already a subscriber? Please accept a sincere thank you for being a fan of
Black Rose Writing authors.

View other Black Rose Writing titles at
www.blackrosewriting.com/books and use promo code
PRINT to receive a **20% discount** when purchasing.